MW01047162

Invisible Girl

Cherise Craney

ISBN 978 – 1-927848-09-8

First Edition – Hard cover
Victoria, BC, Canada
filidhbooks.com
Copyright 2014 – Cherise Craney

For Bronwyn

Chapter 1

I don't like oatmeal. Mummy says it's all we have for breakfast today. I'm eating it at the coffee table. Finn is sitting beside me, reading a comic book. Mummy is in her chair reading a book for school.

She's always reading.

She's obsessed with reading.

I'll go to her school and tell her teachers not to give her so much homework.

No one is paying attention to me.

"Mum," I say.

I have something to tell her.

"Mmmm?" she says.

"Mum."

"Yes, Maeve?"

"Mum."

I can't remember what I wanted to say.

"Mum."

"Oh my god, what? What?"

"Am I a medical miracle?"

"Well, I don't like the word miracle. You were very sick when you were born."

"What's wrong with miracle?"

"It implies magic saved you. Doctors saved you."

"Oh. Was I almost dead?"

"You were very sick."

"With seizures?"

"You inhaled meconium, which hurt your lungs. Then there were seizures."

"What did I look like?"

"You were huge, the biggest baby in the special

care nursery."

I like hearing that.

"And?"

"And they kept shaving your head to put in IVs. You had a Mohawk. You looked like a turtle. I need to read this, Maeve. Please eat your breakfast."

She's obsessed with reading.

"Mum."

"Yes, Maeve?"

"Mum."

"What? Please, finish what you want to say."

"Mum."

Mummy makes a growling noise. Finn sits up and touches my arm.

"Maeve, come on. Let Mum read. Let's go get you dressed."

"Okay. Mummy's mad at me." I can feel my face starting to cry.

"No she isn't, Maeve, she just needs to do her work. She has a test. Let's go get dressed."

Finn takes my hand, and we go to the bedroom.

***

Finn looked at the clock and realised he had ten minutes left to pick up Maeve by three. Mr. Addel had his back turned, writing instructions for the class assignment on the board in bright red marker. The marker squeaked with the start of each new letter. It made Finn anxious as he closed his notebook, quietly, and leaned down to unzip his backpack.

The zipper made a huge sound.

Mr. Addel's back went stiff and his marker stopped mid-squeak on the board. Without turning he said, "It's not time to pack up yet."

All eyes turned to Finn, frozen in his chair.

Finn released a puff of air. He hadn't realised he had been holding in his breath.

He coughed nervously. "I'm sorry Mr. Addel but it's ten to. I have to go."

"Go where?" Mr. Addel asked, still without turning around or lowering his arm, his sparse white hair seeming to stand on end in anger.

Finn felt his face burn hot. He hated having attention drawn to him, everyone looking at him expectantly, some with pity.

"You know why I have to leave."

Someone giggled at the back of the room and Finn felt his jaw tighten. His fingers grasped his backpack, the tips white with pressure.

Mr. Addel turned from the board, his eyes fixed on Finn in a squint. He capped his pen and then put his hands in his pockets and rocked back on his heels.

"Mr. Lynch, perhaps you and your mother don't care about grade ten social studies, but this is an important class; I expect you to attend the whole thing. You need to pay attention in class and do your work or..."

"I do *do* my work," Finn broke in. "I do pay attention in class, but there's nothing I can do about needing to leave early. Do you want to talk to my mum about it? She said she'd come in and talk to you if she had to."

"Fine, tell your mother to come in. Make sure she does, and I'll explain it to her."

Finn thought that would likely be the other way around, but he shut his mouth, got up, and left, careful not to let the classroom door slam. He heard Mr. Addel say something to the class, followed by some nervous laughter.

"Jackass," Finn said under his breath. He seemed to get at least one every year, one teacher who made him feel bad for needing to help his mum with his sister. He shouldered his backpack, wiped his long bangs out of his face, and ran through the door at the end of the hallway. Outside, a fine rain made him shiver and zip up his hoodie. He now had less than ten minutes to walk the eight blocks to Maeve's school.

***

I'm in the hallway of my school. The hallway is empty except me and my worker. Jani's looking at me. She wants me to do something. Maybe she wants me to say something.

Did she ask me a question?

I don't know, I don't know. I don't know how we got here.

I feel so sick. My tummy hurts and I want to throw up. Jani's shoes make a squeaking sound as she turns toward me. The sound hurts my head.

"Maeve, do you have something to put in here?" She's holding my backpack open. She comes closer to me. "Are you alright?"

I want to say no. I want to scream it at Jani. I feel horrible.

Jani pushes me to a bench. "Here, let's sit down for a minute."

I try to say okay. I sit down next to Jani and close my eyes. I feel dizzy.

The bell rings and freaks me out. The other kids come out of their rooms. It's so loud. I hate how loud it is. I want to hide my head. I keep my eyes closed.

I feel shaky. I'm shaking very fast.

I hear Finn's voice. "Did she have one?" he asks Jani.

"I think so," Jani says. She moves away, and I can feel Finn sit next to me. I don't open my eyes. I hug him.

"Hi, Maeve. How are you?"

"I want to go home."

"Okay, let's go home."

***

Finn worried about Maeve on the way home from school. The walk only took five minutes normally, but Maeve looked ill and confused. He had to keep a hand on her jacket sleeve, helping her navigate the sidewalk. She walked slowly.

Maeve wobbled up the front walk of their building and Finn opened the large, glass front door to the lobby for her. They lived on the ground floor, in a two bedroom apartment. The main hallway had industrial grey carpet. It smelled of long dead dinners and stale cigarette smoke.

Maeve stood listless and quiet as he opened the front door of the apartment. He got her into the living room and made a space for her to lie down on the couch. Finn sat with her, holding her head on his lap and stroking her cheek while she slept for a half an hour. He couldn't let her sleep for too long. When he thought she'd had enough, he shook her gently awake.

"How are you feeling, Maeve?"

"Okay," she croaked. She wiped her eyes.

"Would you like to go sit at the picnic table and play with your dinosaurs? It's sunny now. I'll make some snacks. How about peanut butter and jam sandwiches?"

"Okay."

Finn helped her find her bucket of dinosaurs in the front hall closet, then led her out the sliding glass door to the picnic table in the courtyard. He dumped them out for her, and then went back in, leaving the door open so that he could see and hear her. He set to work making peanut butter and jam sandwiches, glancing at her once in a while as she fed the dinosaurs fallen leaves.

As he put the sandwiches and juice boxes on a tray to take out, he looked up to see Maeve clutching a dinosaur to her chest, and staring around with big, scared eyes. He knew that she didn't remember where he'd gone. He walked quickly back out the door with the tray.

"Hey, Maeve. You okay? I was only gone for five minutes. I was watching you through the doors."

"Oh, yeah."

Finn laid out the sandwiches and drinks. "Here you go, PB & J and grape juice."

"I don't want sandwiches. I liked peanut butter when I was four."

"Maeve you *just* said you'd like peanut butter and jam sandwiches."

"Oh, yeah. I was just kidding." She grabbed a sandwich half and shoved it in her mouth, tears dancing in her light grey eyes. "I'm sorry. I'm an ass-hole."

Finn looked at her. He sat down, his legs facing the outside of the table, and wrapped a gangly arm around her chest. He pressed his chin to her forehead, mashing her eyebrow. .

"No. You're good. You're a good little sister."

She leaned into him. "Yeah," she whispered.

6

***

Ever since her daughter could walk, Siobhan had found little Maeve nests around the house. They contained toys, blankets, pillows, combs and brushes, and scraps of food. Siobhan would find the nests in closets, behind the couch, in different rooms.

Maeve liked small places. She would go into the bathroom, close the door, and stay there for hours, singing, talking to herself in the mirror, or jumping and twirling. At school this caused a problem. She'd disappear in there for hours, liking the solitude.

Siobhan never saw her making the nests, and neither did Finn. They would just find the nests. Siobhan had bought her a tent for her room four years ago. Maeve loved it. Everything that she could carry ended up in it, and Siobhan would have to make sure to check it regularly for mouldy items and laundry. She found the hamster once. It probably thought it had truly escaped to a beautiful rodent paradise, tunnelling through the debris and making a nest of its own.

As Maeve got older, the nest-building became a habit of hiding things in the bed. Siobhan would crawl in next to her, stretch out an arm, and find a plastic shovel, a package of Twizzlers, or any number of items that don't belong in a bed.

"Honey, why is there a vegetable steamer under my pillow?"

A look that says, *I have never seen that before.*

"I don't know, Mummy."

"Did you think Mummy might wake up in the middle of the night and want to steam some broccoli right here in bed?"

"No! That's silly!"

"Yes, yes it is." Siobhan laughed, and hugged her, and smelled her hair.

"Okay, Mummy, say it again. You say, 'Why is this here?' like you're mad, and I'll say, so you can make broccoli in bed!"

They did it again and again, until Siobhan said, "Okay, enough. It's time for sleeping."

"Okay, Mummy, just one more time."

"No. Jeez, we've done it a hundred million times. It's time for sleep."

"Okay. Cuddle me!"

Siobhan pulled Maeve's slight form over to herself and sang. She only knew three songs all the way through. She sang *Suzanne*, *Oh Lord Won't You Buy Me,* and *You Are My Sunshine*. The rest of the performance consisted of snippets from Schoolhouse Rock shorts and old TV ads. Just as she sang, "Turtles, Turtles, yeah, yeah, yeah, Turtles, Turtles, ha, ha,ha, MMMM I love Turtles," she decided that Maeve had fallen asleep.

Siobhan laid for a while, stroking Maeve's hair, and rubbing her back. Then she carefully got up, stepping on books and toys, and went into the kitchen. She passed her son at the table. He sat doing homework, a science book open before him, one knee up, absent-mindedly eating a pencil. She ruffled his greasy hair on the way by.

"Have a shower tonight, okay?"

A grunt.

"Do you want tea?"

Another grunt. She knew this meant yes.

She cleared just enough space on the counter for the teapot, filled the kettle and then plugged it in. While she waited, she put the fresh carrots back in the fridge and rinsed the worst of the dishes. The sink overflowed as usual, but it would have to wait. She stood for a bit staring at a fridge covered in alphabet magnets, and saw that Maeve had spelled out, "Soon doom will come," on the door.

The kettle boiled and she poured the water into the teapot, then got the cups and put milk and honey in them. She missed the cups when she poured the tea, and poured half of it on the counter. It ran off and dripped on her bare foot.

"Shit!" She jumped back from the hot tea and stepped firmly in the wet cat food on a plate on the floor, "Shit!" Her foot squished the cat food and the plate broke. "Ew. Crap."

"What are you doing?" her son asked, and peered through the opening between the kitchen and the dining area.

"I'm practising my Dance of Burnt Foot In Cat Food. It's all the rage on campus."

"Mum," he said with that rolling eyes voice.

"I spilled hot tea on my foot then stepped in the cat food."

"Ew."

"Yeah, ew. Bring me some napkins off the table, please."

"No, you come get them."

"Finn, I've got what looks like poo all over my foot. Please don't make me walk on the carpet. If I walk and it gets on the carpet, I will tell everyone who comes in to not step in the poo spots. I'll say they are your creative expression."

"Ugh. You would, too. You're sick."

"Not sick, just petty and vengeful. Now please bring me some napkins."

"Fine."

A sullen face appeared around the corner. A thin arm thrust napkins at her.

"Thanks."

Siobhan wiped the globs of cold, wet food off her foot and saw some blood. She wiped her foot the best she could, then hobbled to the bathroom and ran cold, stinging water over her foot. It made her have to pee, which she did as she put a band-aid on the small cut. The band-aid had *Buzz Lightyear* on it, the theme of the bathroom décor. Very chic. The bubble bath, toothbrushes, and shower curtain all had pictures of *Buzz Lightyear.*

Siobhan went back to the kitchen, walking gingerly. She took her text books out and put them next to her son's, then brought the partially filled cups of tea out. She sat with a sigh, stretching out her legs, and put her feet up on the chair across from her. She sipped her tea and looked at her son, who pointedly ignored her.

"What's up, Mr. Moody?"

"Nothing."

"Bull."

"I have homework."

"And this depresses you? You like homework."

"I do like homework. It isn't the homework."

"Well, then, spill it. Why are you all emu?"

A sigh. "It's emo, Mum."

"I like large birds better than sulky kids. Besides, you're in a fowl mood. Heh? Heh?" she reached out and jostled his arm.

A groan. "Right."

"One day you'll appreciate my genius." Siobhan sipped her tea. "I'm not going to leave you alone until you tell me."

He dropped his head on his book with a thump. His cup

jostled and tea slopped out. Siobhan found a t-shirt on the floor and wiped the mess up, then dropped the shirt back on the floor, kicking it under the table to ensure it wouldn't be found until the next time she cleaned.

She leaned forward and rubbed the back of Finn's head, his dark hair sticking in the direction of each caress, "C'mon, Hon, tell me."

"It's just Mr. Addel was bugging me today, again," his muffled voice said. "He made everyone look at me. I hate that."

"But you're cute, who doesn't want to look at you?"

"Mum! I *hate* it." His head came up, and his blue eyes looked pained. "I really hate it. I've explained and explained. I gave him your note and everything."

"Okay, okay. He doesn't get it. People don't get it, all the time. I'm sorry you have to go get her, I just didn't have a choice this semester."

"I know. I *know* that. Mr. Addel doesn't. I don't think he can understand that you're in school. Or why."

"Judging you or me isn't his business. If he's so old fashioned that he can't understand why a woman my age is in university, maybe I'll say you need to come home early to bring in the crops."

"We live in an apartment."

"Finn, Finn. What have I told you about being pedantic?"

"Oh, *you* are a weirdo and that's *my* fault?"

Siobhan took his hand. "I was completely normal before I had you. A good, Christian girl with dreams of Thanksgiving and folded linen."

"Right."

"So, I need to go talk to him?"

"Yeah."

"What day is your next class?"

"Wednesday, after lunch."

"Okay, I had to skip class that day anyway and go to the food bank, I'll come after that."

"Thanks, Mum."

"You're a good boy, Finn. And you're a good big brother. I'm sure Maeve felt better today knowing you were there."

"She never remembers having them, does she?"

"No, which makes it harder and better at the same time. You know what? I'm tired. Tristram Shandy can wait until tomorrow. My paper isn't due for a couple of weeks. I'm going to bed. Remember to shower, okay?"

"Okay, Mum. Thanks."

Maeve was playing in bed when Siobhan got to the room. She was startled by Siobhan's reappearance, and immediately lay down and closed her eyes.

"Hon, you should be asleep."

"I am an idiot!"

"No, you're just a kid who isn't asleep. Being awake doesn't make you an idiot. I'm awake, am I an idiot?"

"No. But what if I accidentally fall off a building?"

"Well, that would mean accidentally going into a building, accidentally going to the roof, and accidentally breaking onto the roof. That's sort of like me accidentally making a cake. No one accidentally makes a cake."

"What's happening tomorrow?"

"School."

"I hate school! Can't I go with you to your school?"

Siobhan hugged her tight. "But you hate school."

"I only hate mine."

"Well, you'll already miss two days next week for your EEG, so maybe not."

"I have an EEG next week? Do I get to stay up all night?"

"Yes."

"Why?"

"You need to be sleepy for it. Now, it's time to sleep, okay? I'm going to turn off the light."

"Okay."

Siobhan turned out the light and lay there. She felt Maeve fidget. First Maeve rubbed her face, then chewed her nails, then adjusted her toys. Then the cat jumped on the bed. Maeve giggled and talked to her.

"Maeve, it's sleeping time."

"I am an idiot!"

"No, you're just a kid who isn't sleeping."

"What is happening tomorrow?"

"School."

"I hate school. Can I go with you to your school?"

"We'll talk about it in the morning. Now we need to sleep. Lie down, and no fidgeting."

"Okay."

Maeve laid down, and she fell silent for a few minutes.

"Mum, what's happening tomorrow?"

"Roll over, and I'll rub your back."

"Okay. My back has been hurting all day."

Maeve rolled over on her tummy, and Siobhan put her hand under her pajama top and lightly rubbed her soft back. Maeve settled down, and Siobhan began to feel hope that she'd finally fallen asleep. Her hand slowed down and rested on the small of her daughter's back. Siobhan's eyes slowly closed, and her breathing became regular.

"I wish I never had a stroke."

Siobhan pulled Maeve toward herself, and held her tight.

"I know," she whispered. "It isn't fair. But you have me, and Finn, and we love you."

"Why did I have it?"

Siobhan had answered this a thousand times.

"You had a clot. Remember I showed you that video about strokes?"

"When I was born?"

"Yes. You developed a clot in a vein in your umbilical cord, just before you were born. That's what the doctors think caused your stroke. We can talk more about it tomorrow."

"Okay."

Siobhan continued her back rub, staring in the dark at the dim outline of her daughter. Silence.

"Mum, did you know the gigantosaurus was the largest of the known sauropods?"

"Uh, no. I did not know that. But you need to sleep now. You can tell me in the morning."

"Okay."

Deceptive silence.

"What is happening tomorrow?" Siobhan buried her face in her pillow.

"Tomorrow we are packing up and moving into a pumpkin."

"Mum! Really!"

"Tomorrow I am inventing nuclear toilet paper."

"Mum!"

"School. Just school. Now, go to sleep. I'm tired, Hon."

"Okay."

Siobhan lost hope at this point. Maeve had never slept well. Finn hadn't had such a problem. Even as a toddler he'd just announce when it was bedtime for him. He'd fall asleep within two minutes. But Maeve fought sleep; her mind became stuck in loops, going over the same ground over and over.

14

Siobhan cuddled her close and started singing again. Finally, around three, Maeve slept. Siobhan knew that Maeve would miss school in the morning.

Chapter 2

Finn woke in the morning before his mum. He could hear her snoring in the next bedroom. He lay in his bed, listening to her. It made him feel safe, like no one would break in because they obviously had a rabid water buffalo in the apartment.

He'd set his alarm early because he hadn't taken his shower the night before, and he hoped to have it before his mum woke up. Also, before Maeve woke up, of course, because she would follow him into the bathroom and want to talk to him, or read him a book, while he showered, and he wanted some privacy. Maeve liked to ask him about his body: why did he have hair, why did he pee standing, did he wish he was a girl, too? The answers didn't matter, because she'd just ask him all the same ones again the next time. She would ask them forever.

Finn got up and went to the bathroom, closing the door softly, and then sniffed the towels hanging on the hooks to find the freshest. He stepped out of his boxers and started the shower, peeing while the water heated.

After drying, he got dressed and padded softly into the kitchen. The smashed cat food plate and cat food were still there. He threw them away, and the cat, an old fluffy black one, ran in and mewed, so he fed her. His mum had named the cat Labia, and for years he'd been innocently calling for the cat out the window, not knowing what the name meant until a couple of years ago. He'd gotten quite mad at his mum.

"But I got the cat before I had you, Hon. The name wasn't a trick on you."

"Well, you could have told me, Mum. All those weird looks I got from people on the sidewalk! Jeez, I'm never calling her that again!"

And he hadn't; he'd called her "cat" ever since. He didn't want to be the neighbourhood teen pervert. His mum still called the cat by name, and when she'd shout out the window for her his face would go red, and he'd shut himself in his room.

His mum never got embarrassed. "It's just a name and just a body part. Honestly, who raised you? Have you ever even met me? When we finally get a dog, I'm going to name it Tree, so I can yell, 'Here Tree! Here Tree, good Tree!' in the park. I'm only going to get worse."

Finn scratched the old cat under the chin. "It's not your fault she named you that." The cat drooled on his hand. He wiped his hand on his pants.

Finn made some coffee and then went into the living room with a cup and turned on the television. He heard his mum's alarm go off, heard her smacking randomly at her bedside table until she finally killed the alarm clock, then heard the sounds of her getting out of bed, the trudge and shuffle of her feet in the hallway. Siobhan appeared, wobbly and mussed, in the living room.

"Hup?" she murmured at him, and he laughed at her. "Hey, shut up," she whined. "Coffee?"

"Yeah, I made some."

"Okay, then. I won't trade you to Kurdish yak herders today. But watch it tomorrow." Siobhan went into the kitchen and he heard her fill a pot and put it on the stove, then pour a coffee. She shuffled into the living room and plopped into the chair. "Oatmeal is on!" she announced, with a strange air of accomplishment.

"It's just oatmeal, Mum"

"Ha! Just you wait. It will knock your socks off!"

When the oatmeal had cooked, he got them each a bowl, spilling milk as he handed hers to her.

"What did you do? This just looks like regular oatmeal. You ruined my oatmeal! Where are the fresh fruits, the nuts, the expensive Quebec maple syrup?"

"We have canned pineapple, Mum. You'll have to pretend."

"Well, that totally sucks!"

"Yeah. Are you going to wake Maeve?"

"No, the little monkey stayed up till three last night. I don't think she'll make school today. She'll have to come with me, I only have one class at eleven today. You go and have fun, maybe hang out after school?"

"Hang out doing what?" he asked with genuine puzzlement. He never just hung out. Anywhere.

"I don't know. Aren't you supposed to do sports? Get all sweaty with other boys, and whack each other with jock straps? Or skip last period and harass the clerks at the 7-11? Don't ask me, I'd quit school by your age, but I know it's supposed to involve something like that, some sort of public mischief."

"Uh, well, I don't want to whack boys with my jock strap, and I feel bad for the people who work at the 7-11. Can't I just come home?"

"What about Terry? You haven't hung out with him for awhile. Why not go play Nintendo at his house?" Siobhan slurped her oatmeal.

"Mum, no one plays Nintendo anymore. Besides Terry hasn't really been talking to me lately. He's sort of Goth now."

18

"Well, do something irresponsible and appropriately hedonistic. If you're home when I get home, I'll be unhappy. You need some time just to flake out."

Siobhan often felt bad for needing his help with Maeve, but Finn really liked being responsible for Maeve. He liked how the people in the building treated him like an adult, and how Maeve's school treated him like a responsible person. Most of all, Finn liked his sister and how he felt needed by her, important, her favourite person. Just being a flake didn't appeal to him. But Siobhan worried about Maeve's inability to connect with the kids in her class, and worried about Finn's lack of interest in his classmates. He didn't hate them, he just didn't have much to talk to them about.

"Okay," he said, finishing his breakfast and gathering his books and coat together. "I'll find something to do. But not sports or public mischief." He headed towards the door. "Bye Mum."

"Finn!"

He stopped dead in the door. "Damn, almost made it," he muttered to himself.

"Where's my kiss, you sneak?"

Finn surrendered and walked over to her chair. She put her bowl next to her on the end table. Finn tried to dodge in with a quick peck, but Siobhan grabbed him and pulled him into a bear hug on her lap, holding his arms down and smothering his face in kisses. He struggled at first, but then gave in to her embrace, her affection. She was warm, and solid. She was strong, and for a moment he let himself enjoy the mothering, feeling the pulse in her neck where his cheek lay, smelling the lotion she used, her arms holding him mushed up against her breasts. In moments like that he felt perfectly at ease, like he had when he was little. She rubbed his forehead and whispered, "I have a secret to tell you."

"What?" he asked. He smiled at the old game.

"Take the golden *an*, and give to Stan in the tan van. Wait. That's not it. Oh yeah, yeah wait. I love you. Shhhh. Nobody knows."

"Everyone knows, Mum."

"Oh, yeah. Then tell them."

"I will. And I love you, too." Finn squeezed her, and kissed her cheek.

"Okay, go on monkey boy. And Finn?"

"Yeah?"

"No hiding in the library today. I'm on to you."

***

Maeve got up with only the usual amount of grumpiness and disgust, then became slightly happier once Siobhan had assured her twenty times that she would be going with Siobhan for the day. Eventually fed and clothed, Siobhan had to pare down Maeve's take-along wish-list to only what Maeve herself could carry

"Can I bring the cat?"

"No."

"Can I bring the race track for the cars?"

"No."

"Can I bring the spatula?"

"Why would you bring the spatula?"

Outside, Maeve bounced along beside Siobhan, cheered by a bright, late morning, she prattled on endlessly.

"Okay, Mummy, I'm a dragon, I'm a purple dragon, and you can be a green dragon. Green is your favourite colour!"

"Yes, it is."

"Okay, you are a northern dragon, and you can fly, so when I count to three, you fly! One, two, three!"

"I'm afraid I can't actually fly."

"Aw, it's okay Mummy, it takes time to learn to fly. Why don't you be a green dragon? Is green your favourite colour?"

"Yes, it is. Please watch the road!"

"I *am* watching the road!"

"Maeve! Stop!"

"Oops, sorry, I didn't mean to step into the road. You should watch me, Mum. When I was four I almost got hit by a car."

"Okay, I will certainly do that," Siobhan took her hand.

"You know, tomorrow I'd like to go to school with you."

"We're going to my school today."

"I forgot. Do I have all the stuff I brought?"

"You mean the stuff you're holding? Right now? In your arms? Yes."

"Good. I had to check. Tomorrow...tomorrow...can we...we...can we pretend to be dragons?"

"Sure"

"Do you know why I read so much? Because it is a good way to get information! To get it in your head. How else would you get it?"

"That is certainly a mystery."

"Are we catching a bus?"

"Yes."

"To where?"

"I told you, to my school."

"Oh yeah, I forgot. Is green your favourite colour?"

"Yes."

"You want to know what I would do if a stranger tried to

touch my vagina? I'd say, 'Hey, what's that over there?' and distract him, and then I would kick him in the penis."

"That sounds like a good plan. I'm sure he'll be fooled."

"Why do boys have penises?"

"Uh, well, they need them for sex for one thing."

"Oh. Are we catching a bus?"

"Yes, for the hundredth time, yes," Siobhan answered, sounding annoyed but not meaning to.

"This bus?"

"No, not that one."

"What number then? The four?"

"No. The twenty."

"Okay."

"I like reading! Reading gives me information! I love you. You're my squishy. If the doctor tells you to lose weight, you tell him NO!"

"I'll try to remember that, although I think it's a bad idea to take medical advice from children."

"What bus again?"

"Let's sit here at the bus stop".

"What's your favourite colour, Mum?"

"Green, Honey."

Maeve kept this up while the bus arrived, and as they boarded and looked for seats. They found two at the back and Siobhan distracted Maeve from her endless stream of conversation with some books from her bag, saying a silent thank you to Roald Dahl.

Siobhan gave her a hug and then concentrated on her own reading. She made messy notes in the margins, trying to jot down things whenever the bus had stopped.

The bus followed a direct route to the university and quickly filled up with students. Siobhan noticed no other older students on the bus, and certainly none with a child in tow. She felt bad for people so young forced to choose what to do with the rest of their lives. Eighteen year old kids should be living out of vans and doing Dead tours. Education could come later. She worried that Finn would not take time off to explore and would insist on going to university right away because he felt so responsible, especially for Maeve. He'd want to help out.

Siobhan sighed. Finn had a good heart, but he had too much to worry about at such a young age. She didn't want him to give up his youth to worry and responsibility.

She returned to her reading.

***

Mummy is taking me somewhere on the bus. I'm not sure where. I have a book and she has a book. I like being squished between her and the window.

Maybe we're going to Children's Hospital. I like it there, the play rooms have little houses in them.

"Mum. Mum. Where are we going?" I ask.

Mummy leans forward and puts her head in her book. The book covers her face. "I told you, we're going to my school."

Mummy's pretty funny sometimes.

I can't tell where we are when I look out the window. There are people sleeping outside here.

"Mommy, is this the bad side of town?" I ask.

Mummy looks out the window. "People call it that but it isn't bad it's just where the poor people are in the greatest numbers. Poor people aren't bad. We're poor. Are we bad?"

"We're poor?"

"Yes."

"But why are they sleeping outside?"

"Because they have illnesses and addictions that mean it's hard for them to get housing and stay in housing. Most of them are disabled. Unfortunately, poverty is too often the fate of disabled people, and it's very wrong. I never want you..."

"What? Want me what?"

"Want you to quit asking me these questions because they're important and you should always ask them. I have to read now, Maeve. You read your book okay?"

"Okay."

I wonder where we're going.

***

When the bus got to the university Siobhan waited for the other people to get off before taking Maeve off. Crowds confused Maeve. Siobhan's only class today started in about an hour, so she thought that they would have their packed lunch outside, to enjoy the sun. Walking across the road to the sidewalk, Siobhan held Maeve's arm out of habit, steering her to a free spot among all the milling students.

"Stand here, Hon. I am going to see how much money I have. Maybe I can buy you a hot chocolate."

"Really?"

"Yes. Just stand right here." Siobhan put her backpack on the ground and started a methodical search of her pockets, bag, and wallet, pooling change in her hand. She counted it into the other hand, removing lint and hair and paper, and then counted it again to the first hand. She removed the pennies. She always found using all change embarrassing, especially pennies. At home she would simply let Maeve collect all her pennies and then Maeve would offer them to her whenever she would say that she had no money for treats, or a bill, or rent. Unfortunately, Maeve's knowledge of money was not as advanced as her willingness to help.

"Three seventy-five, four seventy-five, five, sixty, seventy, eighty. Five eighty, Hon. Enough for a coffee *and* a hot chocolate." Siobhan looked up with a smile.

Maeve no longer stood there.

"Maeve?" Siobhan turned around in a panic, looking down the sidewalk toward the recreation centre, then behind her to the field, then toward the student union building. "Maeve?" she yelled loudly. Some of the students turned to look at her. Siobhan turned back toward the buses. Maeve had moved off in that direction about ten feet, walking in a tight circle with her head down. People walked past her and gave her dirty looks for not looking where she went.

Siobhan shoved the money in her pocket and grabbed her bag. She moved quickly up to Maeve, forcing people out of her way. She grabbed Maeve's arm and said, "Okay Hon, okay, I'm here." Siobhan didn't try to stop her, just tried to keep contact with her. Maeve's face looked blank, and a long string of foamy spit hung from her mouth. All of a sudden she stopped walking and seemed to collapse in on herself, holding her stomach.

"Oh, no, Mummy, I'm sick." She started spitting on the sidewalk. "I'm going to throw up." She started to cry a bit.

"No, Hon, it's okay, it was a seizure, it's over, let's sit down, why don't we sit down, okay?" Siobhan pulled Maeve tight to her, helping her stand. These moving seizures had just started recently, usually she had absence episodes.

Siobhan would have to take her to the neurologist.

"Yeah," Maeve groaned. She let Siobhan move her over to a low retaining wall. The other people moved aside only reluctantly and Siobhan had to use her size to physically take over space, making them move.

They sat down and Maeve fell into her, her eyes closing. She fell asleep. Siobhan held her, and rocked her, and talked in low, soothing tones. Maeve would need to recuperate. The seizures exhausted her, even though they usually only lasted a minute or two.

People walked by, some staring, most not. Siobhan wished they had a more private space, but the seizures never came at convenient times, never gave her any time to prepare. Seizures don't care about privacy.

She touched Maeve's hand and found it cold. Her head lolled on Siobhan's arm, and Siobhan rubbed her cheek gently. She held her on the retaining wall and stopped noticing the people around her, and she waited for Maeve to wake up.

***

Finn sat hidden in the library, feeling like his mum could see him. He kept looking behind himself, just checking that she hadn't magically appeared in the stacks. He felt silly, since he knew that as soon as he saw her tonight she would ask what he had done, and would know exactly where he had gone.

In front of him lay biology and anatomy books. He found this kind of stuff endlessly fascinating. Siobhan would usually let him accompany her to Maeve's various doctors' offices where he would ask a million questions that the doctors would bemusedly answer.

Today he had trouble concentrating though, as the field outside the window radiated with sun, clean and clear, and the grass shone a rich green. Other kids milled around outside, chatting, laughing. Usually he didn't feel like hanging around with them, not that he usually could even if he wanted to. Most of them didn't seem very interesting. He didn't even have the excuse of having been bullied in school, he really hadn't been. Mostly the other kids found him polite but aloof, and after some brief conversation they would just wander away. He felt happy to let them.

However, today he wished he knew some of them better. Not to whack them with a jock strap, but just to hang out, have an idle conversation, maybe have someone to watch a movie with instead of his mum, who liked cheesy horror films. Today, now, he wished that he had some friends to hang out at the 7-11 with.

He got up and distractedly closed and stacked the books, his attention focused on the window. He gathered his books in one hand, his bag and jacket with the other and made his dreamy way out the door, dropping the books on a re-shelving cart.

The hallway sounded quiet, currently thin on students, only a few slouched and chatted at the far end, waiting outside a door to a classroom, perhaps waiting for some club to start. He walked past them and out the large double doors, the sun making his eyes water and squint as he stepped outside. He looked around to see if he actually knew anyone enough to approach them. His eyes slid around, noticing familiar faces, occasionally coming up with a name, but not really making a familiar connection with anyone, until he saw the group of black outfitted, long limbed skulkers half hidden in the bushes to his right. A group of Terry's friends, but no Terry. He had talked to some of them a few times, on the rare occurrence of Terry having a chat with him. He closed his eyes and tried to think of some names. The tall, painfully thin one he knew as Luther. The large girl standing like an obelisk of self-consciousness beside him, Neka. The other, shorter boy had PE with him and Terry, but the class had split into two groups for the first semester, so Finn didn't know his name.

Finn felt a little awkward about just walking up to them. He stood watching them, their voices muted. He wondered if maybe Terry had asked them to wait for him and maybe he might show up soon. Then Finn would feel better about approaching them. Had Terry been at school that day? Finn tried to recall if he'd seen him. The only class they shared, PE with Mr. Mackelin, hadn't happened today. Finn opened his eyes and looked at the little group of death kids and decided maybe today he wouldn't manage to find something to do. Maybe he'd just head back to the library and see if they had any good DVDs. He turned to go and heard the big door behind him thump open. There stood Terry, tall and thin, arms bare in a black t-shirt despite the cool air, a long black coat tucked under his arm. He slouched in a way that made him seem shorter, but he stood easily six feet tall already, and loomed over Finn's five foot four.

Finn coughed and squeaked, "Hey," at him.

"Hey, Finn. What's up?"

"Oh, you know, just hanging out. I got some time to kill."

"You don't have your sister today?"

"Naw, she went with Mum today, so I have some time free."

"That's cool. So what are you going to do?" Terry pulled a

pack of gum from his pocket and started shoving pieces in his mouth. Finn watched him with amusement. He seemed to not know that eating ten pieces at a time might seem extreme to others. He'd done it as a kid, too. Terry caught Finn's eye and motioned an offer of some gum.

"Thanks," Finn said, sliding a piece out. "I don't know what I'm going to do. I have a couple of hours. What are you up to?"

"We're going to head over to Neka's. Her parents are away, so we're going to hang out there, maybe raid their liquor cabinet. Do you want to come?"

"Uh, sure. I probably won't drink though. Stomach problems," he lied. His mum didn't like drinking, and although she likely wouldn't get mad at him, they would have to have a talk about it if she smelled it on him. He liked to avoid those talks.

"Whatever, we aren't going to force you. C'mon then."

They walked over to the group together, and the other kids gave him the once over.

"Hey, Scary," said the little one whose name Finn couldn't remember.

"Fuck, Jono. Quit calling me that shit," Terry said, gum smacking.

"Yeah!" Neka joined in, and punched Jono in the arm, hard. Jono fell to the side a couple of steps.

"Ow! Fuck Neka, lay off," he whined, rubbing his arm. "What are you, his body guard?"

"No," Neka laughed. "I just wanted to whack you."

"Well don't do it." Jono turned his annoyed face to Finn.

"Who's this?" he asked, looking at Finn but asking Terry.

"It's my friend, Finn. He's going to hang with us for a bit. That okay, Neka?"

"Yeah, sure," she nodded.

"Cool, thanks," Finn said. He followed them from the school, the two tallest boys loping in front, Neka and Jono behind them, with Finn trailing.

To Finn's surprise, they had to catch a bus to Neka's house. "Where are we going?" he whispered to Terry at the bus stop.

"Over the bridge, is that okay?" Terry asked. "Neka lives out of bounds. They used to live here, though."

"Oh. That's fine. I don't know if I have bus fare." He searched around in his pockets and found a dollar. "I have a buck." The others weren't paying attention, they argued about some band Finn hadn't heard of, about whether they warranted the price of a ticket to see.

"Oh, we can handle that. Neka. Neka! Hey, can you front Finn some bus fare? He doesn't have enough."

They all stopped and stared at Finn.

"Uh, okay, sure, no problem." She reached into a large and scraggly bag she carried and produced a couple of loonies. "Here." She thrust her fist at him, and her hand was warm and moist as she shoved the coins into his hand. Her awkwardness made him feel even more awkward.

"Thanks," he said quietly. He worried that she felt pushed into doing it, but Terry said, "You're the coolest," to her, and a large smile spread across her full cheeks as she blushed. Terry had that effect on people. People just liked him and wanted to be liked by him, and not just his Goth friends, either.

They all got on the bus and the trip took just twenty minutes over the bridge north. The size of Neka's home surprised him, accustomed as he was to the apartment buildings and bungalows of his East Vancouver neighbourhood. He usually only saw such houses from the outside, on rare trips to the ferry, or the occasional outings through North Vancouver with his mum.

Neka's house had three floors, and the bottom one had large rec room with a pool table, huge TV and a bar. They went in and Neka told them to do whatever they wanted. Terry put on the stereo, and the other two started up an Xbox, slumping down on pillows on the floor. Neka went behind the bar and took out a book with plastic covered pages and began to flip through it. Finn felt a bit out of his depth and just stood in the doorway, watching everyone and staring with curiosity around the room.

"Well, are you coming in?" Neka asked from behind the bar. "Shut the door."

"Oh, yeah. Thanks." Finn shut the door and sat on a stool by the bar. "What are you looking for?"

"I don't know. A drink recipe to try. Unless you just want a beer?" She blinked her mascara and eye-liner coated eyes at him.

"No, I'm fine. Maybe you have a Coke or something?"

She gave him a strange look and then opened a fridge behind her and handed him a can of Coke. He thanked her and opened it and took a few sips, feeling it remove the top layer of skin from his throat. He coughed. Neka occupied herself with bottles and shot glasses, measuring out different coloured liquids. "Your parents don't mind you drinking this stuff?"

"Mind? Well, they would if they knew, but they're almost never home, so they don't notice. And it's not my parents, it's my mum and her husband."

"You're here alone?"

"The cleaning lady comes two times a week, but she's

usually gone when I get home. Now leave me alone while I make these, you're distracting me."

"Oh, sorry. I'll go over there." He pointed to Terry on a large sectional in front of the TV, sprawled watching the video game. Luther sat in a jumble of limbs on the cushions on the floor, all sharp elbows and knees, and he obviously had the better gaming techniques, since Jono swore nonstop beside him, scowling over his low points. The constant sound of gunfire from the game fought with the music Terry had put on, and Luther just kept laughing at Jono and telling him to learn to play. Finn sat next to Terry with his drink. "What game is this?" Finn asked Terry.

"I don't know, some first person shooter. Hey Luther, what game is this?"

"Uhhhh," Luther drawled, "I'll get the case."

"Will you all shut the fuck up! It's seriously hard to play with all this yapping and music and shit, god-damn!" Jono shouted.

Terry reached out a long leg and kicked Jono lightly in the ass. "Calm down, it's just a game, and it's not our fault you suck at it. Luther always beats you. He always beats everyone because he's good. So relax or quit playing and let Finn have a go."

"I know it's just a game! And I beat Luther once!" Jono growled at Terry.

"Yeah, when Luther was on acid and kept staring at the screen and asking where the colours were going. Doesn't count."

Luther laughed, "Hahaha, what a night that was. Remember I started saving worms that had crawled out on the side-walk? Phew."

"You did what?" Finn asked.

32

"Well, I was worried they would bake when the sun came up," Luther laughed. Terry laughed as well.

"No, I mean, you were on acid?"

"Well, sure I was. Who does stuff like that straight?" Luther shot him a quizzical look.

"You've never done it?" Jono snarled, not looking away from his game.

"No. No I haven't," Finn answered and took a big drink of Coke that made him cough when it went down his throat wrong.

"Never mind," Terry said, pushing his long dark bangs off his forehead. "It's no big deal."

Neka came over with a tray with drinks on it. They had umbrellas and fruit on swords and maraschino cherries in them.

"What the hell are these?" Jono asked, pausing the game and poking his with his finger.

"Um, well, I sorta screwed up, so it's a new drink. I call it...Fruity Hell."

"Looks toxic," Luther mumbled around a mouth of fruit. "We're probably going to need insulin."

"They might be good," said Neka, sitting on the couch next to Finn with hers. "What are we listening to besides you guys bitch about the drinks?

Terry had eaten his fruit and was picking his teeth with the little plastic sword. "Johnny Cash. He's cool."

"Isn't he country?" Neka said, grimacing from her drink.

"Yeah, but still cool," Luther opined from the floor, his drink between his legs as he pushed the controller madly.

"Will you shut up!" Jono yelled as his soldier exploded into little bits. "I'm trying to play here!"

Terry looked at Finn and rolled his eyes, then leaned forward and with a long hand pulled the controller from the smaller boy's hands. "You're cut off. You have issues about games, we aren't going to shut up and sit here and watch you lose. Let someone else play for a bit."

"What! But, I...You. Oh, fine! Fine! Fuck this. It's a stupid game anyways," Jono said. He grabbed his drink and flopped down in a chair to the side, slopping some of his drink on his shirt, then angrily trying to brush it off. He sat there looking miserable.

Terry held the controller out to Finn. "Wanna try it?"

"Me? Uh, sure. I won't be much good, I don't play them often anymore." Finn squirmed a bit in his chair. He felt out of his depth and a little bit like Terry thought he had to protect him, like a special case. He took the controller and sat on the pillow on the floor, carefully putting his pop beside him.

Luther unfroze the game and at first the split screen confused Finn. He kept looking at Luther's side and thinking that he controlled that action. He died three times in a row, which amused Jono, who kept making snide comments. Terry had to keep telling Jono to shut up.

On his fourth try, Finn had a breakthrough and managed to fully concentrate on his side, and to his surprise he managed to keep going for a reasonable amount of time. When he did finally die, Luther paused the game and turned to him and said, "Not bad, Dude," to which Terry and Neka added their approval. Jono had grown completely silent during the game, and he grunted in a non-committal way.

"Thanks." Finn felt himself blushing. "Someone else want to play? I've got to head home soon." He looked at his watch.

"Naw, Luther can play solo if he wants," Neka said, pulling a cherry stem from her mouth. "Why do you have to go?"

"I've got to help my mum with my sister. Mum has lots of homework to do, so I usually watch my sister."

"Your mum has homework?" Jono asked sharply. "Why does she have homework?"

Finn turned to him and contemplated not answering, but everyone except Terry was looking at him. Terry had stopped tapping his tooth though, and sat still waiting for the answer. "She's in university."

"What?" Jono squawked. "How old is she? Did she have you when she was five?"

Finn felt angry at Jono's question, "She's 39. She just decided to go to university," he answered, trying to sound stern.

"And how old is your sister?"

"She's nine."

"And she can't watch herself?"

Terry sat tapping his knee, purposely not looking at anyone now.

Finn took stock of Jono, his messy, long, dyed hair, small frame, his greasy face. He decided he might be able to beat him up if he needed to, and decided to tell him to go fuck himself, but then he heard his mum in his head say, *People don't get it, all the time*, and so he exhaled slowly instead and looked at Jono straight in the eye. "No, she can't. She had a stroke just before she was born. She also has a bad seizure disorder, so she can't be alone for most things. Like having a bath. If she was left alone in the bath and had a seizure she could drown."

They sat for a minute and then Luther said, "I didn't know kids could even have strokes."

"So, you're sister's retarded then?" Jono growled from his chair.

Terry shot forward and grabbed Jono's arm. A sudden and satisfying look of fear clouded Jono's face. "You watch what you say. You're being really fucking ignorant," Terry cautioned.

"Let go of me!" Jono sputtered. After a minute, Terry let him go.

"No," Finn said coolly, "she's actually quite bright in many ways. She has a lot of seizures which affect her memory, and she has trouble understanding people because she can't read body language. But it wasn't the part of the brain that processes higher cognitive functions that was affected."

"Wow," Luther said, "I have no idea what you just said, but it sounds complicated and messed up."

"Yeah," Neka said weakly from the couch.

They fell silent for a few minutes while they watched Luther. Terry tapped a front tooth with his little finger, Jono sulked, and Neka tried not to look as if she kept glancing at Terry out of the corner of her eye. Terry still had his long black coat on and Finn wondered how long he planned on staying. The silence felt awkward to Finn, and he found himself longing for his mother's lack of self-consciousness, her ease at talking to people.

Finn cleared his throat, Terry tapped, Neka snuck looks, Luther shot and killed enemy combatants, and Jono sat and stared daggers at the lot of them.

Finn finished his Coke and squeezed the can, causing it to crumble. "Well," he said, getting to his feet, "thanks for having me over, Neka, but I have to go."

"Whatever," she said. "I guess you can come back some time, I'll see you around school anyways."

"Sure," Finn made his way to the door. "See you guys." Luther grunted at him, and Jono snarled a goodbye.

"Wait, Finn, I'll go with you." Terry got up and strode to the door.

"You don't have to go, Terry," Neka said, startled, rising to her feet. "I was going to make you dinner."

"Naw, thanks anyways, but I have to go. I'll come back tomorrow maybe, okay?"

"Yeah, sure." Neka looked sad and flopped back down on the couch. "I'll see you later." She kicked at the coffee table leg.

Terry and Finn left, Finn trying to keep up with the tall boy's longer stride. He felt relieved that he wouldn't have to figure out how to get back on his own.

***

My eyes are closed. It looks pink and bright with them closed.

My head hurts. It seems very loud here. It keeps getting louder. I hate it! Shut up!

My arms are around something soft. I squeeze. It feels like Mummy. I smell. It smells like Mummy.

I'm so happy she's real. I'm happy I'm not dreaming her.

I can't open my eyes. I'm just going to stay here, I want to say to her. I'm going to stay here. I'm going to hold you.

But I can't say anything.

"Shh," Mummy says. "Shh, I'm here. I'm here."

Don't go away.

***

After about twenty minutes, Maeve had recovered enough to walk slowly into the student union building. Now they didn't have enough time to eat and drink outside in the sun. They had to get their drinks and make their slow way to Siobhan's class. Siobhan carried both her bag and Maeve's bag over her shoulder, and Maeve's now cold hot chocolate in her left hand, and guided Maeve around with the her right hand. She watched her carefully and paid attention to all obstacles in her path, offering directions: step up, mind the bump, watch out for the pole. While Maeve usually did need direction, she was particularly clumsy after a seizure.

They arrived at Siobhan's class, a large one with amphitheatre seating so that everyone looked down on the professor. Siobhan manoeuvred Maeve to the very back and settled her in with her drink which Maeve drank with bleary determination. Siobhan pulled some snacks and books out of her bag to keep Maeve content.

Maeve had great deal of experience in university classrooms. She knew the main rule: keep quiet so everyone can hear the professor. For the most part she did very well at this, although occasionally she felt compelled to share a thought about the book she read. Siobhan whispered, "Shhhh," and wrote a note to her about being quiet, then gave her the pen to write her own note. This started a lengthy exchange, with Maeve writing laboriously in her shaky block letters.

be quiet, the teacher is talking
WANT TO KNOW HOW TO BE A FIREND???
a friend you mean? how?
DONT B A BULLY
that's good advice. now be quiet and read so I can listen
I AM BORD OF THIS BOOK
read another one
WANT TO DRAW WITH ME

okay, you start by drawing the evolution of dinosaurs
OKAY

Maeve sat and drew figures of different dinosaurs that looked like they'd suffered from horrible nuclear accidents. Siobhan watched out of the corner of her eye. She added a flower or cloud when prodded by Maeve and furiously scribbled notes in between contributions.

Maeve finished her drawing. Siobhan took the note pad and started to write Maeve another note when Maeve suddenly slid under the desk and crawled under Siobhan's skirt. Because they sat far behind everyone, no one saw Maeve do this. Siobhan sat and blinked straight ahead, trying to figure out what to do. Even though no one saw them, Siobhan felt conspicuous about being the only student with a small person wedged into her clothing. She tried to reach under and pull Maeve out, but Maeve giggled, and several nearby students turned to look.

Siobhan sat.

Maeve started to tickle her knees.

Siobhan slapped a hand over her mouth and started to move her knees around, which just made Maeve more excited. The professor looked at her curiously and stalled in his lecture. Siobhan reached under and grabbed Maeve's hands and clamped her shoulders between her knees. Then, as quietly and nonchalantly as possible, she pushed her chair back which pulled her skirt off Maeve. Maeve looked very pleased. Siobhan gave her a stern look, or what she hoped would pass for one, and then calmly pulled her out from under the table and deposited her in her chair.

Maeve looked deflated.

Siobhan gave her a hug and wrote another note to her:

just a few more minutes Honey. please read a
book

U R A FUN BLOCK

Siobhan smiled sadly at her. Certainly, sitting in lectures
didn't offer much fun for a young girl. She pulled Maeve
close to her, opened a bright picture book, and pointed at
it. Maeve settled into the embrace and went back to
reading.

Finally, the class ended and all the other students filed
out while Siobhan packed up her table. The professor, a
young man likely her junior by at least ten years, packed
up his stuff as well. As she made her way down the stairs,
holding Maeve's hand, he looked up at her and said, "Can
I talk to you for a minute?"

"Sure," Siobhan said, moving in front of his desk.
Maeve tried to push open the heavy wood door to leave,
but couldn't budge it.

"Mummy! Let's go!"

"Just wait while I talk to the teacher, Hon." She turned to
the professor. "Yes?"

"I just wanted to say that you shouldn't bring, um, guests
to class with you."

"Well, she's not a guest. Sometimes I have to bring her
or miss class. I did approach you at the start of the
semester and ask if that would be okay."

"You did? I don't remember that."

"I do it with every professor at the beginning of each
semester." Siobhan looked calmly at him. It had become
routine for her to do this every semester, and she had not
had a professor yet that had said no. She always made
sure that Maeve remained as unobtrusive as possible, and
willingly removed her on the one occasion where she'd
gotten too noisy. Most professors ignored Maeve, but a few

40

had gone out of their way to talk to her. One had kindly ignored Maeve while she played with a magnet set a couple of steps behind him the whole time. Maeve had been younger then, of course.

"Sometimes she's unable to attend school for a good reason, but I like to miss as few classes as possible," Siobhan said.

"Well, if she's ill you should drop her at a daycare. There's one here on campus."

"Daycare?"

"I understand it can be hard to be a mother attending university, which is why you and your husband should consider putting her in a daycare."

"I think you might be a tad confused about daycare."

"What do you mean?"

"Well, first, Maeve is nine. Daycares are for preschool children."

"Oh."

"Also, you don't just drop a child, let alone a sick one, at a daycare. People can wait years for a daycare spot. And the kids go full or part time, not casually."

"Oh."

"And the daycare here on campus would be completely unaffordable to me, I'm a single parent."

"Oh."

"And, most importantly, Maeve is highly special needs. I've never just dropped her anywhere. When she started Kindergarten, I had to sit outside her class all day for two weeks or they wouldn't let her go. Simply walking in and saying, 'Here's my high needs, sick child for one day,' will never work."

"Oh. I didn't know, she doesn't look like...anything...I

mean she looks..." he trailed off.

"Mummy! Now!"

"Just a minute, Honey." She looked at her professor, who shuffled papers on his desk. "She doesn't look like anything might be different about her? I know. It's been the story her whole life. It's okay, but lots of things can be happening that you can't see. Do you have kids?"

"No."

"Yeah. Well, I will miss time if she's sick enough, but if she's able to go with me, I need to bring her because I can't miss too much time. Luckily, it always ends up that she only needs to go to each class once or twice at the most. If she gets too rambunctious, I'll take her out, but there are people in the class who talk through the whole thing and she's not that bad."

"Well, okay. Just, you know, some of the students might have wondered." He coughed.

"Do you want me to send out a class email and explain?"

"Yes, that would be good, thank you."

"Okay, I'll do it tonight."

Siobhan said goodbye and moved toward the door.

"Finally!" Maeve said as they were leaving.

"Honey, you're being a bit rude. I had to talk to my teacher."

"I'm sorry, Mum, I need to go to the bathroom."

"Okay, it's right over here."

Maeve ran ahead and completely overshot the bathroom. Siobhan had to shout, "Stop!" at her and usher her into the bathroom. She pushed Maeve toward the handicapped stall and they both went in. Maeve needed help getting her pants down and then sat with her feet off the floor.

"Mummy, why do you always come in with me?" She asked this every time.

"You know why, Maeve. Why?"

"Because of my seizures?"

"Exactly. Mummy's too fat to slide under the door, and who wants to slide around on the bathroom floor?"

"I hate my seizures."

"Yeah, I can understand that. Now hurry up, Mummy has to go, too."

"I'm hurrying. Jeez, you are so bossy."

Siobhan wiggled waiting for Maeve to finish. She felt a great deal of pressure in her abdomen, but when she sat down to pee, she didn't feel relieved. She tried shifting on the seat and it lessened slightly, but didn't go away. It felt like pre-menstrual bloating, but she'd just had her period. She pushed on her lower belly, but felt no pain. After they cleaned up and had walked for a bit, the feeling went away and she forgot about it.

Maeve, always a walking calamity, needed constant direction again on the way to the bus stop. She ran too far, or turned down the wrong way. She fell and skinned her knee, and then after crying over that, promptly walked into a pole. Siobhan held her and sighed. *This girl simply cannot be left to her own devices.* Here, in the middle of campus, a million seemingly harmless items presented an obstacle course for her.

Maeve stopped crying, and Siobhan kissed her all over her face.

"I love you," she said.

"I know! You tell me all the time! You are obsessed with me."

Siobhan smiled and they walked to the bus.

From: School Board Office, District 36
Re: Entry into after school program

Dear Ms. Lynch,

This letter is to inform you that we have reviewed your request to reassess our decision to not allow your daughter to attend the after school program, Excel, at her school, Herbert Elementary.

While the program is intended to support students who need extra help with school work and social skills development, we are afraid that we cannot accommodate Maeve's health concerns, specifically her seizures. We cannot accept the liability that she would present to the staff, some of whom are volunteers.

Thank you,
Mr. Husik
District Superintendent

***

When Siobhan and Maeve got home, much later than usual, Finn had not arrived yet. This fact surprised and pleased Siobhan, who had expected him to break his promise to find something to do after school.

Siobhan went through the cupboards to see what bastard dinner she could put together and came to the immediate conclusion that she should go to both the regular food bank and the university one this week. She hadn't tried the university one yet. She worried it would mostly have Ramen noodles and Kraft Dinner, which didn't hold much promise for a family of three. How many ways could she even prepare those? She feared she might well find out. She'd go on Thursday if she could remember to phone them first.

She felt the same pressure in her lower belly that she'd felt earlier in the day. She slammed the cupboard door shut and ran to the bathroom, nearly killing herself on Maeve's shoes in the hallway.

"Ouch!" she shouted.

"What? What's wrong Mummy?" Maeve shouted from the living room, where she lay flopped on the floor reading a book.

"It's okay, Hon, I'm okay. Just come put your shoes away." She ran in pulling up her skirt and sat down. The pressure remained after she was done, so she just sat and waited for it to pass, pushing on her abdomen.

The front door opened, Siobhan could hear it from the bathroom.

"Finn!" Maeve said and ran to him, jumping on him.

"Hi, Maeve." He gave her a big hug.

"Who's that?" Maeve asked, pointing at Terry.

"Finn! Is someone with you?" Siobhan asked from the bathroom.

"Yeah, Mum, Terry's here."

In the bathroom, Siobhan quickly rose and slammed the bathroom door shut. She sat and listened to the conversation out in the hall.

"Maeve, this is Terry. You remember Terry, my friend?"

Maeve looked blankly at Terry, still wrapped around Finn's neck, even though she had grown too big for him to hold her.

Finn extracted himself from Maeve's arms, and Terry

looked down at her and smiled. "Hey Maeve. You got very tall. Do you remember me?"

Maeve shook her head no. "You know what? I have a dragon collection."

"Oh, yeah?" he said, then realised she expected more. "How many do you have?"

"How many do I have?" she whispered to Finn.

"Twenty," Finn whispered back.

"I can go get them. But I don't know where they are. Where's Mummy? She knows."

Siobhan yelled through the door, "I'm in here, Hon. They're in our room, on the shelf in the closet."

"Thank you. I'll be right back!" she shouted at Terry and ran off down the hall.

"I'm sorry, the dragons are very important to her," Finn murmured to Terry.

"It's okay," Terry shrugged, and they both went in and sat on the couch, pushing things that had been heaped on it aside. They heard the toilet flush and Siobhan came out.

"Hi," Terry said from the couch.

"Hey, Terry, good to see you. We haven't seen you in awhile."

Siobhan looked over his head to toe black outfit, dyed black hair with blonde roots, and spiked arm jewellery. "I see you've accepted death and chaos as your personal saviour. Good for you."

"Mum!" Finn looked wide-eyed at her, but Terry just started laughing.

"I never heard it put that way before." Terry smiled at her.

"Would you two like some tea? I was just about to start dinner."

"What are we having?" asked Finn.

46

"I don't know. We may not know even when we're eating it." She looked over her shoulder into the kitchen.

"Sure, some tea would be nice," Terry said.

Maeve came into the living room with a large stuffed poodle. "I thought you were getting your dragons?" Siobhan stroked Maeve's arm.

"Oh. I forgot. Where are they?"

"In your closet, on the shelf."

"Okay!" Maeve bounced back out of the room. Siobhan went into the kitchen. With some effort, and the lucky discovery of a can of stewed tomatoes, she managed to start preparing a dish she hoped resembled pasta. *Do people usually put chickpeas in pasta? Oh well, if you can't go for tasty, you have to go for healthy.* She put the kettle on and listened to snippets of murmured conversation from the boys in the living room, to Maeve bouncing in and out of the living room as she repeatedly forgot her mission to get her dragons, and to Finn's good humour at having to get up eventually and help her get them. They both came out holding dragon figures, Maeve with one in each hand and Finn with the front of his t-shirt used as a sling to carry the rest. He dumped them on the floor and earned a lecture from Maeve on proper dragon transport. Maeve set them up on the floor, giving careful information about their various types and habits. Siobhan felt impressed with Terry's patience as Maeve repeated herself often, not remembering which ones she had already covered.

Finn and Terry eventually left Maeve playing with her dragons and wandered off to Finn's room. Siobhan took their tea into them and found them playing Finn's ancient PlayStation and laughing together. She felt happy that Finn had finally gotten some regular kid time and left them to themselves.

She went back to the living room where Maeve sat playing with her dragons, and picked up a text book and highlighter and read while dinner cooked. Maeve continuously interrupted her to ask questions and share important information about dragons. She forgot immediately each time Siobhan would ask her to let Mummy read. Either Finn would need to watch her, or she'd need a movie put on for Siobhan to get any real work done in the evening, but she resolved to not interrupt Finn tonight. She wondered if Terry would stay for dinner. She knew the boy lived with his grandmother a few blocks over, she would likely expect him home soon.

Siobhan made sure she had enough clean dishes in case Terry stayed, and put the pasta on to boil. Pasta from the food bank always came bulk, in bags with twist ties. Siobhan had a whole half a cupboard full of mostly empty bags of pasta. She kept meaning to consolidate them, but they made her depressed to look at. She had gone to a single mother's food bank once, much harder to access than the regular ones, and had felt so happy when she'd gotten lots of dairy products, yogurt and cheese, until she'd gotten home and realised all of it had a thick coat of mould covering it. Three containers of yogurt and not one edible one. Two of her friends had discovered the same thing. She'd never gone back. Instead, she made do with the random offerings at the regular one: hot dog buns, no hot dogs, bags of bulk dried chicken noodle soup, random wilted vegetables, and interesting mixes of beans and lentils. She had come to despise the saying that beggars can't be choosers, implying that they shouldn't complain. Whoever had coined it had obviously never gone to the food bank. You had to have genius skills to make a meal out of what you received.

With dinner ready, she took Maeve to the washroom to wash her hands and had to ask her repeatedly to stop washing random items sitting on the counter. If she left Maeve to her own devices, Maeve would stay in the washroom for the evening, completely unaware of the passage of time. Siobhan manoeuvred Maeve to the coffee table and set her up sitting on the couch, pushing the coffee table closer to Maeve. Then she went down the hall and knocked on Finn's door.

"Yes?" he shouted through the door.

She opened the door and found both boys slumped on the bed playing a video game. Terry's legs stretched almost clear across the room.

"Dinner's ready. Terry, it's not much, but you can stay if you want, unless your grandmother is expecting you."

"Well, she won't be expecting me, but no thanks, I think I'll head out. Thanks though."

"Okay."

She left and a few minutes later Finn and Terry followed her out, Terry carrying his long trench coat which he put on near the door.

Finn looked a bit nervous as he said, "Okay. Well, nice to see you Terry."

Terry looked down at him and said, "Yeah, you too. Later."

"Later," Finn stammered back. Siobhan knew this meant, "Let's do it again, soon. Your presence is pleasant to me, and I feel we will have a continued friendship based on mutual respect and camaraderie." Siobhan smiled to herself, thinking of all the subtext that lay under their general grunting and stunted language.

"Well, that was nice," she remarked to Finn in a casual manner.

"Hmm?" Finn tried to look nonchalant as he served himself dinner.

"What was nice?" Maeve asked, a fine tomato sauce moustache on her face as she sucked up noodles.

Siobhan turned to Maeve where she sat next to Siobhan on the couch. "That Finn found something to do. That he hung out with his friend. We need to make it so that he can do it more often." She turned back toward Finn's direction. "What were you doing before you got home?"

Finn came out of the kitchen and sat in the chair across from them with his bowl and looked at her, his pale blue eyes, so like Maeve's, looking a bit sheepish. "We went with some others to Terry's friend's place. Neka."

"Where was that?"

"Over the bridge in North Van. Her place is huge."

"Her parents were okay with that? Just having new people show up?"

"Uh," he stalled, shoving in a mouth full of pasta and then looking down, disgusted, at his bowl. "Mum, did you put chickpeas in here?"

"Um, maybe?"

"Well, that's just gross." He started fishing chickpeas out with his fork and shoving them to the side.

"Hey, they're full of fibre and protein. Besides, you should just be happy I didn't serve them for breakfast with milk! Chick-ee-Os I call them. They start soggy, they stay soggy."

"Ew, Mum, really."

"Okay, okay, don't appreciate my culinary visions. See if I care."

"I appreciate you, Mummy," Maeve chirped and spat a chickpea out on the coffee table.

"Uh-huh, I see that." She leaned sideways and gave

50

Maeve a kiss on the cheek.

They ate in silence for awhile. "Finn, you didn't answer my question."

"What question?" he asked innocently.

"Did her parents mind her just bringing you over?"

"Well..."

"Well?"

"They weren't exactly there."

"What does that mean? Parts of them were there?"

"No," he sighed, exasperated. He felt like withholding the information, but he wasn't sure why. "They weren't there. They're on vacation somewhere, so Neka stays by herself."

"How old is she?"

"I think she's fifteen."

"But that's so young to be by herself. Is she lonely, all by herself?"

"I don't think so, I think she has her friends over. And there's a cleaning lady."

"Well, now I'm worried about her."

"Mum, you haven't even met her."

"Still. Feel free to invite her over for dinner or a movie sometime."

"I'll get right on that. I barely even know her, Mum."

They finished eating and Finn took Maeve to the couch to read with her a bit. They read health pamphlets from the pharmacy. Every time they went to the drug store Maeve loaded up on pamphlets, which she read voraciously and then discussed ad nauseam. She had pamphlets on acne, diabetes, menstruation, osteoporosis, ageing, and breast examination, just to name a few. Tonight they were reading one on spinal cord injuries.

Maeve grabbed hold of Finn's arm and said earnestly, "If

I fell off a waterfall I would crack my spine."

"True, you might get really hurt," Finn answered.

"You know when a good time to crack your spine is?"

"No, when?"

"Never!" she said, shocked that he hadn't thought this through.

"Well, what about International Spine Cracking Day?" Siobhan volunteered from the kitchen table, where she was organising class notes and planning her schedule.

"Just don't attend that. Also, I don't want to ever have anaesthetic." Maeve held up a hand in emphasis.

"Anaesthetic?" Finn asked, to clarify.

"Yes, anaesthetic. It's a perfectly good word, Finn, I learned it when I was four. And what about that clear thing?"

"What clear thing?" Siobhan puzzled.

"You know, the clear thing with the two big things?"

"What on earth are you talking about?" Finn's eyes narrowed in controlled humour at her.

"You know! When the doctor yells, 'CLEAR!'"

Siobhan and Finn both started laughing. Maeve sat smiling happily, not sure what had made them laugh, but enjoying it just the same. When she had gone off to read in bed, Finn told Siobhan that maybe Maeve shouldn't be allowed to read all those pamphlets, maybe they made her worry too much about her health.

Siobhan looked at his concerned face, impressed with the maturity and concern he had for his sister.

"You know Hon, I think it makes sense that a little girl who has so many doctors and regular testing done would be acutely interested in health issues, I think it actually helps her to understand that lots of people have health issues. Plus, she has so much curiosity. That's a very good thing. No, I think it's good for her to learn all this stuff."

"Okay, Mum. I guess it is better than feeling alone in the world."

Siobhan hugged him. And he actually tolerated that for ten whole seconds before squirming away and heading off to his room.

Chapter 3

The next morning was gloomy, a wind howled, and rain cycled through torrential to merely soaking and back again. Maeve had trouble getting out of bed, but Siobhan had to get her up and moving early to go register for a time slot at the food bank. Maeve grumbled and groused, so Siobhan unearthed the old beat up wagon from the storage closet, wrapped her up warm and dry, and gave her an umbrella to hold. She'd have to take her down to register, then back up to school, then head back down to the food bank to wait to be called in. If she missed the call she'd lose her place.

The wagon had one wonky wheel that made it hard to pull, as she faced into the wind and slogged through large puddles, hoisting the wagon over curbs with no cut-outs, or around them on the soggy ground. Siobhan kept her head down, switching arms back and forth as each one complained under the strain.

Maeve weighed about ninety pounds, and with the uncooperative wagon it felt like a hundred and fifty. Finn would've come along to help, but he had farther to go than Maeve, and Siobhan didn't want him to get to school late when there was a choice.

Siobhan arrived at the community centre soaked to the bone. The place already had a great number of people in line to register. Siobhan pulled the wagon over to a heat register where she would be able to see it from the line-up, and left Maeve happily reading a book while she stood in line. They asked for verification of income, address, family size, proof of children, and proof that she didn't get child support. That last one caught her off guard. They hadn't asked that before.

Siobhan looked at the woman behind the table, who looked exhausted already.

"Are you new here?"

"Yes," the woman answered. Her eyes were watery and red behind thick-rimmed glasses.

"Well, is that question listed on your form, because I can't understand how I would prove not getting something."

"Well, it's not listed, but we're supposed to verify income."

"Yes, I understand, and I've given you those documents. Both list my income sources, so I don't know what else to show you. I don't get child support. The only way I can think to show you proof of income, other than those documents, is to get naked and show that I have no child support on me."

The woman looked confused, and very concerned that the large wet woman might hop up on the table and take her soggy clothes off. A supervisor chanced by and, to everyone's relief, it all got sorted out. After getting a number chit, Siobhan started back out. Maeve became even more grumpy at having to leave the comfortable warmth of the heater which had made her grow drowsy.

Finally at the school, Maeve stubbornly refused to go in, saying she wanted to stay with Siobhan, and that school bored her and the teachers yelled at her. Siobhan pulled her out of the wagon.

"Honey, Mummy has to go back down there and pick up groceries. It won't be fun. It'll be much better for you to stay here. And the teachers don't yell at you, you just have trouble understanding the difference between strictness and yelling."

"No, Mummy, I want to go with you. I can help hold the groceries in the wagon."

"No, Hon. I can't pull you and extra stuff, go inside. I'll talk to your teachers and you can spend the morning just reading, okay."

"Okay," Maeve sulked.

Siobhan held her hand and led her in, helped her take off her coat, and sat her at her desk. Then she pulled Maeve's worker aside and explained that Maeve felt grumpy, so they should just let her read and listen.

The rain came on strong again as Siobhan continued her trek, and cars threw up plumes of water as they raced by. Siobhan had to pay attention to where the water had become deep on the road and attempt to time her passage carefully to avoid getting drenched. Back at the community centre, things had wound down to a crawl and Siobhan spent two hours in the lobby waiting to be called. She drank coffee and worried over Maeve's increasing dread of school. It saddened her that Maeve had come to dislike school so much. She'd started daycare at two and a half and, yes, it had proven very difficult for Siobhan to find one. She'd phoned up several and taken Maeve in, a sweet little toddler, so happy, blonde hair shining, and she charmed each one. But as soon as Siobhan mentioned seizures, the interviewer looked scared and suddenly doubted whether the facility could handle that. Did Maeve need medication? How often did they happen? What about liability?

Siobhan could've pushed, but if staff expressed such immediate fear then she doubted their ability to care for Maeve during a seizure. Siobhan finally found one about a mile from where she lived and they welcomed Maeve without fear, a great relief to Siobhan.

She'd faced the same problems when she enrolled Maeve in school, later. Despite having six hundred students, they had no staff trained with first aid for seizures. Things had grown harder as time went on, because many of Maeve's learning and social problems didn't manifest early on, only slowly revealing themselves as Maeve grew older. All of the great services they'd received before kindergarten, such as speech therapy and physiotherapy, had become unavailable when Maeve entered school. Now the only services available were supposed to come through the school, and they proved almost non-existent. Siobhan attended every meeting with the support staff and special needs co-ordinator, sharing specialist reports and assessments on Maeve, but the information grew in complexity and most of it, especially all of it together, confused the teachers and support workers. Everyone saw Maeve through his or her specific experience filter and specialty. They had trouble with Maeve's entirety.

At one o'clock the food bank volunteers called her into line up for food. It didn't usually take so long, but there had been a mix-up with the allotments. Siobhan lined up with other single mums and families. Little babies in strollers, mums packing food in with them somehow, going from table to table and getting handed their quota of dry goods, old bread, canned goods, all of it a jumble of food. Some of the babies cried, dressed too warmly for the long wait inside. The children made it slow going, as women tried to keep track of little ones and the things the volunteers kept telling them. When Siobhan's turn came, she pulled bags out of her purse and tried to pack them as quickly as possible. By the time she finished, it had drawn close to two o'clock and she remembered that she needed to speak to Finn's teacher. Siobhan stopped outside the door, loaded wagon behind her, and puffed out her cheeks in thought. She wanted to drop the bags and wagon at home before going to his school, but realised that she had no time. The rain still came down steadily, so she tied the bags shut and started off.

The rain had stopped by the time Siobhan arrived at Finn's school; she felt damp and hot from wearing her raincoat. She had forgotten to ask Finn what room his class with Mr. Addel was in and so decided to go to the office, looking in whatever doors stood open along the way. Rooms of students sitting in desks staring at teachers. *Just five or ten more years of that ahead of them*, she thought. *Well, the lucky ones, anyway.*

The kids in the classrooms craned their necks to watch her as she passed, the soggy woman with the soggy wagon, squeaking down the hallway. At the office, the receptionist behind the counter slid a glass partition open and crinkled her nose at Siobhan's dishevelled and red-faced appearance. Siobhan just stared back at her and asked for Mr. Addel's room number. The receptionist gave her a second floor room number, and Siobhan glanced speculatively back at her wagon. "Do you have an elevator?" The woman pointed vaguely down the hall and slid the partition shut again. Siobhan wrestled with the idea of standing there and running a wet pink tongue all around the glass, but then thought she might save that for teacher-parent interviews.

She took the creaky elevator up to the second floor and found the classroom. Finn looked out and saw her, and she waved at him. He smiled a grimace at her and she took the cue and stepped out of view. At ten to, he came out. She could hear Mr. Addel giving him a hard time, and the laughter of some of the kids. She'd felt okay about this until now, thinking Mr Addel just needed some information about the situation, but when Finn came out with big red cheeks of embarrassment, Siobhan started to feel anger at Mr. Addel. She gave Finn a quick hug, before he ran off to collect his sister. The bell rang and Siobhan waited as all the kids filed out, chatting and laughing loudly with each other. When the crowd thinned enough to get through, she wheeled her wagon through the door and saw Mr. Addel putting his notes in his briefcase. He ignored her obvious entrance. Siobhan waited for a moment, but when he didn't acknowledge her she let the handle of the wagon fall on the floor with a bang. He jumped and looked at her with annoyance. "Oh, excuse me," she said with exaggerated politeness, "I see I've startled you." She smiled at him.

"Yes," he said. "May I help you?"

"Yes, you may. I'm Finn's mum. Finn told me that we needed to talk about his needing to leave early Mondays, Wednesdays, and Fridays."

"Ah, yes. I feel that we seem to have a misunderstanding. You need to make other arrangements so that Finn doesn't miss part of his class. I understand how hard it must be, being a single parent, but you must make the extra effort, or else change...whatever it is you do on those days," he said, a static smile held on his face.

"There are no other arrangements to make. For this term at school, Finn needs to pick up his sister because my classes run late on those two days. I'm in university, and it takes me time to get back to this side of town."

"Well, put her in an after school program."

"Really, you don't think I tried that?" Siobhan felt her hand tapping against her leg in frustration. "She wasn't accepted in the free after school program at her school because they consider her a liability, and before she can go to the other one, we have to wait for supported child care funding."

He looked steadily at her and she back at him. "Well, then get a neighbour or a babysitter for her."

"Look, Mr. Addel, perhaps you don't understand the depth of my daughter's condition, which is fine, but none of what you suggest would be so easy, even if I had the money to pay for it which I don't. I can't just get someone to look after her. I try very hard to take classes that match her schedule, but it's not possible all the time. Now, I have already cleared this with the principal. Finn studies hard, he does his work, and he doesn't deserve to be made to feel bad about the situation. You don't have to like it, you don't have to understand it, you just need to stop harassing him. I will go to the principal if you keep doing it."

Mr. Addel had stopped looking so haughty. *He usually has all the power in here.*

"Well, school work is important and..."

"Yes," Siobhan cut him off. "It is important, and if he starts slacking then we will have to address that, but he's not slacking now."

Addel coughed and looked down at his briefcase.

"I hope we've reached an understanding here, Mr. Addel."

"Yes, I think we have. Thank you for coming by."

Siobhan left him standing in his classroom and pulled the wagon back to the elevator. She just wanted to get home now, and hoped that this discussion stuck. She didn't want to have it again.

But she would.

***

I'm not allowed on the playground. Except the swings. I can go on the swings. Mummy says that the doctors told her not to let me on high places. Unless her or Finn stay right next to me.

I think the doctors worry too much. And Mummy worries too much,

Jani is pushing me on the swing.

"When is lunch over?" I ask.

"It's not lunch, Maeve, it's almost the end of the day, remember?"

"Oh." I feel so stupid. Why can't I remember stuff? People get mad at me, forgetting all the time. I feel like crying. "Can I go on the slide?"

"I've already explained that you can't Maeve. Find something else to do."

"Okay."

I walk over to a bush. The leaves are green, and when I touch them, they're sticky. They stick to my fingers when I pull my hand back. I have to rub them between my fingers to get them to fall. They twirl down, one after the other, laying on the ground at my feet.

Jani freaks me out by yelling, "Maeve what are you doing?"

She made me jump.

"Oh Maeve, look. You've pulled all the leaves off this branch." "I just did some of them."

"Maeve, look at the bush."

I look at the bush. It has branches at the top. One whole branch has no leaves. I look down at the leaves on the ground. How did I do that?

"I'm sorry I didn't mean to do it."

61

"I know. Let's just not do that anymore. Look, your hands are all sticky. Come, we'll go wash them."

Jani takes me to the teacher's bathroom. I use this bathroom because I can't be alone. I turn on the water and wash my hands. I like the water running. It looks pretty, and it sounds neat when I splash it.

The water is cold. It makes my fingers sting.

"Hurry up and finish, Maeve. School will be out soon."

"Okay."

I wash them some more.

"That's enough now."

"Okay." I feel like Jani's going away.

"Maeve!"

She freaked me out again.

"Sorry. I'm sorry."

Jani shuts off the water. Then she gives me paper towels.

"Okay, let's go back outside."

"Okay. Will lunch be over soon?"

"Remember? It's the end of the day? Your brother should be here soon."

"Oh."

***

Siobhan planned to meet Holly at the student union building at lunch. They both needed to go to the university food bank as well as the regular one, because the end of the semester was always financially difficult. Siobhan idly read the jobs posted on the huge board in the lower hallway. Many student jobs remained vacant at the university, and Siobhan kept imagining how great it would be to have one at the library, or in one of the departments.

But she just didn't have the extra time to do it. Maeve needed so much attention. Extra time away from her mum would really upset her. But still, Siobhan daydreamed of a regular pay-cheque. Receiving it in her greedy hands, running off to the bank to cash it, signing her name on the back after staring in awe at the, hopefully, long string of numbers on the front. Well, most jobs direct-deposited pay these days she supposed. Ah well, she'd ask them to make up a prop cheque for her to work out her fantasies on.

Siobhan had grown used to all sorts of deprivations. Never having money for movies, for dinners out, for days with the kids more expensive than the park or the beach. Only the most basic utilities, and never any new clothes for the kids or her, just thrift store stuff for the kids. All of that had become so normal that Siobhan barely registered it any more, even as she sat in classes with well-heeled eighteen-year-olds who came from middle-class and upper-middle-class families. Siobhan had sat in lectures and listened to professors say things that assumed that they, all the students, had middle-class backgrounds. Siobhan always spoke up to excuse herself from that assumption.

"Uh, I'm not middle-class. I've never been middle-class."

One professor had said, "Yes, we all like to think that."

"What does that mean? Do most middle-class people think themselves higher, or do they want to slum it? I am not middle-class," Siobhan said, feeling patronised.

The professor had just coughed and gone back to his lecture. Siobhan found it darkly amusing how poverty existed as solely academic to most of the people she encountered here.

Siobhan liked reading the ads for housing. Four bedrooms on the West side for $3000 a month, one bedrooms for $1500. Who the hell could pay that? Obviously, lots of the students here, or their parents, could. It would be great to live in one of them though, so close to the campus. Ah, but she had history as a long-time, East Van hippie, not a yoga pants wearing yuppie. Although, some yoga would do her good. She surreptitiously poked her butt cheek. And, let's face it, the Drive had been taken over by yoga people, the hippies had lost.

"Reading the ads makes you touch your butt?" Siobhan jumped at the voice behind her.

"Jeez, you scared me. And yeah, what the hell, we all need a hobby." Siobhan tried to look annoyed but smiled instead.

"Hobbies are for people who can't get jobs. So, yeah, that's us."

"Butt touching could lead to a job. Of some type. I could be a doctor! They touch butts."

"Sounds like you've been to career counselling."

"No, I just picked up a brochure, actually. I'm an English major. Actual career planning gives me hives."

"Right. You're not all focused like us in the art department." Holly patted her arm in consolation.

"Want to get a coffee? I think we have an hour until the food bank said they'd open for us."

"Yeah, and then let's go outside for a bit. This place is about to get all busy for lunch."

They made their way upstairs, got coffees, then wandered outside and found a semi-secluded bench beside the aquatic centre. Siobhan's friend produced two battered and stale cigarettes from a candy tin and they smoked them, feeling light-headed and bad for smoking.

64

Siobhan blew a long streamer of smoke and then coughed. "Do you ever get a sharp pressure below your bellybutton, and then when you pee it feels like something's pushing your guts?"

"Pushing inside?"

"Yeah."

"No, I've never felt like that. Have you been feeling that?"

"Yeah."

"Maybe you should get it checked."

"Lady, I can't go to the doctor for *me*. All my doctor energy goes for the kiddo. Besides, it's probably just gas or something. Or a prolapsed uterus."

"Oh! I hope that's not what it is."

"Why? It could work for me. I could take two seats on the bus. I'd be all, 'Hey, buddy, can you not clearly see my uterus sitting here?'"

Holly laughed at her. "You could get it a jaunty hat."

Siobhan caught the eye of a young man sitting on the next bench, looking at them with fear. Siobhan smiled at him, and he smiled nervously back and returned to the large text book on his lap.

"Did you bring bags with you?" Siobhan asked Holly.

"Yeah," she said and shivered, pulling her coat around herself. She had a long slender body, with long fingers and short brown hair.

"Are you cold?"

"Yeah, aren't you?"

"No. this weather is lovely." Siobhan had a body built for cold weather. Actually, hard work in cold weather: tall and fat.

Holly surveyed the heavy clouds, trying to understand what Siobhan saw as lovely. It would rain soon, and the wind came in cold gusts, bringing leaves down with it. Siobhan stuck her face into the wind. She liked cold wind, liked it strong enough to blow her sweater open and take her breath.

"So, how's Allyssa?" Siobhan asked.

"Oh, good. Having trouble getting to school. I keep having to write her notes, which the teachers say aren't good enough."

"Maeve has trouble getting to school, too, and sometimes they bug us. It's just so hard for her, and I still have to dress her and brush her teeth and stuff for her. She gets really grumpy and I don't like to argue with her or then she goes to school grumpy. School's already hard enough for her."

They sat quietly for a minute.

"Do you ever think about dating again?" Siobhan looked at Holly.

"Dating? Yeah, sometimes, but Allyssa wouldn't like it and I never have free time anyways. Are you thinking about it?"

"Sometimes, too." Siobhan hadn't dated anyone since she'd gotten pregnant with Maeve. Maeve took all her time. After all the time she spent in hospital, in the special care nursery, hooked up to monitors, getting the horrible anti-seizure medications that would make her gag, and the weeks it took Siobhan to get her to breastfeed because she'd had so much sedation. Siobhan hadn't even thought about doing anything but parenting since then. And then school, when she'd decided to go.

"But how would I do it, with school, Finn, Maeve, and Maeve's millions of doctors. I'd be lucky to eke out an hour a week. Month. Year. Although, that might be the perfect relationship for me."

"Someone you never saw?"

Siobhan smiled at Holly. "Yeah."

Holly smiled, too.

Siobhan finished her coffee. "And then there's finding people who are okay with the kids coming first. It's a tall order."

"Yes, I know what you mean."

"I don't want to be a single mum who has a string of partners running through her life, like most serial monogamists. I don't even want people to develop relationships with the kids unless they feel like continuing them if we break up. For Finn it would be very hard to get used to someone and then have them disappear."

"Allyssa would just be jealous. She doesn't even want a brother or sister."

"It's hard to share when you've been an only kid for so long." "Well, it's time to go down to the food bank."

"Okay." Siobhan stood and stretched her arms up. Her knees cracked.

They entered the student union building again, fighting against throngs of students leaving for the next class. They went downstairs and walked around looking for the food bank, which turned out to be in a small, windowless room off a side corridor. A young woman met them.

"So, you're Siobhan and Holly who called yesterday."

"Yes," Siobhan said. "Do you want to see our student ids or something?"

"No, no. It's okay." she pushed her long, blonde bangs out of her eyes, then fished some keys out of her pocket. The door opened and revealed metal shelves stacked floor to ceiling with boxes and cans.

"Holy crap," Holly said under her breath.

"So, on the phone you said you had dependents?"

"Yes, we're single parents." Siobhan couldn't take her eyes off all the stuff in the room. She wondered how much they gave out. Students could only use the food bank here twice a semester. "So, what do we do?"

"Oh, just help yourselves."

"What?" Holly said sharply.

"Take as much as you need. I'll come back in a few minutes, okay?"

"Okay. Sure. Thanks." Siobhan and Holly stepped in and stared, turning in a circle together as the door shut.

"Oh my god, look at all this stuff," Siobhan said, "and look, there's interesting stuff!" She reached out and grabbed a can off the shelf. "Look! Lychee nuts!"

"It's unreal. Does no one ever come here?"

"I guess not. Or else they get a lot of stuff. Who knows?"

They went through each shelf meticulously, filling every bag they had and even filling their jacket pockets. Overloaded and with shoulders screaming, they made their way to the bus loop. Siobhan felt good at the prospect of making a meal for the kids tonight that she wasn't going to have to convince them to eat.

***

Finn had had a good day at school. He'd aced a biology exam, remembered to bring a lunch, and Terry had sought him out to hang with him and the others. Luther and Neka acted friendlier to him today, although Luther seemed the type not to let actual events happening around him affect him much. He seemed to disappear into his own thoughts a lot.

Jono hung back quietly, acting bored with the conversation.

Finn felt more at ease, watching the others smoke,

joining in on the conversation. Terry rewarded him with smiles and winks, and Neka put her hand on his shoulder at one point. Finn blushed, because girls didn't make a habit of touching him. He didn't smoke when offered one, because his mum hated cigarettes.

When the bell rang, they made their slow way in together. Inside the doors Terry said, "So what are you up to this weekend?"

Finn stopped and felt a bit nervous. "Uh, not much. I think my uncle is coming into town. That's all, really."

"Huh. Well, we're hanging out at Neka's all weekend. You want to come hang out?"

"All weekend?"

"Yeah, her parents are still gone."

"Well, I can't tonight. Maeve and I watch movies together Friday nights, but maybe tomorrow, I'll see."

"Okay." Terry pulled a pen out of his pocket, tore off a piece of cardboard from Neka's cigarette pack and wrote down a number. "Here's Neka's number. Give us a call and let us know."

"Okay," Finn said happily, and took off for class.

Finn felt happy through his last two classes, even more so when Mr. Addel only stood still and watched him leave the class room at ten minutes to three. His mum hadn't told him what she and Mr. Addel had discussed, but whatever she said had worked, and Finn felt relief.

On the way to pick up Maeve, Finn stopped at a little corner store and pulled out the five dollars his mum had given him in case he forgot his lunch. He bought some chocolate bars for him and Maeve when they got home. The man behind the counter counted out the change into his hand and Finn thanked him and turned to go. Then he stopped, and for no good reason that he could think of,

Finn turned back and asked if he sold single cigarettes. The man looked at him through dusty glasses and said, "Aren't you a little young to smoke?"

Finn noticed a heavy accent in his voice, European or Russian or something.

"Uh. No?".

The man looked at him a moment longer and then said, "What the hell, I'm not a cop." He reached under the counter and pulled up a colourful cardboard box. "How many?"

"Uh, well, how much are they?"

"Twenty-five cents each."

"Okay, I'll take two." Finn handed him two quarters. The man handed him two cigarettes quickly, like he thought that would make him less guilty. Finn murmured, "Thanks," and left, the two cigarettes held in his hand. He stopped outside, feeling very conspicuous, and fished in his backpack for his pencil case, into which he put the cigarettes. He walked away as quickly as he could,

What did I do that for? He wondered, holding his backpack stiffly on his back as if the contents might burn him.

When he arrived at Maéve's school, he found her on the swings with Jani nearby. Maeve shouted, "Finn!" and looked like she wanted to run to him but couldn't figure out how because of the swing. Finn walked over and grabbed her swing, stopping her movement from behind. She turned in the swing and grabbed him, putting her face against his coat.

"Hi Finn," came her slightly muffled voice. "I'm so glad you came. Are you going to stay at school with me?"

"No, silly," he said, putting his hand on her head. "It's time to go home."

"Oh! Okay."

Jani came over to them.

"Hi Finn," she said, smiling at him.

"Hi," he said shyly. "Did she have a good day?"

"No seizures today, and she was pretty involved. She joined in during class discussion, told everyone about dinosaurs."

"She does know a lot about dinosaurs." Finn smiled at his sister, who bounced up and down next to him, doing her own thing.

"That she does."

Maeve chimed in, "Birds are related to dinosaurs. I learned that when I was four."

"Yes, they are, Maeve." Finn adjusted his backpack which had slid down one arm because of Maeve's bouncing.

"I wanted to tell you that Maeve's teacher is away on sick leave. We don't know how long. We had a temporary sub today, but we'll have a new one on Monday."

"Oh, I hope she's alright. I like Mrs. M."

"I think she is going to be okay. Yes, she's very nice."

"I like her, too," Maeve bounced at them.

"Okay, well Mum will come in and talk to the sub next week I'm sure."

"Yeah, that would be good. I'll tell them. Have a good walk home," Jani smiled at him. "See you Monday, Maeve."

"Okay, bye." Maeve started pulling him.

"Other way Maeve," Finn corrected her.

"Okay."

They walked towards the sidewalk and climbed a small set of stairs. The rain that had only been sputtering came down harder.

"Here, let me do up your jacket." Finn stopped her. After zipping her up they started walking again. Maeve sidled up to him and put a hand on each of his hips, forcing him to walk at a strange angle.

"Maeve, what are you doing?" "I'm carrying you. I'm a dragon."

"Oh."

"We will stop at that tree there, and I will inject dragon DNA into you. Then you will be a dragon, too."

"Okay"

"You will never get the dragon DNA out. I got mine when I was four." She pushed him to the tree, "Okay, kneel down."

"But the ground is wet. Can I just crouch?"

"No," she said with absolute conviction.

"Okay then." He knelt, feeling cold water soak into the legs of his pants. Maeve pretended to ready a needle for the DNA transfer.

"Okay, this might hurt." She looked at him earnestly, her pale blue eyes sparkling at him.

"Oh no. Well, I guess it's worth it."

She put her hand on his arm and pressed, then stepped back. "Okay, now you're a dragon. It might hurt. I gave you DNA."

"Right. Well, actually, I feel pretty good."

Maeve perked up.

"Great, now we can fly home."

"Awesome, let's go."

They flew home.

Chapter 4

Siobhan felt anxious about her brother's visit. Ten years older than her, Thomas had already moved out by the time she'd turned six. Their mother had died when Siobhan was ten, and their father drank himself to death five years later. Thomas and Siobhan rarely saw each other during that time. Thomas had hated their father. He had alcohol and drug problems himself, and was the bad apple of the small interior town they had been raised in. Thomas had been a petty criminal who was often in jail, and he and their dad would have long vicious fights that often ended with them beating each other. Thomas didn't see their father for the last year of his life.

After their dad had died, Siobhan ended up on her own. Thomas had been too messed up to be much help. When she was twenty-one, she received a phone call from Thomas, and agreed to meet him for dinner even though she didn't want to see him. He'd become a born-again Christian after joining AA, and while Siobhan felt happy that he'd stopped drinking and doing drugs, he had grown even more judgemental and bigoted than before. He was worse than their father, and had that moral concreteness that people get when they credit god with their redemption. Thomas' more homophobic sentiments had worn her patience thin the last time he had been visited her four years ago, and they had fought bitterly. He'd slammed out the door with barely a goodbye to Finn, the unexpected shouting making Maeve cry.

Finn had felt the tension between them, and he remembered the fight they'd had the last time they'd seen Thomas. He remembered the yelling in the kitchen, Uncle

Thomas slamming down a coffee cup so hard it broke, the gunshot sound of it making Maeve jump nearly off the couch. After that, when Uncle Thomas called, his mother would say a few things to him then pass the phone to her son.

Finn liked his uncle. He thought he resembled Thomas more than his mother. Thomas never made flip and off the wall comments. He didn't approach everyone in the way his mother did, chatting with anyone nearby, or saying weird things to the cashiers at the store. Once, Finn had stood by mortified as his mother arm wrestled a barista in a coffee shop, both of them laughing and having a good time as everyone turned to watch. Finn felt less conspicuous going places with Thomas.

Siobhan thought that Finn pined for a male figure in his life, and her jeans and mac jacket clad brother fit the bill, with his old Valiant that smelled of stale cigarettes and fishing gear. It used to smell like stale beer, too, before Thomas found Jesus and joined AA. Thomas hunted, and cut wood, and still lived in the small interior town they had grown up in. He felt like a step back in time. She supposed that Thomas' life might appear interesting and easy to Finn, and simpler than a mum in university and a sister who operated on a different level than everyone else. Finn had a complicated life.

Now, after an absence of some years, Thomas was coming for a visit tomorrow, at Finn's request. Maeve didn't remember him, of course, and she didn't like talking to people on the phone. As Siobhan got her ready for bed, Maeve asked a million questions that Siobhan didn't want to answer. Sitting up in bed, an encyclopedia of the human body open on her lap, Maeve swallowed her seizure medication with a sip of water and asked Siobhan, "Is

Uncle Thomas your uncle?"

"No, he's my brother."

"Your brother? Did you play with him when you were little?"

"Not really, he's a lot older than Mummy"

"So he was grown up when you were born?"

"No, but still older." Siobhan lay down next to her and rested her head against Maeve's hip. Maeve's skin was warm and soft.

"Oh. Why doesn't he live with us?"

"Well, adult brothers and sisters don't usually live together."

"Except me and Finn, right? And you. We will always live together, but in a different house. A house with a chimney."

"Oh, yeah, for sure. And you can have your own room and bed."

"No! I will always sleep with you."

"Hon, someday, far away, when you're at least forty-five, you might have a boyfriend, or girlfriend, who knows? And you might want to sleep with them. You certainly can't sleep with them in here."

"Well, they can just leave then! What about my seizures? I need you if I have one."

"Yes, you do, But hopefully one day you won't have them, or so many of them."

"I forget, is Uncle Thomas your uncle?"

"No, my brother."

"Can I write him a letter for when he comes?"

"Can't you just tell him?"

"No, I'll forget and it's important."

"Okay, wait, I'll get you some paper and a pen." Siobhan lifted herself up with a sigh and wandered into the living room. She returned and handed Maeve a notebook and a pen.

"What's this for?" Maeve asked.

"You wanted to write Uncle Thomas a letter."

"Oh. Okay."

Siobhan lay down again and turned her back to Maeve. "You can have ten minutes, then it's sleepy time, 'kay?"

"Okay."

Siobhan lay next to her daughter and let her mind wander. Maeve laboured away at her note. Siobhan could feel her soft leg against her back, hear the tightness of her breathing as she concentrated. She could hear Finn cough in his room down the hall. She looked at the floor near her bed, a jumbled mess of her and Maeve's clothes, books, and a stick from the courtyard. Next to the stick she saw the small grater she used for garlic. She reached down and picked it up. looked at it for a minute, then put it on the night stand to take with her when she left.

"Maeve, are you done?"

"Almost."

"Because it's time for bed."

"Almost!" Maeve panicked.

"Okay, hon, don't freak out. I'm not going to tear the book away. Two more minutes."

"Okay, Mummy." Maeve kept making big block letters, her penmanship awkward and hard to control.

Siobhan lay still next to her, closing her eyes and drifting.

She had just about fallen asleep when Maeve announced she had finished her important letter. Maeve handed it to her. Siobhan's vision blurred at first as she tried to read it, crinkling her eyes and moving the paper back and forth trying to bring it in to focus. She read aloud.

DEAR READER,

I HAVE SEEN MANY CRICERES. I HAVE SEEN TROLLS AND OGERS. I HAVE DEIP MAX DRAGONS. THE LEADER OF THEM ALL LET ME TAKE SOME HOME. I SEND MY LOVE TO MY WIFE AND MY MUM.

"Well, that's very good, Sweetie. I can totally see why you had to let him know this."

"What?"

"Never mind. It's a good note. Now, it's time to lay down."

"Okay, just let me fix this." Maeve began to fuss, fluff, and arrange her collection of stuffed animals and pillows on the bed.

She had a specific system, all the animals had a place on a pillow. Her little throw pillows had to be specifically arranged, one on each side and one under her back. Siobhan knew that Maeve had already done this tonight. She would not remember though, and arguing with her would be futile as it would simply cause her to panic about needing to do it, and worry about Siobhan getting mad at her. Maeve often felt bad, even when things had nothing to do with her. Siobhan didn't like that.

Siobhan waited patiently for her. Well, patient on the outside. Inside she grew more worried about how tired she would feel when she finally got to work on her reading tonight. It always happened that she never got to things until Maeve had gone to bed.

When Maeve had finished fussing, she lay down, slinging a long bony leg over Siobhan's legs.

It's weird how used to being uncomfortable I've become, Siobhan thought, as she adjusted Maeve's leg to a slightly less uncomfortable position.

Thomas appeared in the doorway, broad shoulders, stocky frame, standing about as tall as Siobhan. He smelled like tree sap and motor oil. He wore the same style of plaid flannel mac jacket that he'd worn since he turned fifteen. Finn looked small and awkward standing in front of him in the doorway. Thomas ruffled Finn's hair and grabbed him up in a big bear hug. Finn groaned happily as Thomas crushed all the air out of him. Maeve hung back and chewed on a nail, smiling nervously.

Thomas put down a wobbly Finn and looked down at Maeve. Maeve was nervous, unsure of the identity of the large man in the doorway.

"Hey there, l'il miss," Thomas said, bending down towards her.

"Hi," she squeaked out, still chewing her nail.

"Do you remember me?"

"I'm not sure." She didn't look at him directly. She looked a little bit sad. "Did I meet you when I was four?"

He reached out a large, hairy, work abused hand and rested it on her shoulder. "And other times. It's okay if you don't remember me right now, I haven't seen you in a while. Can I give you a hug, anyways?"

She looked at him hopefully and nodded her head yes, quickly, like she felt afraid he would change his mind. With much more care than he had shown Finn, he gave her a light hug. Finally, Thomas turned to Siobhan who had stayed back and watched from the living room.

"Hey there." She moved toward him awkwardly and punched him on the arm.

Finn felt nervous for them as he watched them in their agony of indecision, each of them shuffling and hemming and hawing, unsure how to proceed. Eventually, they hugged in a way that looked more like wrestling, ending the hug as if they had received a shock.

Well at least they hugged, and nothing was broken this time, Finn thought

Thomas cast a furtive eye around the messy apartment. He cleared a spot on the couch with a sweep of his arm and sat down. Finn sat down cross legged on floor facing him. Maeve stood behind Siobhan, peeking around Siobhan's hip. Siobhan stood aimlessly, unsure of where she should sit. She rarely felt nervous around people, and the unfamiliar emotion just added to her discomfort.

Finn asked Thomas about his trip down, enjoying his gruff voice and the smell of outdoors coming off him. He smelled vaguely like cigarettes and his beard seemed crinkly and stiff.

Maeve wandered over from behind her mum and tried to sit on Finn's crossed legs, which didn't really work now that she'd grown so big. Finn grunted as she sat down on him.

"Are you living in the same place?" Finn asked. "The place in the picture you showed me? A little cabin by the river?"

"Yeah, yeah." Thomas rubbed his beard. "I still live there, been there eight years now. I like it, it's quiet, although last winter the power went out for three weeks. But I managed."

"Men have testicles to make sperm," Maeve said slowly and carefully. "It's all a part of nature."

Siobhan laughed, which made Maeve jump a little bit. Finn shot her a look of embarrassment. Thomas just stared and then said, "Uh, well I guess that's true."

"I know many ways to protect myself," Maeve said. "I

can teach you them if you want."

"Okay, that would be very nice of you, thank you. Maybe we can do that tomorrow?"

"Okay. Do you want to watch a movie with me?"

"Well, maybe tomorrow? I thought I might take you guys out for dinner that be okay?"

"You don't have to do that," Siobhan protested. "Really, I have stuff here to make for dinner."

"But I would like to take you guys out. We haven't seen each other for so long. I don't want you to cook, I just want to visit." Thomas turned to the kids and asked if they wouldn't like to go out instead.

"I do!" Maeve said. "I want to go out."

"Okay, guys, it's settled then. We'll go out." They all turned to Siobhan expectantly.

Siobhan felt weird about having Thomas take them out. She knew he was laid off from his tree planting job last month. He only worked in the spring and summer regularly. He did make pretty good money during the summer, but he had a tendency to think that helping her out gave him the right to comment on her parenting and life choices.

Siobhan took a deep breath, and exhaled slowly as they all looked at her. "Okay, let's go then."

They all got their coats on, climbed into Thomas' old beater Valiant, and went off for dinner.

***

Thomas tried to convince them that he would sleep quite happily on the couch, but Siobhan told him he didn't really mean that. The couch could only seat two people, it wasn't big enough for him to sleep on. No, she put her foot down, Finn would sleep in her large bed with her and Maeve and Thomas would take Finn's bed. Thomas felt happy to see that Finn's room had at least had a brief cleaning lately. This grew more important to Thomas when he found a doll's head, a whisk, a sand covered lip gloss, and a bag of cheezies in the couch cushions.

Nevertheless, Thomas couldn't help but react a bit negatively to the news that Maeve still slept with Siobhan. He had never thought the two of them should sleep in the same bed, or that Finn should've as a baby, either. Babies need cribs, he'd said. This time he only let a passing look of disagreement cloud his face. Siobhan didn't care what he thought about it, and he knew it. She had encouraged Finn to decide when he wanted his own bed, and Maeve slept with her because of her seizures.

Siobhan ignored his look of judgement. Well, actually, she rolled her eyes at it, but she didn't say anything.

So Thomas got Finn's room. The mattress felt saggy beneath him, obviously the thing had little time left before it would end up out beside a dumpster. An old desk sat in the corner, with school books on it, and an old McDonald's Star Wars cup sitting next to them. In front of the long window that overlooked the courtyard hung a spider plant in an old fashioned macramé plant holder.

"Finn, I think the plant's dead. Maybe you could still save it, though," Thomas said, taking it down and poking at it.

"No way, it took that thing forever to die. I hate spider plants."

"Oh." Thomas looked at it, then glanced at Finn to see if the boy looked serious. He did. Thomas shrugged and hung it back up.

Finn removed some towels that lay folded on the end of the bed and then changed the sheets. Thomas milled around the room, looking at the books on the shelf. One thing this family did not find themselves needing: more books. Every room had overflowing book shelves. On Finn's, Thomas saw science books, science fiction books, and the type of books that every English teacher he'd had in high school handed out, Penguin Classics. The mark of boring to Thomas. He pulled one out and looked at the cover.

"*Jude the Obscure*, by Thomas Hardy," he read out loud. "Have you read this?"

"Hmm?" Finn murmured, rising from his sheet adjusting and looking over at him. "Yeah. Mum loves Hardy."

"It looks depressing,"

"Yeah, it's not a happy book."

"Why do you read depressing shit? Why would your mum want you to read it?"

"She read that one for school. She liked it and wanted me to read it. She likes to talk to me about them, it's a thing we do. I don't read everything she reads, but some of it, yeah."

"And did you like this book?"

"Yeah, I did."

"What's it about?" Thomas sat down on the chair at the desk, turned on the light and thumbed through the book.

Finn sat on the bed and took the book out of his hand. "It's about Jude, this man who is poor but wants to go to university, but he can't because he's poor, and then he gets married, and then she leaves him and he still can't change his life. Then he falls for another woman, his cousin, and she marries someone else. And then they get together, have kids, and then everyone dies."

"Jeez, what on earth is the point of that??"

"Mum says it's about class and gender roles and shows that we've always had those same problems. That's why she likes Charles Dickens and Mark Twain. She finds them funnier, though."

"But your mum goes to school, to university, even though she's poor."

"Yeah, but it isn't free. She'll owe about $100,000 when she's done, at least that's what she thinks."

Thomas sat forward in his chair. "$100,000? Really? How on earth does she see that as worth it? Why doesn't she just quit and go get a job instead of doing this silly school thing? Honestly. $100,000? How will she ever pay that off?"

"She wants to give us a chance at a better future. And we'll always have to take care of Maeve."

"Well, why can't she just...learn to cut hair? Or bake? She took those baking courses years ago? Why not stick with that?

"She tried, but that didn't work, not with Maeve. Baking is not a flexible job. You can't just finish your muffins the next day."

Thomas saw that his questioning made Finn uneasy.

"Well, maybe. Anyways, I guess you shouldn't have to answer these questions. Go on, go to bed, I'll see you in the morning." Thomas stood up and pulled Finn up with him. He put his hand on the back of Finn's head and gave him a rough kiss on the forehead. "Go on, go on, you little genius. Sleep well."

"Okay, goodnight Uncle Thomas."

***

The next morning, Thomas awoke first and wandered into the kitchen, thinking he'd make everyone breakfast. The kitchen looked a fright, with dishes stacked precariously on the counters and in the sink. Thomas looked at them in dismay. He'd need to do them before he even attempted to cook. He emptied the sink, washed it out, and filled it full of hot, soapy water. The sound of dishes banging woke Finn and then Siobhan. They wandered in and Finn gave Thomas a hand while Siobhan sat in the living room looking annoyed.

With all the dishes washed, Thomas asked Siobhan what she had available for breakfast. Siobhan said, "Oatmeal."

Thomas hated oatmeal. He told Finn to grab his coat, they'd have to go shopping, and together they piled into Thomas' car.

Finn and Thomas pulled into the store parking lot and found it packed. They drove around the huge lot trying to find a spot, Thomas' jaw grew tight and stiff as he talked to Finn.

"Did I do something wrong by doing the dishes? I didn't mean to make her mad." He looked at Finn who craned his neck around looking for a spot.

"Well, I think she just feels bad that the house is such a mess. I think she wanted it better for your visit."

"Humph," Thomas sniffed. "Housecleaning is a mother's *job*."

He caught Finn's quick take of what he had said, "Well, it's supposed to be, anyways. It was that way with *our* mother."

This made Finn feel bad, but he didn't know exactly why, and he did not disagree with people unless he knew exactly what to say. "She does a lot," he managed, feeling awkward.

"Maybe she does too much."

Finn looked at him and shrugged. "Just maybe don't say housecleaning is her job to her. No one needs the rant *that* will bring." Finn looked earnestly at his uncle.

"Yeah, I think we can agree on that." Thomas puffed his

cheeks out. He knew how stubborn his sister could get when they butted heads.

In the store, Thomas walked quickly through the aisles, grabbing exactly what he wanted off the shelves with no comment, merely putting the items in his basket and heading to the next aisle. "Am I going too fast for you?" Thomas asked, thumping things into his basket.

Finn was a bit startled by the question. Had he been moving slowly? "No, no. I like it. I wish Mum shopped like this."

"How does she shop?"

"Well, you know how she is. She talks to everyone, and...to a lot of *things* as well."

"She talks to *things*? What *things*?" Thomas stopped and looked at Finn.

Finn smiled self-consciously. "Well, the last time we were here, she argued with a box of cereal because it was nine dollars."

"She argued with cereal? What did she say?"

Finn felt bad for mentioning it. Obviously his uncle didn't like some of the things his mother did. "Uh, you know, why was it nine dollars, how good could it possibly be, would it rub her feet while she ate it? That kind of stuff."

"Uh, huh, okay." Thomas whistled slightly through his teeth. "And what did you do?"

Finn smiled some more. "I became immediately and intensely interested in the price of the granola bars down the aisle."

Thomas laughed and grabbed Finn a one armed, manly hug, crushing him then releasing him with a strange intensity.

"And what about Maeve?" he asked. "How does she react to that kind of behaviour?"

"She either doesn't notice because she's flying around, or she laughs at Mum being silly. Usually the first."

"She's a different little kid, that's for sure. How does she do at school?"

"She hates it. Wants to spend all her time with me or Mum. It's hard for her, she doesn't understand the other kids and usually ends up doing her own thing. She'd rather read or colour."

"Does she have friends there, at school?"

"Well, the other kids are friendly to her, but they don't get her either. She's the queen of the non sequitur."

Thomas squinted at him. "What does that mean?"

"You know, she says things on a tangent. You'll be talking about something and she's usually just talking about something else. And she perseverates."

"And what does that mean?"

"She repeats herself, over and over, because she doesn't remember that she told you already."

"Oh, yeah, I noticed. Last night at dinner, the dragon stuff she told us over and over."

"Exactly."

"And why does she keep saying that everything happened when she was four? She must've said that fifty times last night."

"We don't know exactly. Mum thinks that she doesn't have memories but she knows other people do. She wants to be normal, so she makes up memories."

They turned down an aisle and found two young men it laughing about something they had found in the freezer. One man leaned heavily on the other and casually kissed his cheek. Finn heard his uncle make a grunting sound of disapproval, and turned to see him with his lips pressed firmly together. Without saying anything, Thomas turned on his heel and went to the next aisle. Finn looked at the two young men, who now saw him, and made an apologetic smile before following his uncle.

They made their way to the till and Finn helped his uncle put things on the conveyor belt.

Thomas paid. The checkout girl flirted with him, drawling a little bit and sort of letting her hand linger as she handed him the change. Finn noticed, but when he mentioned it to his uncle, Thomas looked surprised.

"No, she wasn't." He looked back through the door at the the girl, who smiled sweetly out the window at him, not looking at what she did as she scanned the next customer's goods.

"Yeah, she was totally hitting on you."

This made Thomas blush. "C'mon, let's go," he said gruffly.

Finn laughed and looked back at the girl, who now had angry customers glaring at her as she looked after Thomas.

As Finn turned back to Thomas, from the corner of his eye he caught a glimpse of a figure sitting against a pole in the parking lot, looking tired, with make-up smeared on her eyes.

"Hey, hold on," he said to his uncle and walked up to her. "Hey, Neka, how are you?"

She looked startled and seemed not to know him. The sun shone in her eyes and she put a hand up to her brow to shade them.

"Oh, hey. Finn, right?"

"Yeah," he said, "what are you doing out here so early?" Her face crumpled a bit and she looked choked up.

"I lost my keys and no one is there to let me in. I've

been trying to get a hold of the cleaning lady, but she's not answering her phone."

"Oh," Finn said.

His uncle, who had hung back, now walked up and stood beside Finn.

"What's going on? Do you know each other?"

"Yeah, this is Neka. We go to school together. This is my uncle, Thomas."

They both said hi to each other.

"Where are your parents?" Finn asked Neka. "Can you call them?"

"Not really. They're in Brazil."

"Who are you staying with then?" Thomas asked her.

"I just stay by myself, at home."

"Oh."

"Well, you could maybe come to my house. We're just hanging out. Uncle Thomas is going to make breakfast."

"Ah, that would be weird."

"My mum and sister are home, so it's guaranteed to be weird, but it will be okay. C'mon." Finn looked at his uncle for confirmation.

"Uh, yeah, sure. It'll be fine. Great. C'mon," Thomas said.

Neka sighed. "Okay, thanks. Beats sitting in the Safeway parking lot all day."

She got up and Finn was amused to see that she stood as tall as his uncle. They went together to the car.

***

Siobhan sat after Thomas and Finn left, feeling judged by Thomas' kitchen clean-up. She pulled over a nearby box and started tossing random articles in it. A book, a jar of pennies that Maeve had collected, some loose paper. Then she forced herself to stop, and sat back with a sigh. *Why do I care?* Her house existed in chaos. She didn't like it, but she normally felt at least some peace with it. She'd enrolled in school four years ago, and she'd accepted this trade-off not long after. It hopefully would change after school ended this year.

She didn't like the way she reacted to Thomas judging her. Their mother had always treated housework as the most important thing. She'd cleaned their house immaculately, the kitchen floor on her hands and knees, the dusting done daily. The smell of bleach had always lingered in the air. Her mother washed everything but them in bleach. And she'd acted like the two of them, Siobhan and Thomas, had absolutely no idea how to even wipe their own asses. Once Siobhan had approached the washer with some sheets and her mum had materialised out of nowhere, hearing the scream of cotton threads about to get abused, and torn the sheets form Siobhan's hands. Siobhan had never even attempted to do laundry again until after her mother died.

What I really should do is just toss most of this crap out. Just leave the couch, and one plate each. Plus forks and spoons I guess. She sat back and closed her eyes for a minute. *Just let it go. So what, if he did the dishes? I'm still doing the right thing by going to school. I hope.*

Siobhan laughed to herself.

She opened her eyes, got up heavily and shuffled down the hallway to her bedroom. Maeve lay snoring in the bed. Siobhan got in next to her and wrapped an arm around her slender body, pulling her close. Maeve stirred a bit then fell back to snoring. The little girl started jerking for a minute and Siobhan lay breathless, watching the seizure until it stopped. Then she drifted off to sleep, her chin buried in Maeve's hair.

She awoke to Finn standing at the end of the bed, shaking her foot by the toe.

"Mum, Mum, wake up, we're back. Uncle Thomas is starting breakfast."

Siobhan ran a hand over her face. "Okay Hon, we'll be there in a few minutes."

"Okay. I brought a friend home with us for breakfast."

"A friend? Who? Terry?" Siobhan asked.

"No, Neka. She lost her keys and couldn't go home because her parents are in Brazil. She's trying to get a hold of her cleaning lady. She was just sitting in the parking lot at the store and I thought it'd be okay to bring her home."

"Oh, of course, yeah."

Finn left the room, and Siobhan rolled over and shook Maeve gently. Maeve groaned at her. Maeve did not like to get up unless she awoke on her own, so she could lay in bed and read. Siobhan gave her kisses on her cheek.

"Honey, it's morning time, breakfast will be ready soon."

Maeve rolled on her back and caught her mother in a death hug. "I had a bad dream."

"Oh no, about what?"

"I don't remember."

"Well, I'm sorry you had a bad dream, but it's morning now."

"What's happening today?"

"Uncle Thomas is making breakfast, and then I don't know what will happen."

"Do I have school?"

"No, Hon, it's the weekend."

"What day is it?"

"Saturday."

"And there's no school on Saturday?" Her large eyes looked suspicious.

"No, there's no school on Saturday."

"Good!" she said, with the relief of someone who had just been told they will live.

Siobhan squeezed her tight. "Okay, time to get up."

"Can I lie here and read?"

"For a few minutes, yes." Siobhan reached down to the floor and grabbed some books and gave them to Maeve. The little girl looked very happy.

Siobhan went into the living room and Finn jumped up from where he sat next to Neka on the couch like something had bitten him. Neka gave him a curious look and then saw Siobhan standing there.

"Mum, this is Neka." He swept his arm out like he was demonstrating a showcased item. He took a step back and tripped over a basket of clean clothes and fell on top of a footstool.

"Jeez, Finn, relax a bit." Siobhan gave him a sympathetic look. "Are you okay?"

His face had turned red in embarrassment. "Yeah, I'm okay, I'm okay."

"Good. Hi, Neka." Siobhan said turning to Neka and introducing herself. "Would you like some coffee Neka? I made some this morning."

Finn had started to fold the clothes in the basket to distract himself from his embarrassment.

"Sure, thanks."

"I'll get it." Finn jumped up, knocking the folded clothes off his knee.

"No, Hon, I'll get it. You just sit still. Very, very still."

Siobhan went into the kitchen where Thomas had an array of pots and pans out and stood busily mixing something in a bowl.

"Good morning again," he said cheerily.

"Morning. Jeez, look at this, you're like a restaurant. What are you making?"

"It's a surprise. Out, out." Thomas shook a dripping fork at her.

"I'm just getting some coffee." She got some cups from the cupboard. "I have egg cups, if you want them."

"Oh, yeah. You have egg cups, I know. I washed about twenty of them this morning."

Siobhan smiled to herself.

"Do you need any help?"

"No, no, everything's going good. Is Maeve up yet?"

"Yep. She's reading."

"She likes to read, doesn't she?"

"Yeah, it's about her favourite thing ever."

"Does she understand what she reads?"

"Yeah, although she usually doesn't remember it. Unless it's about the body, dragons, or dinosaurs." She poured the coffees, put all the cups, milk, sugar and spoons on a cutting board, and went toward the living room with her makeshift tray.

"Could you guys clean off the table so we can eat?" Thomas asked as she started to walk away.

"Uh, we usually eat in the living room. The table's a bit of a disaster." She looked through the little pass-through from the kitchen to the table, piled high with papers and books.

He looked disappointed.

"Oh, you know, it's fine, we'll clean it, no problem."

Thomas smiled happily at her. "That's great."

Siobhan carried the makeshift tray into the front room and balanced it on the footstool Finn had fallen on.

"Here you guys go. Add what you want." She took hers and sat in her chair beside the couch. "So, Neka, Finn says your parents are out of town?"

Neka looked a bit uncomfortable about Finn's mum talking to her. She sat with her coffee in her hand and stared like Siobhan's question might be some secret test.

"Uh, yeah. They're in Brazil. They'll be back next week, and then they go to Quebec for a month."

"Is it hard, being on your own?"

"Mum," Finn said, worried about where this line of questioning was going.

"No, not really," Neka replied, sipping her coffee. "They leave me a credit card and money, and they phone once in awhile. I have friends over a lot, and the cleaning lady is okay."

"What's her name?" Siobhan tried to ask casually.

"Anna. She's Filipino, I think. She comes twice a week."

"And she has keys to the house?"

"Yes, she usually comes while I'm at school." Neka started picking at her leggings.

Siobhan found herself mesmerized by Neka's hair, which had all sorts of bits sticking off in every direction.

"How long does it take to do your hair like that?"

Neka laughed self-consciously. "Oh, about half an hour." She reached up and smooshed some flat.

There was a terrific thumping in the hall and Maeve burst in, wearing one of Siobhan's long skirts pulled up to her chest. She ran up to Siobhan and launched herself, slamming the edge of Siobhan's chin with her head and causing Siobhan to abandon her coffee in midair to catch her daughter. They went crash, the coffee went crash, and both of them ended up coffee-soaked and moaning over their respective injuries.

Thomas stuck his head out of the kitchen. "What the hell are you doing in there?"

Siobhan held her chin and tried to comfort Maeve, who had started crying. "Oh, nothing. Maeve just felt a tad exuberant this morning. Are you okay, Honey?"

"I'm sorry, Mummy, I'm sorry."

"It's okay." Finn reached over from the couch and rubbed her back. "It was an accident. Let's go and wash your face and get some real clothes on. You aren't big enough to wear Mum's skirts."

"Okay." Maeve let him take her off while Siobhan held her chin and picked up her coffee cup.

"Are you okay?" Thomas asked her.

"Oh, yeah, happens all the time. She doesn't process spatial information very well. She's always splatting into something."

"What information?" Neka asked.

"Spatial." Siobhan wiped her shirt with a cloth from the laundry basket. "She's missing that area of her brain."

"Oh, yeah, Finn said something about that, about her being retarded."

Siobhan's spine stiffened at the word. "No, she is not retarded."

Neka looked embarrassed and stared down at her coffee. "I'm sorry," she stammered,.

"It's okay, you didn't know and I told you, that's all." Siobhan tried to sound conciliatory. "Maeve does have some delays but we don't focus on them, and we try to

94

enable her gifts, which she does have, just like anyone else."

Finn and Maeve came back with Maeve wearing a ladybug costume she'd had since Halloween three years before. Finn caught his mother's look and shrugged. The legs of the costume rode up six inches, and the arms had a similar awkward fit. Finn, in turn, noticed the increased awkwardness in Neka's frame. Hoping to dispel it, he brought Maeve over in front of Neka and introduced them.

"Neka, this is my sister, Maeve. Maeve, this is my friend, Neka."

Neka looked up and said hi unenthusiastically. Maeve looked back and didn't respond.

Finn jostled her a bit and said, "Maeve, say hi."

"My mum says it's okay to masturbate, because everyone does it," Maeve said.

Finn and Neka froze, and for a minute a shocked calm settled in the room. Finn put a hand to his face and slid it down his nose. Siobhan started laughing and gathered Maeve in a hug.

"You know, Hon, you are very right, but generally that shouldn't be the very first thing you say to someone you're meeting for the first time."

"Oh," Maeve said, and laughed because her mum laughed.

Neka and Finn tried very hard not to look at each other, and when Siobhan said that Thomas wanted the table cleaned, Finn shouted that he would do it. He busied himself finding new dumping grounds for the vast accumulation presently cluttering every square inch of the surface. Neka just sat and concentrated on her coffee.

Breakfast had surprised Siobhan, who had expected scrambled eggs and bacon, Thomas' usual fare, and the only thing he'd ever cooked for her before. But he'd made crêpes, a little mangled but light and tasty, and stuffed them with whipped cream and fruit. When Siobhan enquired as to this sudden, and surprising, capability, he admitted to having taken some courses.

"Because I got bored with my usual stuff and besides, in the winter, when I'm laid off, the only other thing to do is drink." He looked embarrassed in the face of Siobhan's and Finn's compliments.

Maeve sat quietly while she ate, feeling shy and tense around Thomas and Neka. Siobhan and Finn kept prodding her to talk. If only Finn and Siobhan had been at the table with her she would've had an inexhaustible discourse on any and all of the things that Maeve found important.

"Mummy, what day is it?"

"Saturday."

"Is that a school day?"

"No, sweetie, no school today."

"Good."

And then, five minutes later, "Finn, what's going on today?"

Thomas kept saying, "Maeve, you already asked that," until his voice took on a characteristic terse tone. He did not have a great deal of patience under the best of circumstances, and Siobhan knew Maeve could present quite a challenge even to people more experienced with children.

After the fifth time Maeve had asked, Thomas said, "Maeve! Stop asking that, you know what the answer is!"

Siobhan put her hand on his arm and said, "I know it's trying Thomas, but she honestly doesn't know, because she doesn't remember she's asked this question. She's perseverating."

"Oh, right. Finn was telling me about that."

"Right, well, I understand that it's hard when she's doing it, but she can't help it. She keeps thinking about something that's making her anxious, but she doesn't remember asking."

Maeve looked sadly down at her plate while Siobhan explained this. "I'm sorry, I just forgot," Maeve said to her plate.

Finn leaned over and plopped some whipped cream on Maeve's plate, which had the desired effect of distracting her from the conversation. Thomas looked at her sadly.

Siobhan turned to Neka and started asking about school. She watched as Neka tried to eat as little as possible, and she felt bad for the girl. She kept offering more food, and ate with more gusto than she usually had for breakfast in reaction to the girl's self-denial.

Neka tried her housekeeper again, and this time made contact with someone who said that Anna wouldn't be back until the afternoon. She relayed this as if she'd let them down somehow, but Siobhan just said, "Well, then, I guess you're stuck with us a little longer," and the girl smiled tentatively at her. Finn gave Siobhan a thankful look and asked Neka if she'd like to play on his old gaming console.

"I know it's nothing like yours, but it's still pretty fun."

"Oh, sure, I guess that would be okay." Neka followed him down the hallway. Siobhan heard his door snick shut.

"I want to play, too," Maeve said, excitedly.

"No, Hon, you hang out with us, and your uncle will

colour with you."

"You will?" Maeve looked at him.

"Uh, sure. I guess so." Thomas looked at Siobhan with surprise. "I haven't done that in a long time though. I'm probably not very good."

"You just need practice!" Maeve said earnestly.

"Okay, you go get the crayons and Mummy will clear the table." Now Siobhan looked surprised. Thomas grinned at her.

Maeve asked Siobhan where to find her colouring books and crayons.

"In our room on the bookshelf." Siobhan pointed down the hall behind her. "Go get them."

"Okay," Maeve said and ran into the bathroom.

"Honey," Siobhan said loudly, "you're in the wrong room."

Maeve stepped back into the hall and turned slowly around in a circle.

"Your crayons are in our room. On the bookshelf."

"Oh yeah," she said and walked into the bedroom. Siobhan and Thomas could see her standing in there, looking around.

Siobhan turned back to the table and began gathering dishes, stacking the plates. She carried them to the kitchen and started the water running. Maeve came back into the living room carrying Winnie-the-Pooh. Siobhan said, "No, honey, your crayons, go get your crayons."

"Oh, yeah." Maeve skipped out again.

"Why don't I just get them?" Thomas stood from his chair.

"In a minute, I'll go get them. We have to let her try first. Sometimes she surprises me and does the thing she's told."

Thomas looked at her, unconvinced. Siobhan could tell that he thought this a little bit cruel.

After five minutes, when Maeve still had not returned, Siobhan went down the hall and found her sitting on the bed reading a book.

"Did you get your crayons, Maeve?"

Maeve looked up at her blankly. "No. Where are they?"

"Right here," Siobhan said and pointed at the bookshelf right ahead of her, "and here are your colouring books. C'mon out and colour with your uncle."

"He's going to colour with me?"

"Yes."

Siobhan took her hand and picked up the box of crayons with the colouring books and led her out to the table, where she handed everything to Thomas. Maeve sat down happily, selected the pictures they would colour, and then spent the next half hour telling him what to do. Siobhan did the dishes, then went and sat in the living room to do some reading, and listened to Maeve's instructions to her uncle, which Thomas took with unusual good grace. The sounds of videos games beeped and clanged in the background. Siobhan enjoyed all the sounds. She sat and read, making notes in the margins with a pen. Even when Thomas and Maeve finished colouring and came and sat in the living room to watch The Iron Giant together. Thomas had never seen it, but it had long been one of Siobhan's favourites, and she half watched it while she read, until her eyelids grew heavy and she dozed off and on.

"You're snoring," Thomas said to her, pulling her out of a fog.

"Oh, sorry," she said, wiping her face. "I need more coffee."

"Can I have a drink, Mummy?"

"Sure, come get it." Siobhan got up and Maeve padded after her. Siobhan poured her some juice and handed her the glass. She watched Maeve as she went to the living room again, then turned to the coffee maker.

"Maeve!" Thomas shouted, and there was a thud and a splash as Maeve's glass hit the floor. Then Maeve made a long, low moan. Siobhan walked quickly back into the living room, and saw Thomas trying to hold Maeve in place, but Maeve swayed and started turning to the left.

"Let go of her, Thomas."

"But, she's fainting."

"She's having a seizure, and you shouldn't restrain her."

He looked at her, scared. Siobhan walked over to Maeve just as Finn came in, followed by Neka. Siobhan ignored them and just started rubbing Maeve's back and talking to her in a low tone. Maeve turned slowly in a circle, moaning and whimpering. Then she started opening and closing her mouth in a strange way, grimacing. She spit a few times on the floor.

When she came out of it, Siobhan lowered her to the couch. She sent Finn to get a blanket. Maeve fell asleep instantly.

"What was that?" Neka asked, staring at Maeve as if she expected her to start vomiting pea soup.

"It was just a seizure," Finn told her. "She has them all time."

"Doesn't she have to go to the hospital?" Thomas asked Siobhan. "We can take her."

Siobhan stood bending over Maeve, rubbing her daughter's head. "No, she has them all time, there's nothing they can do. When she has a very long one, they can give her medication, but we'd get there, wait for hours while they watched her, and then be sent home."

"Will she be okay?" Neka asked.

"Yes, she'll sleep, and then she'll be okay."

They all stood and watched the sleeping girl. Then Siobhan sat at the edge of the couch, and Thomas sat on the chair. Finn looked at his mother and said, "Neka got a hold of her cleaning lady, so she can go home."

"Oh, good." Siobhan smiled at the girl. "It was nice meeting you, Neka. Come over any time. Well, except during finals."

"Thank you for letting me hang out."

"Do you need a ride?" Thomas asked, wanting to get out of the house for awhile.

"No, no, I'm fine, really." She turned toward Finn. "Are you going to come over tonight?"

"Maybe. Can I call you later?"

"Sure, bye." She turned and headed for the door, looking back and giving a slight wave as she went through it.

The rest of them sat and watched Maeve sleep.

Eventually Finn turned the TV on and Maeve woke up.

"What day is it?" she asked Finn.

Chapter 5

Thomas packed up to leave on Monday morning, hugging Finn and Maeve, and even giving his sister a brief hug. He pulled away in his old Valiant, and Finn stood on the sidewalk and waving goodbye, then headed off to school.

In the apartment, Siobhan laid out Maeve's medication and they sat down to eat together at the still clean table. On Mondays, Siobhan had a two hour class in the afternoon, the only class available for a mandatory course. Maeve's worker started late on Mondays and Siobhan didn't like her at school without a worker, someone to walk her around and keep her involved in the classwork. Siobhan tried to do some reading during breakfast, but Maeve prattled on in her usual style. Siobhan would respond to Maeve's statements and questions, then ask her to eat and let Mummy read. A brief silence would occur, and then Maeve would start back up again.

Siobhan realised the futility. With a sigh, she laid her book down on the table.

"Do I have school today?"

"Yes."

Maeve furrowed her eyebrows. "Can't I go with you?"

"No, not today. I have to meet your new teacher today."

"Why?"

"Your regular teacher is ill. Now eat your breakfast, Hon. You still need to get dressed."

Siobhan looked at her daughter, staring honestly and openly at her mum. She reached over and grabbed Maeve's hand and pulled her gently out of her chair and brought her to sit on her lap. Maeve straddled Siobhan's legs, and Siobhan wrapped her arms tightly around her daughter, kissing her cheek. She let Maeve's head rest on her chest. "It's going to be alright."

"What will?" said Maeve's muffled voice. Siobhan rubbed her cheek on Maeve's short, dirty blonde hair.

"Everything."

"No. It won't."

Siobhan just sat and held her for awhile, then helped her finish her cereal. Last year she had a teacher and a worker who had decided that the best treatment for Maeve's memory and ADD symptoms would be to punish her for them. Siobhan thought that they'd had good intentions and had at first gone along with them, deferring to their experience. They would stick Maeve in the hallway, and when Siobhan came to collect her at the end of the day, they would list her transgressions to Siobhan, with Maeve standing nearby, hearing all the ways in which she had failed.

Siobhan knew Maeve forgot the particulars of those conversations and the realities of being in the hallway, but the feeling of shame and of being singled out had stuck with her. It hadn't taken long for Maeve to become a hysterical mess who dreaded going to school. You couldn't punish a brain injury away. Siobhan had managed to stop the teacher and support worker from doing it, but the damage to Maeve had become permanent. And, even worse, at the end of the school year Maeve had had an EEG that showed she experienced seizure activity continuously, even when she did not exhibit, outwardly, signs of a seizure.

Siobhan had sat blankly while the neurologist told her this, staggered by the idea. He outlined a complex schedule for new medication, taken twice a day.

Siobhan had taken Maeve home from the neurologist's office, put on The Iron Giant for her, and gone into her room and cried. She didn't cry a lot, self-pity took time and energy that she didn't have. She felt great shame about letting the teacher try to punish the brain injury out of Maeve. Maeve, who had the equivalent of a remote control flicking madly through channels in her brain. She hadn't known it, hadn't known the how often the seizures were happening, and how much it was affecting Maeve's memory and development, but she had known that Maeve didn't do it on purpose. She didn't have behaviour problems. The seizures stole time away from her, time and experience crucial for development. Maeve was emotionally younger than her chronological age as a result. She had a sweet nature and honest compassion for others. She just didn't understand them.

After breakfast, Siobhan helped Maeve get dressed, trying to get her to do as much as she could, but Siobhan needed to show her the front of her underwear and shirt, put on her shoes and do them up, and brush her hair for her.

"You are obsessed with brushing my hair," Maeve said, watching her mother in the mirror.

"You mean, 'obsessed with having a child who looks like someone cares for her'? Yes, yes, I am." Siobhan looked back at her in the mirror, "Now, go get your coat off the couch and we'll go to school."

Maeve skipped into the kitchen.

"No, Hon," Siobhan said, standing in front of the door, "go in the living room."

Maeve slung the coat onto her shoulder and walked to

Siobhan, who took it and held it out for her. After Maeve had the coat on and the zipper up, Siobhan gave her a granola bar. "Here, you want this for the walk to school?"

"Yes." Maeve took it from her.

They went out the door, Siobhan directing Maeve as the child skipped along ahead of her.

"No, Hon, the other way. Open the door. Push. Good girl. No, Hon, wrong way, this way, remember? Okay, stop, look for cars. Wait for me. Okay, let's cross."

Maeve stopped in her tracks in front of the school door.

"Keep going, honey, we're almost there," Siobhan said as she overtook her daughter. Once she'd drawn parallel, she saw Maeve's wide-eyed blank stare. Maeve made a low growling noise. She started turning to the left and swaying slightly. Siobhan threw an arm around Maeve and steadied her as she started walking the way she had turned.

"Okay. It's okay," Siobhan said, even though Maeve couldn't hear her. Maeve started opening and closing her mouth in an exaggerated way, still moaning, and Siobhan realised she had a mouthful of granola bar. She tried to bend Maeve forward, worried that she might choke, but Maeve felt stiff and unyielding. Siobhan hooked her finger into Maeve's mouth and quickly scraped the food out, flicking it on the ground. "It's okay, Mummy just needs to clear your mouth out. It's okay."

Maeve went even more stiff, and a long strand of drool ran out of her mouth. Siobhan just kept murmuring to her and rubbing her back and shoulders. Maeve suddenly went slack, whimpering. She leaned heavily into her mother.

"I feel sick," she moaned.

"I know, I know. You just had a seizure. It's okay. Lean against me."

They stood there together, Siobhan holding her and stroking her hair, rocking her gently.

"Oh, Mummy, I don't feel good," Maeve's face looked pale and pained.

"I know, let's go in the school and sit down for a bit, okay?"

"Okay."

Siobhan slowly directed her through the large doors. They found a low bench in the hallway and sat down. The classroom doors stood open, and Siobhan could hear different sounds coming from the three immediately near her. A teacher talking, with sporadic squeaking of chalk, students talking and laughing in another, and some low music from the third. It smelled like elementary schools had always smelled to Siobhan, of play dough, bologna sandwiches, and little kids' farts. Siobhan leaned back against the wall and helped Maeve lay down with her head on Siobhan's lap. Maeve fell asleep.

Siobhan sat and gently stroked Maeve's back. She leaned back and closed her eyes.

The sound of footsteps slapping against the linoleum made her open her eyes and sit up a bit. Maeve's worker came down the hall, smiling at Siobhan.

"Hi!" Jani said. "How are you?" She looked down at Maeve."Oh no, did she have a seizure?"

"Yeah, out front." Siobhan looked down at Maeve. "Let's just give her some time to rest, then I'll bring her in."

"Okay, yeah, just bring her in when you're ready. It'll be recess soon."

Twenty minutes passed, and Maeve still slept, but Siobhan knew that the bell would soon ring for recess and the hallway would lose its peaceful feeling as children and

106

teachers swarmed out. She woke Maeve gently and got her sitting up. Maeve still looked a bit disoriented, but she responded to Siobhan's questions and urgings.

Siobhan decided the best plan meant a move to the office, where Maeve could have some time to fully awaken. She got the girl to her feet, shouldered her pink backpack, and led her down the hall. The receptionist looked up when they came in. "Oh, hello, did you need something?" she asked.

"Just a calm place to sit for a minute. Maeve had a seizure outside, she's still a bit out of it."

"Oh, sure, sure, come in. Have a seat. Take as long as you want," she said, and waved at the chairs in the corner.

Siobhan tried to move Maeve to a chair, but once again Maeve had a blank stare. She started moaning again and turned slowly to the left, this time actively spitting on the floor.

When she finished, Siobhan directed her to a chair and sat her down. Maeve slumped, unresponsive. After a few minutes, Siobhan looked at the receptionist and waved a bit to get her attention.

"I think Maeve will have to come home with me for the day, she's just had another seizure. Will you let her teacher know?"

"Oh, dear. I hope she's alright. Yes, I'll let the sub know." She didn't need to ask which teacher Maeve had. They knew her well.

"Thank you." Siobhan got Maeve carefully to her feet and they made their slow way home. No school for either of them today.

***

Finn sat on a bench in the gym and cupped his

throbbing nose, thinking of things he'd rather do than play dodge-ball. Severing his own leg with a butter knife ranked high on the list. The whir and bang of the balls as they hit the walls made him jump. The wiz and dull thump of the balls meeting flesh made him cringe. This was a very unpleasant start to his afternoon.

Terry took this class with him. Finn watched as the larger boy deftly plucked balls that hurtled toward him out of the air and sent them sizzling back to the opposing forces. His aim was excellent as well. Finn felt some envy for his friend's general competence.

The PE teacher finally blew his whistle and the torture came to a slow end as some of the boys still tried to score extra points. Then the big wire bins were rolled out and the boys ran around, tossing the balls in, laughing and swearing. Terry wandered over to him.

"How's your face?"

"It hurts a bit, but I'll live. I guess."

"Well, that was a big hit you took. You should've seen yourself go flying back there. It was really amazing."

"I'm pretty sure Jono aimed at my face on purpose."

"Wouldn't surprise me. He's a bit of a dickhead. Also, I'm pretty sure he's pissed that Neka was flirting with you the other night." Terry sat down heavily next to him, his long legs jutting out twice as far as Finn's.

"What? That's ridiculous, she was not," Finn protested.

"Whatever," Terry shrugged.

The other boys filed slowly out of the gym, whacking and pushing each other. Jono turned at the door and yelled, "Hey, next time duck, you girl."

"Shut the fuck up, Jono," Terry yelled back. Jono shot them the finger and ran out. Finn heard the phone ring in the teacher's office off the gym.

108

"Idiot," he said under his breath.

"Yeah," Terry agreed. "So, what are you up to after school? Want to head downtown with me? I want to get a new CD."

"I have to pick up Maeve today."

"Oh. Well, why don't you bring her along?"

"Really?"

"Yeah, sure. I like her, she's a cute kid."

"Well, sure then. I'm sure she'd like that."

Mr. Mackelin stuck his head out the office door. His face shone beet red as always, and his baseball cap looked too small for his enormous head. "Finn, phone call for you in here."

Finn was surprised, but he got up and walked over. He picked up the receiver and said, "Hello?" His mother's voice came back, sounding strained.

"Hey, Sweetie. Look, I'm just phoning to tell you that you don't have to pick up Maeve. I've got her, and... Look, I don't want you to worry, but I'm taking her to the hospital."

"What? Why?"

"She's been seizing all day, for like four hours now. She seizes, then she sleeps, then she wakes up, then she seizes again. She's had five or six now."

"I'll run home right now and go with you."

"No, Hon, you know the drill. They'll just give her some meds, watch her for a while and send her home. There's no point to you coming."

"But Mum, what if you need me?"

"Honestly, we'll be fine. Just go home after school and I'll phone you."

Finn didn't feel okay, but he said, "Okay. How will you get there?"

"I think I'll phone an ambulance. I don't want to take her

like this on the bus."

"Yeah, that would be hard. Okay, if you're sure. Phone me,"

"I will. You're a good brother, Finn."

"Thanks," he said, and heard her hang up. "You're a good Mum," he said to the dial tone. He put the receiver down and just stood there for a moment, thinking that he'd run home anyways, fast as he could. Then he realised that she had probably already called the ambulance and phoned him second. They'd likely be gone by the time he got home. He felt useless and he didn't like that, even though he knew that she was right about what would happen. In truth, the hospital couldn't do much for Maeve.

He felt sad for Maeve. She'd spend all of tomorrow recuperating and then Wednesday she already had an EEG scheduled, so that meant most of her week had already disappeared.

Finn turned out of the office and mumbled his thanks to Mr. Mackelin standing outside. Terry had disappeared into the showers. He hoped to find him in the locker room so that he could explain the change of plans. He felt disappointment over that, Maeve would've enjoyed time with the two of them.

***

I don't know where I am. The walls have picture of baby animals. I sit up and see Mummy sitting on a chair next to the bed I'm in.

"Mummy, where are we?" I ask.

"At the hospital, Honey," she says.

She gets up and gives me a hug and too many kisses.

"Mummy, your breath stinks."

110

I recognise the hospital now. My bed has metal rails on it. I can hear other kids and babies crying,

"Why am I here?"

"You had a lot of seizures. The doctors need to check you out."

A woman comes in. She has a shirt with monkeys on it. She wants to take my blood pressure.

"Hold as still as you can, Maeve," she says.

The thing around my arm squeezes tight. The machine beeps.

"Good," the woman says. "You were very good." She takes the thing off my arm. To Mummy the woman says, "I'll tell the doctor she's awake."

"Thank you," Mummy says.

The woman leaves out a glass door. Mummy shuts the curtain after her. She comes back over and sits on the bed.

"How do you feel?"

"I don't know."

"Are you hungry?"

"I don't know."

"Okay. Would you like me to put on the TV for you?"

"Yes."

Mummy finds the remote and looks all over for the on button. Mummy flicks through to a kids show. She lays down next to me and I can feel her leaning against me. It feels nice.

A man comes in. Mummy gets up to talk to him. I wish they would stop, because I can't hear the TV. Then Mummy says we can go now.

The outside is cold and dark. Mummy says that the hospital visit took hours. Now the night has come. The moon shines brightly down.

"Mummy, look! The moon."

"Ah, it's beautiful, Honey."

I get on a bus with Mummy. She tells me to sit in the front seats. There's an old man with a big moustache and a shirt that shows his belly. He tells Mummy that old people and the disabled get the front seats.

"We're just leaving the hospital, she needs to sit," Mummy says to him.

The old man gets angry. Then the bus driver yells at Mummy, too. Mummy tells me to stay sitting. She fights with the bus driver and the old man until she wins.

Mummy tells them that I am invisible. Or something.

I feel invisible.

I want to be invisible.

Am I invisible?

***

Finn volunteered to stay up with Maeve for awhile the next night but Siobhan said, "No, you get some sleep. She'll be happy staying up reading beside me in bed."

Finn felt bad, though, about going to bed. He knew Maeve would feel happy, staying up all night reading and colouring, but he also knew that she'd ask Mum a million questions.

Siobhan caught him lurking in the hallway, resistant to going to bed. "Honey, really, it's okay. There's no sense us both being tired tomorrow. Go to bed."

Siobhan sat with her in the living room, Maeve happily colouring and firing a constant monologue at her, with Siobhan uttering the odd noise in answer while she tried to work on her essay, her books and notes spread around her and balanced on her knees, while she pecked diligently away on her ancient computer. Finally, with her eyes blurred and her back aching, she decided it might serve her to get some sleep before taking her daughter for the EEG in the morning. She wished that she had a kid who would sleep for the EEGs without having to stay up the entire night before. Even if they gave Maeve a mild sedative, she would sit there bright-eyed and interested in the procedure.

"Okay, Maeve, it's time for me to get a bit of sleep. You come and read in bed for a bit while I lay down."

"Why can't I stay up with Finn?" Maeve asked, staring up from the floor and the huge pile of markers.

"Because there's no sense in both me and Finn being tired tomorrow. Now come on, you can even play his old Gameboy for awhile, if you want."

"Yay!"

In the bedroom, Siobhan undressed and then helped Maeve get her clothes off. She got Maeve into bed and gave her a stack of books and Finn's old Gameboy. Maeve looked through the books and found a sticker book that she'd forgotten about.

"Mummy, can I use these?"

"Stickers? On what?"

Maeve looked around and then back at her mum. "You."

"Me?" Siobhan yawned at her.

"Yes."

"If I let you, will you be quiet so I can get some sleep?"

"I promise."

Siobhan closed her eyes for a minute. "Okay, but just a couple."

Maeve happily sat and put stickers on Siobhan's cheeks, nose and forehead, pushing down just hard enough to hurt a bit.

"That's enough," Siobhan croaked, her skin itching from the glue.

"Okay." Maeve felt pleased with her work.

"Let mummy sleep now."

"Okay, but first some kisses."

"Yes, some kisses." Siobhan let Maeve kiss the few bare patches where no stickers covered her face. "Now read or something."

"Okay."

Siobhan closed her eyes and listened to Maeve start up the Gameboy. She had just drifted off when a horrid buzzer sound ripped into her sleeping ears. She woke up with a start, confused that her alarm had gone off, and what the hell had happened to the radio setting? Had she changed it?

But she realised, after hitting her alarm clock soundly three times, that the alarm had not gone off. Maeve laughed at her, Siobhan turned towards her and saw the egg timer in her hands.

"It's okay, Mummy, you can sleep for two more minutes."

"Maeve," Siobhan groaned, "where did you get that?"

"I don't know." Maeve looked at the timer like it might have some sort of magic properties.

"Maeve, do not use the egg timer to time me sleeping, okay? That makes me want to jump out the window and run around screaming."

"Okay, sorry."

"So don't do it again."

"Okay."

Siobhan's heart slowed down, and she started to drift off. She heard Maeve crank the timer so that it went off again.

Siobhan opened her eyes. "Okay, give me the egg timer, Maeve."

Maeve hid it quickly under the quilt. "No."

"Yes. Now." Siobhan held out her hand. Maeve looked at her for a minute, then slowly pulled it out and put it in her hand, looking put out. "Now let me sleep, I'm tired." Siobhan's voice sounded froggy and miserable.

Maeve opened up a book and started reading. Siobhan finally got to sleep.

Siobhan's real alarm clock seemed to go off immediately, and she whacked it with the palm of her hand. Maeve sat, still awake beside her. The window showed that the sun still slept. *Five a.m., that's so sick.*

Maeve leaned her face over into Siobhan's. "Ew, morning breath," she said, and clamped a hand down on Siobhan's mouth.

Siobhan moved her hand away. "Mummy, you snore."

"Yes, I've been told."

"You sound like a hippopotamus."

"Thanks."

"Do you want me to read you a book?"

"Okay," Siobhan squeaked as she stretched and tried to force her eyes open.

"How about this one?" She picked up one of her books and showed it to Siobhan.

"Mars Needs Moms. Okay, but read it quickly, we need to go soon."

After the book, Siobhan got them both up and dressed, although Maeve struggled more than usual, tired even though she would never admit it. Finn got up just as they headed out the door.

Finn stood in the hallway in his boxers, all angles and

sinew. "Are you sure you don't want me to come? You might need me."

She went to him and hugged him. "I do need you. But not to come with us. Why don't you take some money and pick up some groceries and make dinner?" Siobhan handed him forty dollars.

"Okay, what do you want?" He folded the money up in his hand, glad to have a task to do.

"You decide." She went back to the door, then turned to him. "Not hot dogs, though."

He smiled at her. "Not hot dogs."

***

The hospital was still quiet from the night when Siobhan and Maeve arrived at seven a.m. Only a few people sat outside the coffee kiosk in the lobby, the large windows dark and reflective. Siobhan breathed in deeply the smell of the coffee, and wished she could have a cup right then, but if she did then Maeve would want a hot chocolate. After the EEG they could have one.

They padded down the hallway together. Maeve held Siobhan's hand and asked repeatedly what they would do today. Siobhan grew more impatient with each repetition, which made her feel bad.

"You know honey, I understand that you don't remember asking me those questions, I do. I'm just tired. I'm sorry if I sounded mad."

"I don't mean to ask them. I'll stop."

Siobhan looked at her, her face serious, her blue eyes determined. Siobhan knew that she would start again with the questions in two minutes.

"I know you will." Siobhan gave her hand a squeeze.

116

"I will make you into a ghost!" Maeve's shout was a painfully loud thing in the barren hallway. She laughed at herself.

"That had absolutely nothing to do with what we were talking about," Siobhan said and laughed, too.

"Yeah."

The nurse at reception greeted them and asked them to sit and wait for the technician to call them. Maeve sat and watched the cartoon that played on a monitor over the door. A sign on the receptionist's window asked parents to rebook if their children had head lice. Siobhan wondered why people would have to be told that.

A small and efficient looking woman came to the glass door, and it whooshed open. She call out Maeve's name but Maeve ignored her. Siobhan touched her hand and said, "We're up, honey. Let's go," and she pulled her mesmerized and reluctant daughter to her feet.

"Hi, Maeve, I'm Gale, I'll be doing your EEG today."

"Maeve, say hi."

"Hi," Maeve said, shyly.

"Would you like to watch a movie in the room?"

Maeve looked at her mother. "Sure, that sounds good," Siobhan prompted her.

"Yeah," Maeve said.

They went into a small, windowless room where Siobhan helped Maeve off with her coat and shoes.

"Okay, you lie down Maeve. What movie would you like?" Gale listed off some movies she had.

Gale put on Maeve's choice and then went to work attaching the electrodes to her head. First, she measured and marked off the positions with red wax pencil, leaving red x's all over Maeve's head and onto her face. Maeve just ignored this part. Then Gale took a Q-Tip and rubbed each x with alcohol vigorously to make sure all the oil came off of Maeve's skin so the electrodes would stick.

Maeve did not like this part. It always came as a surprise to her, because she didn't remember the last time. She cried, and Siobhan had to help hold her, trying to distract her with the animal pictures on the wall. Maeve protested and tried to pull away from the technician, her face red with dismay. Slowly, they got through it, Siobhan keeping up a cheerful banter about otters, and baby bears, and all the animals they could see in the pictures. As a baby, Maeve just nursed through these things.

The girl had managed to get through anything as long as she could nurse.

Gale started attaching the electrodes and soon Maeve looked like a weird robot child, in for some recharging. The brightly coloured wires ran to a panel on the wall that showed the outline of a head. The wires from Maeve's head ran into corresponding sockets on the panel.

The tech sat down in front of the computer. Her screen showed Maeve's brainwaves in bright green on a black background. She asked Maeve some questions, flashed a light in her eyes, and had her blow hard on a pinwheel. Siobhan sat and watched, trying to clarify things for Maeve when she could, and encouraging her when she wearied of the tasks.

Then the tech turned off all the lights and the room went still and dark except for the computer screen. Siobhan found herself struggling to stay awake in the warm, quiet, dark room. Her chin kept falling forward and she kept waking herself with her own snores, keenly aware of them in the silent room.

Maeve appeared to sleep, a rare occurrence during an EEG for her. After Gale got what she needed, she turned on the lights and Siobhan sat bolt upright, trying to pretend she had not fallen asleep. The technician woke Maeve up and performed a few more tests, even though Maeve did not want anything more to do with testing.

"I remember when they used spirit gum for this and it took forever to get off each time," Siobhan said, watching Gale remove the electrodes.

"Oh, yeah, I remember that stuff," Gale agreed.

Siobhan got Maeve dressed again and Gale led her to a treasure box, where Maeve could not decide what to choose. Finally, a strange, tentacled sticky ball called to her enough for her to choose it and they went down the hall to the coffee kiosk together.

Half an hour later they sat in the neurologist's office. They would have to wait over two more hours for their appointment. Maeve got up and made her wobbly way around the play area, determined not to give into sleepiness lest her mother whisk her away to a bed. EEG time equalled party-time to Maeve, and Siobhan would have to pry it from her warm, unconscious fingers.

Siobhan sat watching her daughter through half-lidded eyes. The waiting room began to fill with people who Siobhan thought of as lifers, the parents and children who would spend their lives seeing specialists. You could tell them apart from the emergency and surgery parents because they didn't look panicked or lost in the huge hospital. The parents of the children in the terminal wards mainly stayed apart, probably from needing to stay germ free, but also because they experienced a special kind of pain.

The patients in the neurology clinic waiting room represented a wide spectrum of disability. From those like Maeve who didn't show their injuries much, to children in wheel chairs with supports for their heads and straps for their legs. Siobhan always felt frustrated when she came to the hospital by the general attitude that asking other parents about their children's health violated privacy concerns. As if the children and their parents did not live their entire lives in public. It felt bad to Siobhan, that the attitude of the world still leaned toward disability as a private shame, not so far removed from having a child, or aunt, or parent "put away" in a home. The intention may have been to serve the politically correct need for privacy, but the result of not encouraging parents to connect, to organise, felt unfair to Siobhan. In all her years with Maeve they had not met one other child who had experienced a stroke. That she knew of, of course, not having had the opportunity to ask. She didn't know how or where else to meet other families like hers. Parents like her had little time or energy to look for each other without the support of hospitals and other services.

She had mentioned her desire to have Maeve meet other infant stroke survivors several times to various doctors they'd seen. One doctor had said, yes, introducing the families of children who'd had strokes to each other would be great. The doctor had said they wanted to work on that. Siobhan never heard from her again.

Maeve got called into her appointment two hours later. Siobhan felt groggy and fuzzy, having drowsed in and out while sitting for so long in the waiting room. A nurse weighed Maeve and took her blood pressure, and then showed them into an examination room. Unlike the corridors and waiting room, the exam room felt bare and utilitarian. No pictures of baby animals festooned the walls. Maeve sat beside Siobhan and leaned into her side, a habit she had started a few years before. It made

Siobhan's back hurt, trying to hold up the extra weight. When it happened while they walked together, Siobhan would have to push Maeve up and away from her to get her to stop.

"How much longer, Mummy?"

"Not long, then we'll eat lunch and go home." Siobhan stretched and yawned,

"I'm hungry now."

"Well, we have to see the doctor first."

The door opened, and the doctor came in. An efficient older woman with short white hair and an accent Siobhan could never place. Scottish? Irish? English?

The doctor exchanged brief pleasantries, then got down to business. How often did Maeve have her seizures lately? What happened during the seizures? Had she had any colds or flus? Did she sleep well? She made notes as they talked. Then she put Maeve on the table and examined her, asking her to flex muscles, follow her fingers, get down on the floor and stand on her toes.

She asked them out into the hallway so she could observe Maeve running up and down in the hallway. Maeve demonstrated some very slight differences in the way each side of her moved. The left side did not move as fluidly, the gait showed some restriction. Maeve could have had so much more impairment. The doctors had always appeared to expect so much more impairment, though they never said so outright.

Neurologists did not like to speculate. At least not to Siobhan. And she had long since stopped asking them to. The answer always came back, "We don't know. Wait and see."

Siobhan told her that Maeve had not enjoyed a terrific school year so far. She still withdrew, still didn't make friends, and still remained solitary except for her and Finn.

They went back into the exam room and the doctor sat quietly thinking for a while, rubbing her chin and looking at her notes.

"Maeve's seizures are not being well controlled. She's at the maximum doses of the medications she is on," she checked her notes, "I think we should try her on a different one, and replace one of these."

"Okay," Siobhan said. Changing to a new medication presented difficulties. Maeve would need careful weaning off the old medication while they added the new medication. And there was no guarantee the new medication would work.

"I also want to send her for a full assessment at the health centre. I would like her to get educational, psychological, and physiotherapy assessments. There might be quite a waiting list, but I'll see if I can push to have her in sooner."

"Oh." Siobhan had not expected that. "Okay, well, she's not had a psycho-educational report for a few years. Sure, that sounds good."

The doctor pulled out her prescription pad. Maeve sat and ignored both of them, reading a book Siobhan had brought and leaning heavily against her mum.

The nurse came in and the doctor left. The nurse explained the new medication schedule and wrote it all out for her. Then Siobhan and Maeve left, walking out into the windswept rain.

***

Finn found himself standing with Neka next to some bushes at the far end of the school field at lunch. He'd

122

wanted to find Terry, afraid he would be mad at him for cancelling their plans on Monday, even though Terry had been polite and concerned about Maeve when he had caught up to him in the change room.

"I'm sorry she's having trouble," Terry said, putting his hand on Finn's shoulder. "It's okay, we'll do it another day. Would you like me to come over and keep you company after school?"

Finn thought about it for a minute, then shook his head. "No, thank you. Mum and Maeve will be tired when they get back."

"Okay, let me know if you change your mind."

Finn had not talked to Terry since. He'd come out at lunch to look for him, but he'd only found Neka, standing by herself, listening to music and smoking a cigarette.

"You're not supposed to smoke on school grounds," he said to her, but her music blared out of her headphones loud enough for him to hear it three feet away so she hadn't noticed him yet. He reached out a hand and tugged on her black, raggedy hoodie, and she made a choking sound and jumped.

"Fuck, Finn, you freaked me out!" she shouted.

"Sorry," he said, as she took off her headphones.

"Well, make some noise if you're going to come up behind like that."

"I'd need a full marching band to be heard over your music."

She looked at him steadily for a minute, then shrugged her shoulders. "Well, that's true. Maybe you should carry a trumpet or something."

"Yeah, I'll get right on that. Have you seen Terry today?" "No. He didn't come to school this morning. Him and Luther got a little bit puking drunk at my place last night. I was making green drinks."

"What are green drinks?"

"I don't know, I just mixed stuff until they were green."

"Oh." It sounded like something his mum would say.

"He'll be at my place later, after school. That's where him and Luther are, sleeping it off. You can come over tonight if you want."

"No, thanks though. Maeve is having an EEG today and Mum asked me to make dinner. She had to keep Maeve up all night, so when they get home they'll sleep.

"Oh." Neka looked at him for a minute, took a puff her cigarette, then flicked it on the damp grass. "What's an EEG?"

"They measure Maeve's brain waves to see how many seizures she's having. The brain runs on electricity. Maeve has problems with hers, and that's why she has seizures."

"Wow, I didn't know that. We have electricity in us? Or just her?"

"Nope, everyone."

"That's weird."

Finn just shrugged, and they stood quietly for a moment. "Does it bug you to have to do so much?"

Finn looked at her, his face earnest and open. "No," he said, "that's just the way it is. Maeve needs me. My mum needs me. It's the way it's always been. Besides, if I make dinner we'll get pork chops. If Mum makes it, we'll have some horrible chick pea dish. The woman is crazy for chick peas."

Neka laughed. Then with no warning she leaned down and kissed him on the lips.

124

"That's sweet," she said. "See you later," and she turned and walked off toward the school.

Finn just stood there, watching her go. *She must really love pork chops;* his mother's voice sounded in his head.

He laughed to himself as he watched Neka walk away.

Chapter 6

Siobhan checked her cell phone repeatedly on the way to university, nervous that Maeve's school would phone. Maeve had had five seizures since her neurologist visit last week, a result of the change of medication. Siobhan could expect a few more weeks of needing to dash back at any moment to pick Maeve up. The seizures had started coming in groups of two, and the school grew too nervous at that point to keep her. They'd become pretty comfortable with one seizure, but two in a row scared them. Siobhan decided to keep her hand in her pocket with the phone, in case it vibrated.

Siobhan pulled out her notes on her final essay for her English class this term. She had arranged to meet her professor after class to discuss the essay and then meet Holly for lunch before her afternoon class. They likely wouldn't see each other again before Christmas, especially once the kids got out of school. They were so busy during the semester that whenever there was a break, they would spend all their time off sleeping, doing long neglected housework, and hanging out with their kids. Maeve would likely have a total collapse this year, school having proved increasingly difficult for her.

The bus pulled up and Siobhan shuffled off with the other students, rain pelting her. She loved this time of year.

The classroom felt too warm and Siobhan stripped down to her shirt, her jacket dripping on the floor. Her books felt damp as she pulled them out of her bag. This class was philosophy and, as usual, Siobhan sat at the front. Most of the students, twenty years younger, sat quietly through the classes, even when the professors asked them questions. The silence drove Siobhan insane. She'd wait as long as she could stand it, then answer the questions.

Siobhan had been surprised at how much she enjoyed university. She did all the readings and she worked hard on her papers, because the work was interesting and exciting. And she wished her classes lived up more to her dreams of what university should involve. Having quit high school at fourteen, she had never thought she'd go to university. She still didn't have a high school diploma. After a certain number of years out of school you didn't need one. When she'd started, she'd felt like she had accessed an off-limits area, a place where few people she'd grown up with, or had previously known, had gone. She'd expected that attending university would elevate her out of her class, but in truth it had only served to reinforce the wide gap between her and her fellow students.

The readings for today's class involved essays written by people who suggested that persons over a certain income level give thirty percent of their income to charity.

Siobhan put up her hand and said, "Well, the thing is, poor people don't want charity."

A young man at the back exclaimed, "Of course they do." Siobhan turned to him slightly. "No, no. They really don't. What poor people want is opportunity, not handouts given through various auspices. They want decent jobs, decent pay, decent housing, and access to school. They want their share."

The young man looked angered by her rebuff, and Siobhan meant to say more but the class ended with people looking uncomfortable. Siobhan stayed seated as the other students left. When the room had emptied, she leaned back and stretched, rubbing her hands over her face. *Damn it, I had a whole rant worked out for that, too.* She put her head on the desk.

She sat like that for a minute, then gathered her stuff and headed out the door. She had her appointment with her English professor and it would not do to miss it. Siobhan had some good ideas written down and she looked forward to sharing them with the professor, who had praised her presentation for the class three weeks ago.

When she found the office, the door stood slightly ajar and she saw the professor, a short, serious woman with frizzy hair, sitting inside. Siobhan knocked lightly and the other woman looked up from the papers on the desk, her eyes wobbly under her glasses.

"Oh. Come on in." She cleaned some papers from a chair next to the desk. Siobhan sat in it, and they went over her paper proposal, the professor making suggestions, mainly that Siobhan had too much going on. Siobhan had that problem often. After they had gone over her notes, Siobhan prepared to leave, but stopped and said, "Oh, yeah. I wanted to tell you, I realise I've been late for a number of classes. I'm sorry about that. My daughter has special needs and I can't leave her school in the morning until her support worker arrives. I just wanted you to know that I'm not just lazy, or that I don't think your class is important." Siobhan smiled broadly at her.

"Well, I can't give you special privileges." The professor pushed her glasses up her nose.

"Huh?"

"I can't treat you differently than the other students. It wouldn't be fair."

"I'm not asking for special treatment. I'm explaining my

128

situation in the morning."

"Well, everyone has to be treated the same, or it isn't fair."

"Huh, yeah, I see," Siobhan began to like this professor less than when she'd entered the office. "I guess that's true. It must've been quite a project for you then. Did you go through an agency?"

"What?" The professor looked confused.

"Well, you said everyone must be treated the same to be fair. As everyone else in the class is about eighteen, childless, and middle-class, and I've not lost my children, gotten younger, or become middle-class, then I can only assume you got everyone in the class a disabled child."

The professor just stared at her. Siobhan realised her voice had turned more angry than she intended.

"You know, I've heard this before here," Siobhan said to the woman, her hand gripping the chair in front of her. "My friend goes here as well. She has a kid and a disability, and each semester must go around to each professor with a note from the disability office that asks the professors to give her a bit more time for assignments. The professors don't have to say yes. Usually they do, but not always, and for the same reason you've given."

"Well, I don't..."

Siobhan cut her off, "I think many of you, too many, have confused uniformity for fairness. Uniform is not fair. Not everyone is coming from the same place."

The woman looked down and shuffled some papers on her desk, then coughed twice on her fist.

"I wasn't asking you to do anything about me being late. I just wanted to let you know why. I've never handed in an assignment late, never asked for an extension, but if I did, like anyone else who might come in here, I would deserve to have my particular situation taken into consideration."

The professor didn't look up from her work. Siobhan felt some regret. She gathered her things, said goodbye, and left the room.

Siobhan left the building and walked across the grounds to the student union building, where Holly would meet her. She watched the other students milling around, standing in groups, laughing. She felt foreign, an intruder on campus. She had little contact with any of them because of the limited time she could spend on social activities. She couldn't go to parties or events. She couldn't join clubs or extracurricular activities. She spent her time on campus in class or dragging kids around to work on projects, to the library, to class, because babysitters cost too much, and each semester involved surviving without working. Sometimes it made her question the point of the whole exercise. Would Finn feel this way when it was his turn? She hoped not.

She saw her friend standing outside the main entrance, holding some papers in her hand and flipping through them. Siobhan felt overwhelming relief at seeing her. She walked up, intending to say something terribly witty, but when she stopped and her friend looked at her, Siobhan's throat closed painfully and some angry tears came out instead.

"Whoa, what happened?" Holly grabbed her arm. Siobhan fought to control herself. Public displays of crying felt horrible to her. She swallowed and took a deep breath.

"Oh, just a meeting with a prof." She told Holly what had happened as they walked inside and got a coffee. They wandered back out and found a place to sit, away from others, and Siobhan produced two cigarettes, crumpled, from her wallet. They sat in silence for awhile, sipping from their cups and smoking.

"We're just not supposed to be here. We're supposed to accept menial jobs, or at best a trade or government clerking position, and stay there and be damn happy for it. It's all a dream, that we can get anything better," Holly said, looking around the campus. "Why do you constantly have to explain Maeve to them? Why do I have to go around each semester and explain my disability? It's embarrassing enough when they are nice about it. It's humiliating when they say no, like I'm just trying to annoy them, or get something special with my fancy talk."

"Well, I can't quit. It's cost too much already, not just money, but time with the kids. I have to finish."

"Yeah. And it's certainly better than welfare. Or just taking some minimum wage job, with a boss worse that the profs can be."

"Sometimes they're great. I've had some that actually went out of their way to be considerate, to talk to Maeve when she shows up, to make me feel like I'm not interrupting their classes. I thought the prof I just talked to was like that. I guess I was just really surprised at her. Never mind, maybe I'll write the head of the department about her. And my other prof that thinks I can just put Maeve in any random daycare."

"What if you make them mad?"

"I don't have to name names, just talk of the general problems."

"Sure." Her friend got up and mashed her cigarette out on a trash can, tossing the butt in. Siobhan did likewise.

***

Siobhan barely made it home without peeing her pants. She wiggle danced down the hallway to her apartment door, cursing her overburdened key chain as she flipped through it madly trying to find the key to her door, cursing herself for the millionth time for not marking it for easy identification. She tried two before slamming the right one in, threw open the door with a crash, and then tossed her bag viciously aside as she flew to the bathroom. She tore her skirt up and her tights down and just made contact with the toilet seat in time. A huge sigh escaped her as she wilted with relief.

Then she felt the clunk. Well, what felt like a clunk, like something inside her fell over as her bladder emptied. She sat up straight and pushed on her stomach. She couldn't feel anything from the outside and finally convinced herself that she had just imagined it. She shrugged her shoulders and wiped herself. She stood and looked at herself in the mirror as she washed her hands. Her hair looked a mess, having knotted up where her backpack caught it. She noticed a pen mark on her cheek from some part of the day she didn't remember. She rubbed it away with her wet finger, wondering if she had run around all day like that. She wandered into the living room, grabbed her backpack from where she'd tossed it and sat down hard in her chair. The backpack sat unopened on her lap. *I should read.* Instead she sat and stared blankly at the wall of bookcases in front of her.

She leaned back in her chair and closed her eyes, *I should probably take this opportunity to masturbate or something. Nope, that would take more energy than I have at the moment.* "Sad," she said out loud. She tried to nap, but her neck felt uncomfortable leaning back in her chair and after a few minutes she got up and rubbed her eyes, then stretched, a huge growl escaping her as she did. She never slept well, always on guard for Maeve's seizures and staying up late studying every night. Napping seemed like a hobby she should take up, but in truth it always just made her feel worse to use her time that way. It felt self-indulgent. She wandered into the kitchen instead and turned the kettle on. As it boiled, she filled the sink and made a brave attempt at the dishes that had accumulated since Thomas left, filling the draining board haphazardly and willing the dishes not to crash down.

The kettle switched off and she filled the teapot. She took a cup of tea into the living room and read for awhile, underlining her text. She had trouble focusing as random thoughts kept racing through her mind.

When she read the same passage for the third time, not having retained anything the first two times, she put the book aside. Maybe she could just glean what she needed from the meticulous discussion sheets the prof handed out for each reading.

The phone rang. Siobhan groped around on the floor looking for it, spilling tea on herself.

"Fuck," she said, as she found the phone, trying to wipe the tea with her hand as she cradled the phone on her shoulder. "Hello," she said into the receiver.

"Hello, is this Maeve's mum?" a woman asked.

"Yes."

"This is the Children's Medical Centre. I'm phoning to book Maeve's assessment."

"Oh, okay, go ahead."

"We'd like to see her in February. The assessment will take one whole week, and you need to come to each session."

"Oh? Really, a whole week?" Siobhan felt panicked at the news.

"Yes. She will be seen by a psychologist, a physiotherapist, an occupational therapist, a speech therapist, and a social worker."

"Do I have a choice of when in February?"

"Well, I have you pencilled in for the week of the twentieth."

"Um, that will be a problem. I really need it to be the week before."

"I don't know if..."

Siobhan cut her off. "I'm not trying to be difficult. I realise that that you have a lot to co-ordinate, but I'm in university and I can't just take a week off. If you make it the week before, that's reading week, so that would be okay."

The woman sighed. "I'll see what I can do. I'll phone you back."

Siobhan felt relief, letting out in a gasp the breath she had held in while waiting for a response. "Thank you."

After the call, Siobhan sat with her hand on the phone, hoping the woman would call back right away.

She looked at the clock and realised she had about fifteen minutes left to pick up Maeve. She put on her shoes and coat, walked to the gas station and bought a cheap coffee. It burned her hands as she walked to Maeve's school, so she kept transferring it back and forth, saying, "Ow, ow, ow," as she took timid sips. The sky let down a gentle drizzle, which had made the streets slick and black. The traffic lights glistened off them in the gloom.

The school sat quiet when she arrived, all classes in session. She made her way to Maeve's class and the door stood open, the teacher's voice echoing out into the hall. Siobhan went to the door and slid into the room, making her way to the back. She came into Maeve's class as often as she could, not to disrupt it, but to see what Maeve's day entailed. Maeve couldn't tell her what happened there. Some of the students waved at her and said hi, and she smiled back at them but held a finger to her lips. They had grown used to seeing her in the class, the only parent that still picked up her kid and dropped her off as often as possible. The other children had grown responsible for getting themselves to and from school many years ago, but Maeve needed someone to be there for her every day. She still got lost in the school. Finding her own way home felt like a crazy dream to Siobhan.

Siobhan worried that she spent more time talking to the other kids in the mornings and afternoons than Maeve did for the whole day. When Siobhan was there, Maeve would have conversations with others, but they would have to be guided by Siobhan. Maeve had a lot of trouble interacting, since she couldn't follow the course of a conversation by herself, had trouble understanding when they joked, and became overwhelmed when they talked too much or made too much noise. As a result, Maeve had not made any friends at school, in all these years.

Siobhan had worried about Maeve's trouble making friends her whole life. At daycare and through elementary the most common observation about Maeve reflected her habit of playing by herself. She would fully immerse herself in her activity, playing in sand, or with blocks, or reading, and not even notice the other people around her. She rarely acknowledged the other kids, responding best to adults. She'd spend her lunch and recess with her worker, or alone before her seizures became worse. Except for her mother and Finn, she seemed to never want to spend time with anyone. She never knew the names of her classmates, despite having them in her grade repeatedly. She would read to them most happily. Even in kindergarten she could read, providing voices and reading with emotion, but she never remembered the kids afterwards, nor would she recognise one outside of school if she ran into them.

For years Siobhan had felt dismay at watching her child off on her own, not taking part in the classroom activities. She felt happy any time another child showed an interest in Maeve. In grade three another girl, also quiet, liked Maeve. One on one worked better for Maeve, and so the support workers would take them off together to do work and it seemed Maeve, at last, might make a friend. The other girl's parents seemed quiet, like the girl. They said little when Siobhan approached them outside of class, friendly but hard to talk to. Siobhan stopped trying to engage them, and would simply say hi or wave when she saw them.

One day, they saw Maeve and Siobhan at a coffee shop together. The father walked in with the little girl, and the mother waited outside, smoking a cigarette.

"Hilly would like to have a sleepover," the father said, the little girl smiling broadly at Siobhan and Maeve.

"Well, sure, she can stay over some night, Maeve would like that," Siobhan said, feeling jovial.

"Tonight," the father said, still smiling.

"Tonight?" Siobhan answered, unsure of the exact protocol here.

"Yes."

"Uh, well, that's a bit soon." They both just kept smiling at her, the mother standing outside, smoking, talking on her cell phone, "O...kay...then." Siobhan found herself feeling hypnotised by the smiles and the weirdness.

"Does she have a toothbrush?" Siobhan asked the father.

"No," he said, "just take her to school in the morning." He turned and left quickly, leaving Siobhan with his smiling, silent daughter.

"Okay," she said to herself under her breath. Maeve took her friend by the hand and the three of them walked home.

"So they just dropped her off with you?" Finn asked when they got home, standing with his mother in the kitchen while she made dinner.

"Yeah."

"That's a bit weird, Mum."

"Well, she's a nice girl. She seems a lot like Maeve, so maybe they're just happy she has a friend."

"Maybe. Do we have a number for them in case of emergency?"

"No."

"Do we know their last name?" "No."

"Do we know where they live?"

"No."

"Hmm," Finn thought for a minute. "Maybe we should ask her."

"That's a good idea," Siobhan said, and wiped her hands. Finn followed her to the living room where the girls played, but doing separate things.

"Hilly," Siobhan asked, "do you know your home phone number?"

The little girl stared at Siobhan with huge eyes, not answering for awhile, then slowly shook her head no.

"Well, do you know your parents' names or where they live?"

Again the girl stared at her, then shook her head no.

"Okay, dinner will be ready soon." Siobhan turned to Finn, who gave her a shrug.

A couple of weeks later the whole family had shown up unannounced at Siobhan's door on a Saturday, all smiling and friendly.

"We'd like to take Maeve to a church fair at the park."

"Oh," Siobhan said, standing in her doorway, her hair still a mess because they'd woken her up. "Well, that's very nice of you, but..." and here she faced a dilemma. Did she tell them about her atheism? Did she tell them that nobody could take Maeve until they had trained for seizures and learned about her condition? Did she tell them all of the above including how she found it really weird for them to assume she'd want her child to attend a religious function without her? There may be nothing wrong with it, but sending Maeve off for a day of abrupt Christianity might jar the child a bit. Suddenly, god.

She went with Maeve's health issues. She simply didn't want to offend church people before she'd had coffee, and she assumed they had good intentions even if the approach came across as a bit odd. She'd felt bad though, she rather liked them, probably exactly because of their oddness. *I must remember to talk to the support worker, see if I can get any insight on them.*

Hilly had come over a couple more times and then later that year had stopped coming to school. Siobhan ran into the father sometime later and asked after Hilly. She'd gone to live with relatives on the island, he said, because he and her mother had broken up. Siobhan felt sad for Hilly, and even sadder months later when she saw Hilly's mother on the bus, obviously having started, or restarted, a drug habit. That was a few years ago, and Siobhan had seen none of them again.

Siobhan felt bad for Maeve that the only kid that had been a good fit for her had moved away. The other kids in the class were too much for Maeve, even though they were all nice kids. They were friendly now to Siobhan.

Siobhan found Maeve at her desk with her headphones on, typing slowly on her computer. Siobhan pulled up a chair near her desk. Maeve didn't notice her. Siobhan leaned forward and touched her arm. Maeve turned and saw her. "Mummy!" she said too loudly because of the headphones.

Siobhan put her finger to her lips and said, "Shhhh."

Maeve leaned over and grabbed Siobhan's neck, holding on so tightly that Siobhan couldn't breathe. Siobhan gasped and worked at loosening Maeve's grip, pulling the girl's arms down to her chest.

"Okay, honey, I'm not in fear of floating to the ceiling." Siobhan whispered, "The teacher is still talking, so just do your work and I'll sit here with you."

"Okay!" Maeve said, too loudly again. The teacher looked at them, and Siobhan smiled back.

Maeve's worker, Jani, wandered over after the teacher had stopped talking.

"Hi," she said.

"Hi," Siobhan answered. "I see Maeve's working on her typing program."

"Oh, yeah, every day. How are you?"

"Oh, good. Gearing up for finals soon."

"What are you taking this semester again?"

"Two English classes and a philosophy. All heavy reading and essays." Siobhan took a drink of her coffee. "How's she been today?"

"A little groggy this morning."

"Yep, the meds do that. Just let her take it easy in the morning, they're hard on her."

"This afternoon she did good though. Even played some dodge- ball before it got too much for her."

"Yeah, that game's a bit noisy and busy for her, but it's great that she tried."

"Are you going to hang out and talk to the new teacher?"

"Oh, yeah, that's the plan."

"Good, I know she wanted to talk to you." The small woman wandered away from them to intervene with two other children a few feet away.

Siobhan leaned forward and took off Maeve's headphones. Maeve again threw herself on her mother, like they'd not seen each other a week instead of just two minutes ago.

"I had a bad day," Maeve said into Siobhan's neck, her soft cheek pushed into Siobhan's jaw.

"But Jani said you had a good day. Now, please show me what you've been up to on your computer, let's see your typing."

The bell rang and all the children jostled out the door in a loud tangle, a few shouting out, "Hi, Maeve's mum!" at her. Siobhan smiled and waved back. Siobhan waited for the teacher to finish talking to one or two stragglers.

"Hi, you must be Maeve's mum." The new teacher held out her hand and Siobhan shook it. "I'm Mrs. Blake."

"Yes, good to meet you. I'm sorry that this is the first afternoon I've made it in to talk to you. It's getting close to crunch time at school, I've been busy."

"Oh, you're in school? For what?" Mrs. Blake sat down and Siobhan sat in a chair to the side of her desk.

"I'm working on a Bachelor's in English Lit, and then I'd

like to go on to teacher's college."

"Oh." She looked down at the papers on her desk.

Siobhan felt some amusement at the nonplussed look on her face. People had expressed more interest in her baking training.

"Well, I did have some questions about Maeve, if you don't mind."

"Sure."

"Well, she hasn't completed any of the homework I've assigned."

"Yeah, well she won't. It stresses her out, and I don't like that kind of pressure at home."

"Yes, but all the children get homework."

"Yeah, I understand, but not Maeve. I've put it in her IEP."

"Oh, well, maybe just some math sheets."

"You can give it to her, but I won't force her to do it, especially right now. We're adjusting her meds. Also, she has a really thorough assessment at Sunny Hill coming up. I'll wait and see what they say."

"But how will she keep up with the other children?" Mrs. Blake looked perplexed.

"Well, and understand that I mean no offense here, I just don't care. I'm more concerned that she just comes and participates as much as she can. If she falls behind, if she has to repeat a grade, fine, but she's got enough on her plate right now just trying to control her seizures. I need her home time to be relaxing and smooth, not confrontational. And when she's here, I don't want her pushed. After Maeve has some seizure control, and we've undergone the testing at the health centre, then we can revisit the topic of homework. In the meantime, let's just keep her involved and try to get her to enjoy coming here." Siobhan exhibited more confidence then she felt about this. Pushing Maeve or not pushing her, Siobhan always went back and forth in her mind on that, but stress affected Maeve horribly.

"Okay. If that's what you want."

"Thanks. Is there anything else?"

"Well, yes. Jani told me that Maeve usually comes later in the morning for class, but I'd like her bright and early, to take full advantage of the day."

"Full advantage? I wish that were possible, but since she only gets part time support, that time would be spent by her reading or colouring by herself, not doing any school work. You have a class full of kids, you can't spend all that time just on her, can you?"

"Uh, no. Not right now."

"Of course not. She needs full-time support, or to go to a mini school, where she will learn the skills she needs, which are not met by an adapted academic program. And so that she can access the therapies she needs, and have consistent teachers and workers that don't change all the time. She's supposed to get occupational and speech therapy, but she hasn't since she started school. Instead of spreading the resources so thin that the kids aren't seeing the therapists, we should be concentrating services, in one place, so all the disabled kids have access to them."

Mrs. Blake looked down at some papers on her desk, and Siobhan remembered that this was a new job for her. Siobhan's complaints came from years of experience, but just complaining to individual teachers wasn't the answer she or Maeve needed. Mrs. Blake wasn't the cause of the system's failures. Siobhan took a deep breath.

"Okay, well, next semester I'll be picking her up every day, so I'll be around. Just let me know if you have questions. "

Siobhan stood up and walked to the door. Maeve jumped out from behind the doorway, to scare her like she always did. Siobhan pretended to be shocked, then wrapped and arm around her, and walked her to the door.

***

Saturday morning Finn got Maeve up early and fed her breakfast. Siobhan already sat in her chair, surrounded by books, notes and loose paper on her knees. She didn't respond much to the kids, lost in her studying and note-taking. Finn kept distracting Maeve from interrupting Siobhan. Maeve did not approve of the work Siobhan had to do.

"Mummy," she said to Siobhan.

"Yeah?" Siobhan said, not looking up.

"I want you to take me to your school so that I can tell your teachers not to give you so much work." Maeve's eyebrows furled in determination.

"Oh, Hon, that won't work." Siobhan looked at her and gave a brief smile. "But thank you."

"Eat up, Maeve," Finn said, tapping her bowl. "We have things to do today."

"Oh, give her her pills, okay?" his mum said. "Follow the directions on the papers on the wall in the kitchen."

"Okay." Finn got up and took three pill bottles down from on top of the fridge. He stood and counted out the pills according to the schedule. His mother had marked down the dates of each medication change, and they had to be careful to follow the instructions. Giving Maeve the medicine had become easier now that she could swallow pills. They used to have to crush her medications into juice.

Finn brought the pills to Maeve who took them without complaint, which made Finn a bit sad, that she should have grown used to taking so much medication at such a young age.

After breakfast he went into Siobhan's bedroom and found Maeve's clothes. Siobhan had actually put tape on the drawers, saying what each drawer held, but Maeve still could not find clothes on her own. He took them into the living room and helped Maeve get dressed, doing up her zippers and buttons, putting on her socks, and then headed with her to the bathroom.

He felt quite animated and energetic. Siobhan had managed to give him thirty dollars, having received the child tax benefit cheque early this month, and he planned to take Maeve out for a hot chocolate, followed by meeting Terry downtown to hang out. He'd felt so thankful to Terry for asking him again to hang out, *and* saying to bring Maeve along.

"Where are we going today?" Maeve asked him as he steered her to the bathroom to brush her teeth.

"Out with Terry. Do you remember Terry?"

She shook her head sadly, no.

"It's okay, you will when you see him."

She nodded at him and then took the toothbrush from his hand. Finn brushed her hair for her then helped her with her coat and boots.

"Give Mum kisses," he s aid, and she ran over and threw herself at Siobhan, knocking things off her mum's lap and smacking Siobhan on the chin.

"Ow!" Siobhan shouted.

"What?" Maeve asked her.

"Nothing, it's okay sweetie." Siobhan rubbed her chin. She kissed Maeve on the cheek, and then Finn pulled

Maeve gently away. "You two have fun. And phone me if you need me." She handed Finn her cell phone.

"Okay, Mum." Finn bent and gave her a quick kiss.

Finn and Maeve walked to the coffee shop, Maeve skipping and jumping around Finn like an excited rabbit, and Finn constantly directing her to stop, go, turn, keep up, stop walking right in front of him. Often he had to physically steer her around, something he'd grown as used to as Siobhan. Maeve kept up an endless chatter at him.

"Where are we going?"

"For hot chocolate, then downtown."

"I can fly us downtown."

"Oh, I know."

"I should make you into a dragon, too."

"Yes, that would be..."

"Then we could be a dragon family. If I give you DNA."

"Yes, I..."

"What's that?" Maeve pointed at some black thing just off the sidewalk.

As they drew nearer, Finn could make out the familiar shape. "It's a dead crow, Maeve."

They stopped to look at it.

"Why's it dead?"

"I don't know why. Accident, or poison. Maybe it got hit by a car."

"Oh." She looked at it intensely..

"What do you think happens to dead things, Maeve?"

"I guess, if it's a crow or something, other animals eat it."

"That's very logical." He felt pleased with her answer.

"What about people?"

"Don't touch it!"

"No, Maeve, I meant, what happens when people die?"

"Well, then people have to touch them. To carry them to get buried."

Finn smiled at her, "That's a good answer Maeve." Siobhan would like the story.

They left the crow to its future as a snack and made their way to the coffee shop, where Maeve made a terrific mess of herself drinking hot chocolate. Finn wet a napkin and sponged her off while she complained about his fussing over her.

Finn counted out their bus fare on the table, and they left the warmth of the coffee shop and stepped into a cold wind that had picked up while they sat inside. Maeve had trouble keeping her eyes open in it, so Finn grabbed her arm and steered her where he wanted her to go. They had to cross the street to get to the bus stop. Finn held Maeve at the light, and when it changed he started moving her into the crosswalk. The road had become quite busy, with cars backed up two blocks on either side of the lights. They had made it halfway across when Maeve stopped walking and became a statue that Finn found he couldn't pull. Finn stopped short and turned to her.

"Maeve, you..." and he noticed her eyes, vacant and staring. Her mouth moved up and down, drool hanging out of the corner of her mouth. She started to spit, and then her hand came up and plucked at her jacket.

"Oh, no, Maeve, not here, not in the middle of the street." He looked around, panicked, at the cars. She stood in place and started to moan. Finn wrapped his arms around her, and held on as she started to walk off to the right. He held his arm up, palm up to the cars they stood in front of, and felt overwhelming relief when the large, bearded man in the truck in front of him nodded at

146

him. He could see that something bad had happened.

After what seemed like an hour, Maeve came out of it, and slumped against Finn. The light still hadn't changed and Finn wasted no time in helping Maeve out of the crosswalk. He looked around for a place to sit her down as she moaned that she felt sick. He saw a dentist's office with chairs in it, and he held her up and guided her in.

"Hi," the receptionist said, looking up at them. She wore a green pastel smock, and her hair pulled up in a ponytail.

"Hi. Uh, my sister just had a seizure, can we just sit here for a minute?"

"Oh, is she alright?"

"Oh, yeah, she will be. She has them all the time. We just need to sit for a minute, okay?"

"Would you like some water?" The receptionist stood up and peered over the counter. Finn thought she had pretty eyes.

"Sure, that'd be great."

The receptionist disappeared to a back room and then returned with a styrofoam cup with water in it. Finn took it and thanked her, and held it for Maeve to drink. Maeve didn't want it. Her head lolled on his arm and Finn decided to let her doze for a few minutes. He didn't want to make Terry wait for them though, and he kept glancing at the clock on the wall behind the receptionist.

Ten minutes, I'll give her ten minutes. Finn sat and watched the people passing on the street outside, all covered up in the rain, most of them. Some young guys stood in a pack across the street, outside a convenience store. They all wore tee shirts and no jackets, as if daring the cold rain to do them in. *Instead of looking cool, they just look cold.* Finn laughed at himself for thinking that.

Maeve stirred on his arm, moaning a bit and blinking.

He rubbed her cheek with his finger.

"Maeve, Maeve, you just had a seizure, it's okay."

"I feel sick," she whispered.

"I know, but that will pass. Here, have a sip of water." He held the cup up to her and she took a sip of it. "You just rest for a few minutes, okay. We'll just sit here for a minute."

"I'm cold," she said, even though the office felt warm and she had her coat done up. Finn pulled her tight against himself.

"Better?" he asked.

She smiled a bit at him and then drifted off again.

They stayed at the dentist's office for longer than Finn had intended. He finally roused her enough to head to the bus. She sat next to him, leaning on him heavily, and Finn kept checking the time on his mum's cell phone, grumbling at every light the bus stopped at.

Terry stood outside the museum when they arrived.

"You're late," he said, but not unkindly.

"Yeah, I'm sorry, Maeve had a seizure," he gestured to his sister, whom he had by the hand.

"I'm sorry," Maeve said to both of them.

"It's not your fault," Finn said to her.

"Is she okay now?" Terry asked, bending over to look at her.

"Yeah, she just needed to rest for a bit."

Terry smiled at Maeve, and Maeve smiled back. "Would you like a piggy back ride?" he asked her.

"I'm not sure." Maeve looked at her brother.

"It's okay if you want one."

"Do I want one?" she asked Finn.

"Well, you used to like them, when you were small enough for Mum to give you one. So you can say yes, and then if you don't like it you can get down."

"Okay," Maeve said to Terry. They found a bench, and Finn helped her get up on Terry's back. She grew quiet, looking around at everything while they walked.

"So, what do you want to do?" Terry asked Finn as they walked along. Terry wore a jacket but no hat, and his hair shone slickly wet in the glow of Christmas lights outside the stores. Maeve rested her cheek on the back of his shoulder. She had grown immersed in the lights and the bob of Terry's long gait.

"I don't know. I never come down here. Why not just walk around until we find something?"

"Sounds fine, now that the rain seems to be letting up."

They walked along, chatting off and on. Terry let Maeve down after awhile and she happily walked between them, slowly growing more and more talkative with Terry. They wandered into a used CD and movie place, browsing the stacks on opposite sides, making pithy comments about all the long-defunct bands represented.

"Holy fuck, Poison." Terry held up a disc cover.

"My mum probably listened to them," Finn said.

"No way, isn't she all hippie and free love like?"

"Yeah, now, but in the eighties she was a rocker chick. All big hair and too much make-up. We have pictures."

"Hilarious, fucking hilarious." Terry slipped the CD back. "I think my mum was into country music or something. My grandma doesn't talk about her much."

Finn had always wondered what happened to Terry's mum. This marked only the second or third time Terry had ever mentioned her to Finn. Finn didn't want to ask though. It felt personal and off limits.

"I'd like to meet your mum!" Maeve spouted.

"Well, I haven't seen her in many years, but if I do, I'll let her know that, okay?"

"Okay," Maeve said. Finn took her hand and led her down the aisle.

"Where'd your Mum go?" Maeve asked.

"I don't really know Maeve. She had problems, drug problems. Do you know what drugs are?"

"Yeah, my mummy's friends died of drugs."

"I didn't know that." Terry looked at Finn to see if the topic had gone too far, but Finn shrugged his shoulders to signal it hadn't. "Well, my mum had those problems, and so I went to live with my dad for awhile, and then my grandma."

"I'd like to meet your grandma!" Maeve said, back on the same track she had started with.

"Well, I'm sure she'd like to meet you too," Terry answered her.

Finn felt thankful that Terry showed such calmness with her.

"My mum's fat! But I don't want her to diet."

"Mum could stand to lose some weight, Maeve."

"No! I love her just the way she is." Maeve's face shone with earnestness. "Her morning breath stinks like ass, though." Terry and Finn exchanged amused glances over her head.

"Hey, I know, let's stop talking long enough to eat a doughnut, okay Maeve?" Finn said to her, and the distraction worked. Finn became aware that the counter staff had listened to most of their conversation, as they walked out the door and he caught their amused looks. He smiled nervously at them as Maeve pulled him out the door.

They found a cozy looking coffee house that had chairs near a fake fireplace. Finn sat Maeve down and got her a warm milk and a doughnut. He produced a colouring book and some crayons from his shoulder bag and Maeve went to work colouring farm animals. Terry sat next to him, stretching out and slouching in the chair. Finn noticed that his canvas shoes had holes in them, and they had soaked through in the rain.

"Are your feet cold?" he gestured at them with his mug of coffee.

"Yeah, a little bit. I really need to go to the VV and get some more, but I hate buying used shoes."

"Yeah, they never feel right. My mum doesn't like to buy used shoes. She feels they're more personal than other clothes. I hate shoe shopping with her though."

"Why?"

"Because she puns. She especially likes to pun on themes, and they are just awful puns," Finn rolled his eyes.

"Really? Like what does she say? I'm not sure I know what a pun is."

"You're lucky. It's just word play on similar sounding words and stuff. Like she'll pick up an expensive shoe and say that's the one she would've bought me if I toed the line more often and wasn't her arch villain."

Terry looked blankly at him, repeating the sentence quietly to himself and then thinking about it for a minute until a smile broke through his concentration.

"Ah, I see. That's actually funny, when you think about it."

"Yeah, well, maybe, but it gets old when she does it all the time."

Maeve had stopped colouring and had come over to sit in Finn's lap. He gasped a bit at her weight and then looked quickly at Terry to gauge his reaction, but Terry took no notice. Maeve snuggled down into his chest and he put an arm loosely around her shoulder.

"Hugs!" she demanded. Finn hugged her. He picked up his coffee from the table next to him and took a drink. Maeve's weight had already caused his legs to feel numb and he had just started to move her off when she went stiff again and started moaning.

"Oh, okay Maeve, okay." He held her at an awkward angle on his knee, worried she might fall.

"What's going on?" Terry looked alarmed. "Is she alright?"

"She's having a seizure," Finn said calmly, focusing on holding her.

Terry jumped out of his chair. "What do we do? Should I get something to put in her mouth?" He looked around for something hard.

"No, you aren't supposed to do that." Finn noticed other people in the café looking over at them, some with suspicion.

"You're not? I thought they might bite their tongues or swallow them or something,"

"No, they don't do that, and if they vomit, an object in their mouths can cause them to aspirate the vomit into their lungs. Just pass me a napkin."

Terry handed Finn a napkin and he wiped the froth away from Maeve`s mouth and caught her spit with it. One of the baristas came over, looking angry.

"What is going on here?"

"My sister's having a seizure."

The barista's look changed from anger to fear. "Should I call an ambulance?"

"No, she's stopping..."

"I'll phone an ambulance." The barista took off like a

shot without listening.

"No, really..." Finn called out to her. Maeve slumped against him.

"She's done?" Terry asked, leaning over to look at her. Finn nodded at him. "What now?"

"Well, now we just wait for a bit, and talk to the paramedics I guess," he sighed.

"Do you want me to go tell her not to call them?"

"Yeah, actually, if you could. There's nothing they can do about it."

"Okay." Terry turned and walked to the counter, where the girl spoke on the phone. Finn heard her say that she couldn't do anything now that she'd called the ambulance, store policy.

Terry came back and told him. Finn said he had heard her, and thanks for trying. Then they just sat there in silence until the paramedics showed up.

They couldn't do anything.

Finn phoned his mother while the paramedics checked Maeve out, taking her blood pressure and temperature.

"You should bring her home when they're done," she said.

"I will," he promised, sad to have to leave Terry.

The paramedics finished and Maeve seemed less out of it. Finn helped her get her coat on. They had stopped engaging the interest of everyone in the coffee shop after the paramedics left.

"Well," he said, looking at his friend, "I guess we have to go home now. Mum is worried about Maeve having so many seizures while we're changing her meds."

"Right, well I'll help you home with her."

Finn hadn't expected that. His felt his face blush with gratitude. "Are you sure? You don't have to, if there's something you'd rather do..."

"Nope, I was getting bored down here already. Let's go." He took Maeve's other hand, his sleeve rolled up to show a leather wrist band with metal spikes and a bad, home-made tattoo of a skull on his skinny arm. Maeve looked very happy.

***

Siobhan had packed up most of her studying by the time they got home. She greeted them with tea and biscuits she had just made, leaving the boys in the living room as she attempted to put Maeve down for a nap. Siobhan lay with her and read in the dark of their bedroom for awhile before Maeve finally drifted off, her head on Siobhan's arm. Siobhan waited for a bit then extracted herself from her sleeping daughter and went back to the living room. Finn and Terry sat there, most of the biscuits devoured, looking through the channels on the TV.

"Thanks for taking such good care of her, boys," she said, and sat down next to Finn on the couch. Finn moved away slightly in an effort to ward off any possible hugging. Siobhan noticed his movement with amusement.

"Oh, no problem, Finn's Mum," Terry said.

"I've told you before that you can call me Siobhan," she said, and tossed a scrap of paper at him.

"I don't know," Terry assumed a fake look of contemplation. "It doesn't seem right to call you by your first name, being a friend's mother and all."

"Well, then, you'll be happy to know that I am not his mother. I simply found him one day when I emptied out the vacuum cleaner. I think he's just a dust bunny. That's why I quit vacuuming."

154

Finn sat and shook his head at her, but Terry laughed. Terry had always appeared to like talking to Siobhan. Finn wondered why he always felt so unsure of people, even when they had treated Maeve as well as Terry had today. He wished he could act more like his mum sometimes. She didn't worry about things, just let them go.

Finn and Terry hung out for the rest of the afternoon with Siobhan, turning down the volume on the TV and making up their own dialogue for the shows, Siobhan laughing hard and wiping tears from her eyes. She made them sandwiches and hot chocolate, and Finn told her about finding the Poison CD. He prodded her a bit to get her to show them pictures of her big hair and eighties make-up.

"What did your parents think of that hair?" Terry asked her.

"Oh, they had already died by then," she said, flipping through the photo album pages.

"Both of them?"

"Yep."

"Who'd you live with then?" he asked.

"No one. My father's mother was still alive, but I didn't like her. She was very religious, and neither of my parents were, so I wasn't."

"So you just...lived by yourself?"

"Well, sort of. It was difficult. I was young, it was hard to rent an apartment. I couldn't get welfare. I bounced around. I survived."

"Didn't they make you go into foster care?"

"They tried. And group homes. The group homes were okay. But they can't really hold you, and after awhile the cops just stopped picking me up."

Finn started to feel uncomfortable and tried to think of

something to say.

Terry sat back in his chair and thought for awhile. "I sometimes think of going off on my own."

"Why?" Siobhan looked at him, genuinely puzzled.

"I don't know," Terry shrugged. "Maybe it'd be easier on my gran."

"You're not a baby, Terry. I'm sure your gran has no trouble with you living with her."

"Well, maybe it'd be better to live on my own, grow up a bit."

"Pfft, being on your own doesn't mean growing up. Believe me, I had lots of friends that were really immature and out on their own. So was I, for a long time."

"But you got through it good, look at you, you're fine now."

"Yeah, now. But I had to work at fine. Fine didn't just happen. Yeah, I learned a lot, but I had a lot of damage, too. Stay in your house, with your gran, as long as you can. Until you finish college."

"I don't want to go to college."

"Then don't. But you only have a few years to not have to worry about all that, and a lot longer to worry about it. You have plenty of time to be a prol."

"A what?" Terry looked at her.

"A prol. A proletarian. Working class. Don't be in a rush to go be a wage slave."

Terry just looked at her, then leaned his head back and closed his eyes. Finn worried that his mum had pissed Terry off.

"So, would you do things different then, Mum?"

"Nope. Not at all. But that was *my* life. I had a lot of fun. Most of it I'd do over. Not all, but most. Having you and Maeve, for sure. But, no, hard as it was, I have great memories."

She fell silent for a bit, looking off into space. They all sat together without saying anything.

Siobhan snapped out of it. "So, what are you two going to do tonight?"

Terry and Finn looked at each other. They hadn't planned on anything after going downtown.

"I...don't...know." Finn puffed out his cheeks and tried not to stare at Terry.

"Well, we could go over to Neka's. Her parents are out of town, and..."

"Are her parents ever in town?" Siobhan asked, "Does she even have them? Perhaps she's just a rich old lady who paid for plastic surgery to look young enough to go to high school, huh? Maybe *that's* the truth!".

"Uh, no," Terry said, "I've met them, they're real."

"Crap, another theory blown. Thanks," Siobhan sat back hard in a fake huff, knocking a cup off the table next to her. "Okay, you guys go. Finn, be home by one, 'kay? Do have money left over from today?"

"Yep."

"It's enough?" Siobhan asked hopefully. Finn knew they didn't have much left over right now.

"Oh, yeah. It's plenty. Do you want it back?"

"No, no, keep it."

Terry stood up and stretched. His fingers grazed the high ceiling. "Okay, thanks, uh...Siobhan. It was nice hanging out."

"Thank you for your help with Maeve. You're a nice guy, Terry."

Terry smiled a bit awkwardly at her. Finn gave her a brief hug when Terry turned to the door.

As the door closed behind them, Siobhan let out a sigh

and leaned back against the couch and rubbed her belly. She had her period, and the occasional discomfort she had felt off and on for awhile now had come on full force. She felt stuffed and awkward, and her insides felt constricted. She got up from the couch and staggered down the hall to the bedroom where Maeve lay and crawled in next to her. She lay down in her clothes and stretched out a hand to Maeve's chest, feeling it move up and down. The bed felt warm and soft, and she gave into the sleep pheromones Maeve exuded, drifting off with her head on a Winnie the Pooh stuffed toy.

"Mum, there's blood all over the bed," Maeve woke her by saying sometime later. For a second Siobhan felt panicked that she meant her own blood, but the the feeling of wet legs disabused her of that.

"It's just my period, Honey. Mummy will go have a shower," she said, getting up and kissing her head, "you stay here and read, okay?"

"Okay," Maeve said, taking the books Siobhan tossed up next to her.

In the bathroom, Siobhan stripped off her skirt and sticky tights and ran a shower. *Probably should go to the doctor. After finals.*

***

Finn and Terry walked for a while in silence. It had started raining a bit, but softly, and Finn felt very aware of Terry's breathing in the silent alleyway. This made him aware of his own breathing, which suddenly seemed loud and asthmatic to him. He tried to control it by breathing in through his nose and out from his mouth, an exercise he had read in a book of his mother's once. This just made his breathing seem more obvious to him, so he tried pinching one nostril shut, breathing in through the other, then releasing that nostril and closing the other to breath out. He tried to establish a rhythm that accompanied his footsteps. Step, clasp, breathe in, unclasp, step, clasp, breathe out.

"What are you doing?" Terry suddenly asked him, looking curious and amused.

Finn had frozen mid clasp change, so he held both nostrils shut. He tried to think of something clever to say, but it took too long and he found himself blasting air out of his mouth.

"Nothing," he managed, trying to look ahead.

"C'mon, that was not nothing. What were you doing?"

"I just was trying to breathe normally." Finn smiled and blushed at the same time, as he realised how ridiculous it must have looked. He could hear his mother laughing at him.

"Normally? You 'normally' breathe by manually operating your nostrils?" Terry punched him lightly on his forearm.

"I just became aware of your breathing, which made me aware of my breathing. You know how, suddenly, when you start thinking of something you don't usually think of, you suddenly can't stop thinking about it. Like your tongue."

"What?"

"Your tongue. If you start thinking about your tongue, it becomes this huge, awkward lump in your mouth."

Finn could tell that Terry had started thinking about his tongue.

"Oh no," Terry said.

"Well, stop thinking about it,"

"I can't." Terry started laughing.

Finn laughed, too, and they walked down the street pushing each other and laughing harder with each step, until they collapsed at the bus stop. An elderly Chinese man gave them a wary look and moved to the far side of the bus shelter.

Terry brought out a package of cigarettes and lit one, then offered Finn one. Finn just shook his head at him. Instead, Finn counted out the bus fare he would need, counting it out three times back and forth in his hand. Terry made him jump when he said, "I think Neka likes you."

"What?" Finn said, a little loudly, his heart beating nervously in his chest. "No. No, that's not true. She's got a crush on you, not me."

"Well, yeah, she does have one on me. But she can have one on you, too, you know." Terry blew smoke up and it caught the wind.

"No, no. I don't want that." Finn bent over to pick up a coin he dropped.

"I don't think you get a choice." Terry gave him an odd look. "You don't have to do anything about it, and I could be wrong. I'm not though."

Finn suddenly felt very nervous about going over to Neka's. He looked around at the traffic and then turned to Terry. "You know, maybe I should just go home, I bet my mum could use some help with Maeve," he trailed off.

"Oh, Jesus, don't get freaked out, Finn. Just come on and act like you don't know. I wish I hadn't said anything."

They sat quietly for a minute, and then Finn spoke with a small voice, "She kissed me the other day."

"What?" Terry found this very funny, "and you're surprised that she likes you?"

"Yeah, I didn't think about any reason at the time

160

except pork chops."

Terry stopped laughing. "Okay, I don't understand that, but people don't usually kiss each other because of pork."

Finn laughed a bit and relaxed. "Yeah, that must have sounded really stupid."

"Okay, well, come on, here's the bus, don't get all nervous. Let's go and you can just act like I didn't say a word, okay?"

"Okay, I'll give it a go." Finn stood and collected himself, and then followed Terry onto the bus.

Chapter 7

National Mentoring Program
253 Hugh St.
Vancouver BC

Dear Ms. Lynch,

This letter is to acknowledge receipt of your application for a mentor for your daughter, Maeve. You will be contacted for an interview soon.

We don't wish to discourage you, but we think it will be very hard to match your daughter with a mentor. While we do seek mentors that can match with disabled girls, your daughter has a very complex set of disabilities. Particularly, the seizure disorder will present a problem. She may not match at all.

Yours,
J. Hibbs

***

Siobhan had finally seen her doctor before Christmas, and now had to have an ultrasound. Siobhan really hated holding her urine. She didn't even feel good natured about it as she sat in the waiting room trying to act like she didn't feel like crying and screaming from the discomfort. She would likely start peeing before she got in there.

The receptionist called her, and a dour faced technician led her down a hallway and handed some paper gowns to her, dismissing her request for peeing information and confirmation.

"Get dressed in these and then lay on the table, I'll be back in a few minutes," the woman said, her oddly colourless hair pulled back from her face, and her tech scrubs covered in clowns, which seemed like a terrible misrepresentation.

The tech closed the door behind her. Siobhan moaned a bit, and changed into the gowns as quickly as possible, pressing a hand against her vulva to will the urine to stay put. The table was cold on her legs, which did not help.

The tech came in and squeezed lube onto Siobhan's abdomen. Siobhan whimpered. Then the tech grabbed the head of the ultrasound and started cruelly squishing it around.

Siobhan was trying to choose the correct time to rip the woman's arm off and pee on the plant in the corner, when suddenly the tech said, "You can go use the washroom, we need to use a different wand."

Siobhan did not know what the tech meant, but she bounded off the table and ran like a lunatic down the hallway, not even locking the door as she slammed inside the bathroom and tore her gown up. Some pee hit the floor, but she didn't care. She slumped against the wall.

Back in the room, she said to the tech, "I'm sorry, I just am not good at that. My daughter weighed over ten pounds at birth, and I just have not been the same since."

The tech looked at her. "Okay, we have to use this internal wand. Okay?" She held up a long vibrator shaped wand. "I'm going to put this lubrication on it, and you insert it."

"Really?"

The tech just looked at her and held it out.

"Okay then, but according to my culture, we'll be married."

Nothing.

Siobhan took a deep breath and took the contraption from the technician, shifting around a bit as she put it in herself.

What an odd day.

The tech started to move it around and push buttons on the computer keyboard. Siobhan wished she could see the screen. She lay back and thought of years before, when she'd had dye injected into her uterus to assess the damage from an ectopic pregnancy she'd had at eighteen. She'd lost a fallopian tube. As the dye had entered her uterus, the shape came into focus on the screen above the table. She'd gasped and said aloud, "It looks just like they do in text books! Which makes sense, because why would they lie to doctors about what our guts look like?"

The doctor doing the procedure had just laughed at her.

The tech finally finished up and told Siobhan to get dressed.

Siobhan had had enough procedures with Maeve to know not to bother asking the tech for any information. Instead, Siobhan said to her, "When my daughter was born she had a stroke, from a clot that developed in a vein in her umbilical cord. We had to give her heparin to resolve it after she came home. I took her in for an ultrasound to see if the clot was resolving, and I got up on the table to breast feed her while they did it. They became all excited, and all the techs came in the room because you could see her swallowing, and see the milk going down her throat. It was really amazing."

164

The tech had stopped, and for the first time had some interest in her eyes. Her hand touched the knob of the door, just by the finger tips, and she said, "That would be very interesting."

They looked at each other for a moment, and then the tech left the room. Siobhan got her clothes on, then left into a light snow fall. The buses ran slow.

And she had to pee again.

"Crap," she said to herself, and wished she had a cigarette.

***

Finn had taken Maeve to the freezing parking garage to ride the trike Mum had gotten her for Christmas. It looked like a Big Wheel trike, but larger, metal, and it fit Maeve perfectly. Almost empty, the garage seemed the perfect place for her to zip around. They had tried regular bikes with training wheels before, but it'd always proved too difficult for Maeve who couldn't pedal, watch for traffic, and balance at the same time.

Finn crouched against a wall with a hot cup of coffee before him, watching her as she turned and darted back and forth, stopping often in front of him to tell him important things.

"We should get some stickers, to decorate this trike, like my last bike that I had when I was four." She gestured earnestly with her hands, her eyes looking serious and thoughtful. "We'll just throw the stickers on, randomly."

"Oh, yeah, that's great plan, Maeve. We'll do that."

"And we need to put a horn on here, so that I can honk it to warn people." She pointed at the bike, in case Finn didn't know where the horn would go.

"Well, yeah, you don't want to run people down all over the place."

"No, I do not," her eyes looked huge. Finn noticed her fingers glowing bright red on her handle bars.

"Let's go get you a pair of mittens, okay?" He stood and motioned toward the door.

"You go, I'll be fine right here." She put her legs up to start pedalling.

"Uh, no. That's not going to happen."

"I can do it!" she stomped her foot down.

"You know Maeve," Finn said, and walked over to her and squatted down, "it's not about your ability, I totally think you could stay here by yourself and be fine while I run upstairs, but you cannot control your seizures. You may want to, I know you want to, but they come at any time, and then you can't move where you want, even if a car comes. Especially now that we've got you off the old medicine and started the new one. You're having a lot of seizures now."

Maeve gave him a look of contempt, but allowed him to lock her bike to a bike rack in the bike lockup and lead her upstairs.

He opened the door and she followed him around as he searched for her gloves, moving stacks of papers, and books with pens and notes sticking out of them, sliding piles of clothes around, and opening closets and drawers. He found her gloves stuck on a Winnie the Pooh stuffed bear behind the couch. Maeve laughed when he held it out to her, asking if Winnie the Pooh really needed gloves. Bears have fur, after all.

"I thought Mummy would be up here, concentrating on her studies."

Finn smiled at her choice of words. "No, she went to the doctor's office, remember?"

"Oh, yeah. Will she have another baby? I'd like a brother or sister."

"But I'm your brother," he poked her in the tummy.

She grabbed his hand and held it. "A younger one, that I can help take care of," she smiled.

"Well, I don't think she's planning on any more babies, Maeve. Maybe a dog, later on, but no babies. Remember she had her tubes tied last year?"

"No."

"Well, she did, and that pretty much guarantees no babies."

"I wish she hadn't done that." Maeve took the gloves he offered from his hand and worked at putting them on. "When I have a baby, we'll all still live together. But we'll need a bigger house."

"I'm sure Mum will be thrilled at that news. Here, let me help," he held the gloves open for her small hands. "Okay, let's go."

"Where are we going?"

"To ride your new trike, remember?"

"No. I forgot."

"Okay, well, let me just get some more coffee."

"Okay."

***

The new semester had started and Siobhan's class schedule fit well with Maeve's school day. Siobhan found herself able to drop Maeve off every morning, so she could talk to her support worker, and pick her up every afternoon.

Now that Reading Week had come, Maeve had to

spend the week getting assessed for her psycho-
educational report. Finding the Children's Health Centre
proved a bit harder than Siobhan had anticipated. It took
up several blocks of a residential area, quite far away from
the Children's Hospital, which surprised Siobhan. She had
to pull a reluctant and grumpy Maeve along the sidewalk,
their mood further impaired by the fact that Siobhan
burned with fever and pain from badly infected tonsils.
Each swallow of saliva drove needles of pain into her
throat. She kept trying to save up her spit out of the fear of
swallowing. She would have to go to the clinic after this, for
antibiotics. For any other appointment she would have
cancelled, but arranging and waiting for this set of
assessments for Maeve had presented such a challenge
that Siobhan felt determined, no matter what the obstacle,
she would have to get through it.

Siobhan walked as fast as her fever, lethargy, and
angry child would let her. They stumbled onto a back
entrance, and Siobhan had to work out the way back
around to the main entrance. She read the happy painted
tree signs. She followed different coloured lines on the
floor. Maeve kept asking to sit but Siobhan worried about
the time, and kept trying to prod Maeve along with what
she hoped looked like loving smiles. She did not feel so
very patient today, and found it very hard work not to lose
her temper. They found the reception desk and signed in.
The receptionist directed them back almost to their
starting point, to a happily painted children's lounge filled
with toys and games. Maeve finally looked happy, as she
ran over to a well-equipped playhouse. Siobhan collapsed
in a chair.

They'd not waited more than three minutes when Maeve
got called for her appointment. Siobhan tried to croak

answers at the nurse interviewing them, but each attempt at sound made the nurse cringe. She finally sought to end Siobhan's pitiful attempts at communication.

"You know, you're here all week. Why don't we hold off on the questions until you feel better?"

Siobhan looked thankfully at her.

"Maeve has to go in for testing with the psychologist. It will take several hours, then they'll have a break for lunch. Why don't we find you a quiet room to lay in while she gets tested? Would that be okay?"

Siobhan nodded and let the nurse lead her down the hall to a quiet and dark examination room with a small couch in it. Siobhan hugged and kissed Maeve and watched her walk away with the nurse, looking a bit nervous and glancing back at Siobhan. Siobhan struggled to look like a mum who inspired courage, but she felt weak and ineffectual.

When Maeve had disappeared around the corner, Siobhan went in the room and shut the door. She flopped on the couch and closed her eyes, dozing lightly with many fitful wakings for the next few hours. Whenever she heard a door down the hall snick shut, or the muted voices of people in the hall, or the distant surge of a toilet flushing, she would startle awake and look around accusingly, as if the room had filled with attackers in those brief moments she had closed her eyes.

The waking parts and the sleeping bits meshed to form a constant and fluid state of not quite awake and not quite asleep, which felt a bit surreal when added to the pain and fever. She had no idea of the time at any point, and the overcast and dull day that showed through a small window did not help. She felt suspended. Time dragged out.

Finally, while Siobhan drifted, hot and disjointed, a soft knock came at the door. Siobhan tried to answer, but all that came out was acrid air. She got up and stumbled to the door. Maeve's face lit up and she threw herself at her mum, knocking Siobhan off balance and making her grab frantically for the door to hold herself up. Siobhan tried to smile at her, but even just moving her face muscles hurt.

"You have about a half hour to get some lunch before she goes back in, okay? There's a lunch room downstairs by reception," the nurse told her.

Siobhan nodded thanks to her and then led Maeve down to the lunch room. They found only a vending machine with sandwiches, fruit, and soup. Siobhan had enough change for a sandwich and an apple. They had put out free tea, coffee, and hot chocolate, so she made hot chocolate for Maeve and tea for herself. The tea felt both soothing and painful at the same time. Siobhan sipped it slowly and made her slow and wary way through the middle part of half the sandwich. Maeve told her how bored the testing had made her so far, but couldn't elaborate on exactly what the testing had entailed.

"I don't remember, Mummy, I just want to go home. Can we go home and read a book together?"

Siobhan scribbled, *NO, Must finish test*, on a napkin. Maeve read it and then asked to go home again. Siobhan tapped the napkin. Then, to distract Maeve's continued persistence, Siobhan drew a picture on the other side of the napkin and handed Maeve the pen. It didn't work.

"I don't want to draw. I want to go home." Maeve looked angrily at her. Siobhan shrugged her shoulders and then took her hand and led her back upstairs. She handed Maeve off and then sank back into her stupor on the couch.

170

Mouth and Foot Painting Artists

183 St. Clair Avenue West, Toronto, ON M4V 1P1

www.mfpacanada.com

Flamenco Dancer, from an original mouth painting by Chris Opperman

Schramm Vodka

At three o'clock, after six hours of testing, Maeve and Siobhan left. It took Siobhan a couple minutes of standing in the parking lot to decide on which way to go to get to the clinic Siobhan needed to go to.

***

Siobhan felt so happy that she lived in a time with antibiotics and painkillers, and hot mochas with whipped cream, all of which she arrived with along with Maeve, at the Children's Health Centre for the second day of testing. Her voice still cracked and fizzled, and she still felt a bit of pain, but she felt much better than the day before.

Maeve tested this day with the psychologist again. The same nurse again extended Siobhan the use of a vacant room, and Siobhan managed to get some reading done in between naps. She actually found it quite restful. *Why do hospitals never feel relaxing when you actually have to stay in one?* She supposed the difference lie in how many people came by to check on various parts of your body and in how much string they had used to hold your innards in. No possibly escaping intestines or nurses clucking at your perineum equalled a relaxing day. Just about anywhere, really.

Today she had brought a lunch, and managed to fill out some of the one million very similar yet vaguely different forms they always had her fill out for these things. They gave her seven forms, each with ten to twenty pages, all with statements like, "My child has trouble making friends at school". Her answer options consisted of variations of; all the time, frequently, rarely, and never.

After the testing, Siobhan met the psychologist, a friendly man with short hair and a terribly complicated name from some Eastern European source. Siobhan tried not to say it.

When she came into the room, Maeve had some storyboards in front of her. Siobhan knew the purpose. The story boards told a story, and they wanted Maeve to order and then describe the story. Maeve looked very disgruntled and frustrated.

"Well, I've worked with Maeve for two days now. Mornings are very hard for her, aren't they?"

"Yeah, she really has trouble getting up."

"I think that's from the medications. I think you really should not push her in the morning, and that we should move her appointments this week to a bit later in the day, okay?"

"Okay."

"I think the same goes for school. I think she should go to school each day when she's ready."

Siobhan looked at Maeve. She found this recommendation relieving. Mornings had grown contentious, with Maeve fighting both her and Finn every morning and arriving at school every day in a horrible mood. It ruined everyone's day.

The psychologist then explained to her the testing he'd done. Storyboards, memory tests, having Maeve make up stories to tell him, and puzzles, quite a full two days.

"She has a lot of trouble with memory. Whether that's storing the information or retrieving it, I'm not clear. It could be from her constant seizure activity, or it could be ADD."

Siobhan couldn't see him, because Maeve had climbed onto her lap and sat, mashing her nose against Siobhan's nose, holding Siobhan's head on either side. "Maeve, Honey, the

172

doctor is talking to me. Can you maybe back up a bit?"

"Why?" Maeve asked.

"Because we are not actually the same person. It's okay if you just sit beside me. I'm not leaving you here."

Siobhan pried Maeve's hands off her head and moved her to a seat beside her. Maeve leaned over and buried her head in Siobhan's side.

The doctor had waited patiently. "I also don't think she should get any homework. Just getting through the day is hard enough for her."

"I have already told them not to give her homework, but having you say it would be good."

"Yeah, it will help them plan her IEP. I think that you should focus on the social aspect of school, not the curriculum. Knowing the capital of Spain will not help Maeve as an adult. Developing proper social skills will."

"Will you be giving me a written report of all this that I can give the school?"

"Yes, and there will be a team meeting after she has seen all the therapists as well. But I have one more thing to discuss with you today." He pulled his chair toward the table in a way that let Siobhan know he had something important to tell her. For the first time Siobhan felt a bit nervous. She leaned toward him. She tried to make a noise that sounded attentive, but that sounded more like crazy to her.

"Maeve has anxiety and depression. She needs treatment for them. She also has low self-esteem."

Siobhan actually felt relieved. "Yes, I've thought so. She didn't used to have it, but in the past few years, I've seen her grow less engaged in school, more withdrawn."

"Okay, well, I'm going to refer her to mental health. It may take awhile, there's a waiting list, of course, but she'll need therapy, maybe medications."

Siobhan felt scared at the idea of giving Maeve any more medications. "Really? Meds? But she's on so much stuff already..."

"Well, I'd like to prescribe her an SSRI, for the anxiety, and Ativan for immediate use, as required. Anxiety can be successfully treated with medications. Depression is harder."

Maeve had slid down to the floor and lay under the table singing softly to herself. Siobhan felt thankful that she wasn't usually paying attention, whatever the cause.

***

Siobhan had managed to talk Finn out of accompanying her and Maeve all week. It had made him unhappy. Each morning he tried to talk her into letting him go by highlighting how useful and helpful a second person would prove. And honestly, on the first day, before she had known what the appointments would entail, and feeling so sick and feverish, she'd almost given in. He'd stood in the doorway of her room, while she tried to figure out the deep mysteries of putting on a T-shirt, something she felt sure didn't usually present such a problem, while he pled his case.

"Mum, look at you. You don't even understand your shirt."

"I do," she croaked. "This shirt is just poorly made."

"Uh-huh. You are not even going to make it to the centre. You're going to end up running around, lost and delirious. Let me come, just today."

"No. You go to school. I'll be fine. If I let you go today, it will just be harder to say no tomorrow."

"No, honestly, it won't."

She closed her eyes for a moment and she fantasized about just sending the two of them while she crawled back into bed and slept.

"No, Honey. If you stop bugging me, I will let you come on Friday, or whenever I find out the results, okay? Now go to school."

"But..."

Siobhan ran out of patience. Her throat burned, and she just could not keep talking. She gave him a rare stern look. "Enough. Go to school."

His lip jutted out in a pout similar to her own and he trudged off.

All week Siobhan and Finn had had similar conversations and he trudged off every day, defeated.

"Look, Finn, it will just be you and me sitting in a room, staring at each other for five hours. Really. I promise to stare at you when I get home. You do not need to come."

He looked truly miserable. Siobhan walked over to him and wrapped him in her warm arms. "You're a good brother. I know you just want to help, but really, there's nothing for you to do."

He held onto her for a moment. "Okay," he said in a thick voice and then cleared his throat against her shoulder. When he stood back, his eyes looked bright.

Siobhan had helped Maeve during some of the appointments, like the physical and occupational therapy, helping direct Maeve through the tests. The therapists would direct Maeve to do things, but Maeve would head off in the wrong direction, or grow excited and start jumping, or take a very long time to get into position. Often Siobhan would have to physically move her, muscle by muscle, joint by joint into position, and hold her there, and then help her go through whatever motion the therapists had asked for. Maeve grew frustrated at the painstaking instructions. Well, to her they seemed painstaking. To anyone else they comprised simple directions to stand on a line and walk forward, or hop on one foot, then the other.

By Friday, Finn would not take no for an answer, even though Siobhan had found out that the team meeting would take place a week from that Friday, giving all those who had worked with Maeve a chance to fill out their reports. Siobhan didn't want him to come, but it turned out that the she wouldn't have gotten Maeve through that final day without having Finn help out. Siobhan and Maeve felt completely burnt out by the process by then, and Siobhan had grown snappish, Maeve uncooperative.

But with Finn along, Maeve bounced and skipped along, and he felt so happy to finally get to go that he fairly bounced and skipped as well, which freed Siobhan to immerse herself in enjoying the brisk cold wind that blew. Without the wind the day might have warmed up, and grey clouds made the wind seem even more dramatic. Siobhan enjoyed the brief periods when the wind hit her just right, making it hard to breathe for just a moment. Maeve's cheeks had turned bright red and Siobhan felt compelled to kiss them.

Finn helped Maeve make it through the last of their appointments, helping to turn the testing into more of a game for her. The occupational therapist said to Siobhan, as they left, "Your son is really great with her."

Siobhan nodded at her. "Yes, he is. He's a good kid."

"It's just so nice to see."

Siobhan smiled and walked out.

176

She told Finn what the OT had said and he looked embarrassed but happy. Without talking about what to do next in their day, they ended up walking together for a long while, talking, with Maeve trying to carry her mother and brother in turn. Along the way they petted cats, barked at yappy dogs, and Maeve started to randomly wave at people in cars. The people would smile or look confused and wave back. Siobhan and Finn found it very funny, and Maeve felt happy that she had found something to entertain them. Every time she waved, they'd laugh, and she'd turn slyly back to them and say, "What? Why are you laughing?" because she wanted them to talk about it.

Finally, wind-blown and refreshed, they boarded a bus. Siobhan took Maeve's still red cheeks in her hands to warm them up and realised that Maeve felt very warm, despite having just spent all that time in the cold wind.

"Oh, Maeve, do you feel okay? You're very warm."

"I feel fine, Mum."

"Does she have a fever?" Finn looked concerned. He knew very well what a fever meant for Maeve.

"It feels like it. We'll see when we get home."

By the time Maeve had had a bath and gotten into bed, her cheeks had turned beet red. Siobhan gave her some Tylenol and lay beside her as she slept. Finn kept coming in to check on them, eventually falling asleep on the bed next to Maeve, her small hand resting on the top of his head. Siobhan read and watched her for a long time, and just as she felt like falling asleep, she looked over at Maeve and saw, on her back and shoulders, what looked like a rash. Siobhan ran a hand over her back and Maeve stirred a little.

Siobhan felt scared as she realised that Maeve might have developed a reaction to her new medication.

She turned over in her mind what to do. Maybe Maeve didn't have a rash and the light had played a trick on her eyes. Should she get Maeve up now and look at it, or let her sleep and see how she felt in the morning? How would she get Maeve to the hospital now, anyway? Would she call an ambulance? Did she have enough cash on her to take a cab? She got up and looked in her wallet. Fifteen dollars. Not enough for a cab. She decided to phone the nurse's line. Maybe they'd have a suggestion.

The nurse wanted to help Siobhan more than she actually could.

"I'm worried about Stevens-Johnson syndrome. They tell me to watch for it every time she goes on or comes off a med."

"Does she have blisters on her mouth?"

"No."

"Well, that's usually how it starts."

"But not always from what I've researched."

"Are you sure it's a rash?"

"No, not really without waking her up."

"Well, maybe let her sleep and then check it in the morning."

"Okay. I don't really want to get her up right now."

"Yeah, it's really late. Just let her sleep. Check her in the morning, and phone your doctor if it's a rash."

"Right. Thank you."

Siobhan went back to bed. Finn still slept there and she covered him up with the blanket then slid in next to Maeve. She rubbed Maeve's back gently, and eventually fell asleep. In the morning she didn't remember right away about Maeve's rash, until Maeve trotted out naked to the living room, dragging a blanket with her. What had only looked like the barest suggestion of a rash the night before had deepened into dark red, angry looking blotches, all over Maeve's neck, chest, and back. Siobhan stopped her in the living room and examined her closely. "How do you feel, Sweetie?" Maeve didn't answer. "Hon, how do you feel?'

Maeve looked at her calmly. "Okay? Why do you ask?"

"Because you look like a strawberry."

"Huh? What's happening today?"

"You, my dear, are going to the doctor, right away." Siobhan sat Maeve on the couch and then went in and shook Finn's foot. He looked at her with annoyance, confused about why he had awoken in her bed.

"Wad?" he moaned.

"Get up. Maeve is having an allergic reaction to her meds. I need you to get some clothes on her while I call a cab and get dressed."

Finn's expression changed to one of purpose and he got up quickly and stumbled to the living room to check on Maeve. Then he found some clothes and put them on her, fighting her complete disinterest in getting dressed the whole time.

"Finn, I am trying to read this book," she informed him, in case he had missed all the obvious cues of book reading.

"I'm sorry Maeve, but you need to go to the doctor," he said, struggling to get some mismatched socks on her feet.

Siobhan came in and said, "Finn, I called the cab. I need you to run to the bank machine and get some money out. We'll wait with the cab."

"Okay. Okay Mum." He went to his room and threw on the clothes from the day before. He ran back through the living room and went into his mother's bag and got her card out. His mum worked at getting Maeve's coat and shoes on while Maeve did her best to ignore her. "I'll be right back."

"Okay, we'll be outside."

Rain poured down as he ran to the gas station.

Siobhan pulled Maeve out the door, surprised that Maeve felt okay, but looked so horribly ill. They stood together under the eaves of the front door, Maeve leaning heavily into her.

"What's happening?" Maeve asked.

"We're going to the hospital," Siobhan answered, wrapping her arms around Maeve's shoulders.

"I don't want to go to the hospital."

"Me neither, but you have a rash."

Finn ran up, breathless, his hair plastered to his forehead. His eyes looked large and his cheekbones prominent. He handed his mum her money and card with wet, cold fingers.

"Thanks, Hon. You don't have to come with us if you'd rather head in and dry off."

"No, I'm okay. I'll go with you." He could tell his mum felt scared, even though she tried to hide it from him and Maeve. She smiled at him, thankful to have company.

The cab drove slowly up in front of their building and the cabbie honked. They made their way out in the rain.

***

I hate this hospital. It's so noisy. And full. I want to scream at everyone, but I just hug Finn and close my eyes.

Mummy is talking to someone. I won't open my eyes, but I hear her come over and talk to Finn. Mummy says that we need to go down the hall and wait.

180

"Come on, Maeve," Finn says to me, but I just hold onto him and keep my eyes shut.

"Maeve, it's hard to walk."

I'm sorry. I can't let go.

Now we're in some place quieter. I open my eyes a bit and see a room. There's a bed and chairs. A lady comes in and gives my mum something, then she leaves.

"Maeve, I need you to put these on, okay? I'll help you," Mummy says.

"Okay," I say. She takes of my clothes and puts a weird dress on me.

"What is this?" I ask.

"It's a hospital gown, so the doctor can see you."

"Oh."

"Now hop up in the bed, and I will be right back. You can watch the TV with Finn."

"Okay."

Mummy leaves the room. Finn helps me get in the bed and puts a blanket on me. Then he turns on the TV and finds a cartoon for me.

"Lay with me, Finn."

"Okay, Maeve."

He gets in next to me.

Mummy comes back. She touches my forehead. She sits down. She gets up and looks out the door. She sits again. She gets up again.

"Mummy, you keep blocking the TV."

"Sorry, Maeve."

A man comes in. Mummy talks to him.

He has very dark skin and eyes.

"This is the doctor, Maeve," Mummy says. "He needs to examine you."

Finn gets up, and the doctor looks at my chest and

back. He looks in my mouth. He listens to my heart. Then
he talks to Mummy again.
"You're blocking the TV!"
"Sorry, Maeve."
Finn sits next to me again.
"Does it itch?"
"No."
"How do you feel?"
"Okay. I'm hungry."
"We'll get something after we're done here, okay?"
"Okay.
Finn hugs me.
"You're a good sister, Maeve."
"Yeah."

Chapter 8

The emergency room doctor had told Siobhan to wean Maeve off the new seizure medicine immediately. She hadn't yet started Maeve on the anxiety medicine and they told her to wait until she saw the neurologist. On Monday she received a phone call from the neurologist's office asking if she could bring Maeve in first thing Tuesday morning. Siobhan said yes, first thing, they'd make it. The call came while she rode the bus to school. She sat back and closed her eyes after the call, thinking of the specifics of getting Maeve up to the hospital by nine. She felt happy that she had her own doctor's appointment the following Tuesday, because both appointments on the same day would not have worked, and she didn't want to cancel hers. She wanted to know the result of the ultrasound.

On Tuesday, Siobhan woke Maeve an hour earlier than usual. Maeve did not express gratitude, and tried to hide under the covers. Siobhan got in the bed and started to prod her awake.

"Aw, Maeve, do you feel grumpy and dissatisfied with your mother?"

Maeve moaned.

"Do you think it's time I moved out of the house?"

Maeve nodded her head under the cover.

"Won't you miss me, even a little bit?"

Maeve shook her head under the covers.

"But who will yodel for you while you have a bath?"

"Mum," Maeve moaned from under the blanket.

"Who will make your favourite squid meals for the holidays?"

"Mmmmuuuuummmm," Maeve groaned.

"Who will try to convince complete strangers at bus stops that for a mere five dollars you can psychically connect with their dead pets?"

"Nobody!"

"Okay," Siobhan said in her best fake crying voice, "I guess I'll leave then. Forward my mail to the alley, 'cause that's where I'll be living I guess." Siobhan started sitting up.

Maeve threw back the covers and grabbed her around the neck, making Siobhan gasp.

"No, Mummy, you can stay. Just quit being weird all the time." Maeve kissed her cheek.

"Aw, honey, Mummy can't promise the no weird thing, but I'm glad you want me to stay." Siobhan stroked her hair, and then slowly got her dressed and trundled her out to the living room for breakfast. Just as they started getting ready to leave, Finn came out of his room, shivering in the cold morning apartment.

"I wish I could come," he said, sliding down onto the couch.

"Well, you have that big test today, that's too important. I promise to tell you everything when we get home."

"Okay. Bye Maeve, have fun." He leaned over and hugged her, pulling her off the ground with a great effort.

"Pick me up again!"

"No way! You must weigh five hundred pounds!"

"C'mon Maeve, let's go." Siobhan pulled Maeve out the door, waving at Finn.

The sidewalks had ice on them, making them slippery and treacherous. Siobhan did not feel at all graceful as she minced along with Maeve, trying to stay upright while

holding the shoulder of Maeve's coat to stop her from
bounding off in random directions. Maeve chattered away,
oblivious to Siobhan, the traffic, and the ice. She kept
pulling Siobhan off balance, and Siobhan would swear
under her breath as she swayed and skidded.

The bus came on time, and Maeve insisted they go all
the way to the back to sit. She sat next to the big window
and patted the seat next to her for her mum.

Siobhan put an arm around Maeve, and Maeve leaned
against her and sat quietly for a few moments, looking out
the window. They turned a corner and Maeve sat bolt
upright and pointed to the large, naked, dancing woman
logo painted on the side of a local sex toy shop.

"Mummy! It's you! It's you! Look!"

Siobhan saw everyone turn and look at the dancing fat
woman.

And then they looked at her.

Siobhan smiled,

"Yes. Well, that does look like Mummy, but perhaps we
could not get the whole bus to consider what your mummy
might look like when she dances around naked?" she said
quietly to Maeve, who ignored her.

"And you're throwing products to the world!"

That made Siobhan laugh.

Maeve craned her neck to see the magical naked
mummy as long as she could.

The hospital was jumping with activity when they got
there. A long line of people stood outside a coffee kiosk in
the lobby. The delicious smell of espresso wafted on the
air. Siobhan led Maeve into the neurology office, where a
large Rube Goldberg machine stood in a glassed-in
enclosure at the far end of the office waiting room. The

machine had two wheels to turn, which caused balls to travel up and down a series of buckets, ramps and scoops. Maeve found it enthralling. As she played with it, a young boy about her age came in with his grandmother. He seemed very angry about something, flopping down in a chair, crossing his arms, and giving his grandma a grumpy look. He saw Maeve, turning the wheels on the machine, and he went over and asked if he could play. She said sure, and he sat down and started giving directions, to which she kept replying, "I know that," growing quickly annoyed with him.

"Do you come here a lot?" he asked her. "I do. I'm a haemophiliac. Do you know what that means? It means I have special blood. If I cut myself," he said and drew a hand across his arm, "I could bleed to death!"

She turned to him and said, "Do you know that I had a stroke? Do you know what a stroke is? It is when a blood clot goes into your brain. If you had a seizure, you would scream!"

"Oh," he said. And then they repeated the whole conversation.

Siobhan found the conversation fascinating, sad, funny, and very revealing. Maeve did not usually volunteer so much information and Siobhan found herself thinking that the two of them would make good friends, but grandma did not look very happy and Siobhan didn't want to approach her.

The nurse called them to weigh and measure Maeve, and shortly after that the nurse called them to see the doctor. The doctor appeared more brusque than usual, listening to Siobhan's story of the allergic reaction and making notes in Maeve's file.

After Siobhan had told her the whole story, and the doctor had asked every question she had, she sat and thought a bit then told Siobhan about the new medication they would try Maeve on. After that, she sat back and said, "If this new medication doesn't work, then we might have to assess her for surgery. Have you ever talked to anyone about surgery?"

Siobhan felt a look of shock settle on her face. "No. I have read about it, though. They separate the two sides of the brain?" Siobhan's stomach clenched at the thought. Maeve had her head buried in Siobhan's lap and Siobhan rubbed it, running her finger tips around Maeve's scalp.

"Sometimes. Sometimes they remove the injured section. I think we should have her assessed. Most children are assessed after two or three medicines haven't worked. Maeve has tried six. I'll refer you to the surgeon."

Siobhan didn't know what to say. Her head swirled with thoughts. She just looked at her fingers, running through Maeve's hair. "Well, good luck." The doctor stood up and shook her hand.

"I won't lie, the thought of surgery scares me," Siobhan said to her. The doctor didn't respond, just walked out, leaving Siobhan confused. She had just given her bad news, hadn't she? Scary news?

She got Maeve dressed in her coat and they left, Siobhan walking in a fog of conflicting thoughts, steering Maeve automatically through the hospital and to the bus stop.

I don't want her to have surgery. She looked at her daughter, who slopped through puddles with her boots, and made dragon sounds as they waited for the bus.

I don't want her to have surgery. And I don't want her to have seizures.

Siobhan got them on a bus headed home, but after about fifteen minutes of mulling over what the doctor had said, she realised she would have to tell Finn about the appointment. She didn't want to tell him about the possibility of surgery, it would give him an ulcer to worry about that for the next year, but she also realised that if she went home and didn't take the time to compose herself, when he asked she would likely start bawling. He would not take, "Oh, everything's fine," for an answer. She didn't want to talk to him until she had had lots of time to think.

***

Finn found himself walking around the school soccer field with Terry at lunch. The weather felt warmer that afternoon than it had for the past month, and Terry and Finn were not in a hurry to go in when the bell rang. They ended up standing around outside the fence behind the baseball diamond. Finn hung off the fencing, facing out, his arms pulling painfully out behind him. He half-heartedly kept trying to wedge his heels in the fencing and climb up. Terry squatted with his back against a pole. He kept pulling out grass and biting off the tender white ends.

"You know those little white flowers that grow all over this field in spring? Are those daisies?"

"I don't know," Finn grunted, his left foot sliding back down to the ground. "I don't think so." Finn finally let go of the fence, his hands frozen like claws. He looked at them, and then blew on them, walking over to Terry.

"Mum and Maeve like dandelions. You almost can't go anywhere with Maeve when they turn fluffy, because she wants to pick every one she sees." He sat down next to Terry, cross- legged.

"Aren't they a weed? Don't most people try to get rid of them?"

"Yeah, but Mum's got a soft spot for interlopers."

"What?"

"Things, plants and animals that thrive where they shouldn't and aren't wanted. Like raccoons, coyotes, crows, and dandelions. She likes tenacity."

"I like crows." Terry stood up and yawned, then stamped his feet. "I don't want to go back in today, do you?"

Finn looked at the school. "No, actually, I don't."

"I have some money on me. Why don't we go do something else for the afternoon?"

"Like what?"

"I don't know. Let's go shoot some pool at that Italian place."

Finn had never skipped a class before, unless it had something to do with Maeve. He knew his mum wouldn't get mad about it, and he didn't have any important classes this afternoon. "Sure," he said to Terry, and stood up, too. "But, I'll want to be home in a couple of hours, to hear bout Maeve's appointment."

"No problem," Terry said. "I don't have that much money."

They walked off together, sticking to the alleyways, quiet and deserted in the middle of the workday.

The pool hall smelled of old cigarette smoke, and the back room didn't have any pool players. Terry gave the guy behind the counter some money and got a case of pool balls. Finn followed along behind him and Terry flipped on the bank of lights as they went into the back room. Finn watched Terry choose a stick, turning it back and forth, looking at the tip, hefting it in his hand. Finn pretended to do the same, even though he had no idea what any of it meant.

Terry showed Finn how to rack up the balls and then told him to break. Terry lit a cigarette, and held it in his mouth when he took his shot, screwing up one eye to keep out the smoke.

"You look like Popeye," Finn teased.

"Arr!" Terry stood up and looked at Finn. "Wait, does Popeye say arr?"

"Uh, I don't know. If he doesn't, he should."

Finn had five dollars in his pocket that he had meant to buy lunch with. He excused himself for a minute and went and got them both espressos from the bar up front. The espresso made them jumpy and happy and chatty. The guy at the front counter didn't bother them about the time because they were the only customers and they didn't bug him, so they played and played.

"You know, you're pretty good at this kind of stuff, naturally.Like the video games. You've got good hand-eye coordination," Terry said. He'd still won all the games.

Finn felt very honoured by the compliment. He felt a huge smile grow on his face and his cheeks flushed. He stammered a thank you. Finn glanced towards the front and a small, familiar figure caught his eye. He lowered his voice and said, "Jono just came in."

"Crap," Terry whispered. "Let's be quiet, and maybe he won't see it's us."

They started gathering up the balls as slowly and quietly as they could, but it didn't work. Jono saw them and headed straight back.

"Hey, Scary!" he yelled in the quiet of the back room.

"Jono, I have told you to stop calling me that. I mean it."

"Fuck, okay, calm down," he said, holding his palms out in a back off motion. He barely looked at Finn.

"You guys playing pool?" He started shooting pool balls across the table as hard as he could. They made loud banging noises and clacked together as he shot more across.

"We have been, but we have to head out soon," Finn answered.

Jono gave him a disdainful look, and turned back to Terry. "Hey, play me a game before you go."

"I don't think we have time, and I don't have any more money," Terry answered.

"C'mon, one game. I'll pay and buy you a coffee." Jono whined a bit. "There's no one else to play."

Terry looked at Finn with inquisitive eyebrows. Finn shrugged back.

"Fine, but get Finn a coffee, too."

Jono tried not to look put out by that. "Whatever." He went off to the front.

"Is this alright? Or would you rather go now? I don't know why I said yes," Terry said, sidling up to Finn.

"No, it's fine. I have a bit yet before I have to go. Go ahead, I'll just sit here." Finn sat at a little table in the corner.

Jono came back, followed by the barista, who was carrying a tray with coffees and milk on it. He set them down without speaking and went off.

Jono set up the balls and Terry broke. Jono proceeded to embarrass himself through the whole game and the next by taking on impossible shots and then blowing them. Terry kept shooting Finn funny looks, and Finn kept stifling his laughter.

Jono blamed his bad playing on the table, it had bumps; the stick, it felt slippery; the lighting, florescent lights gave him migraines, which he would get later but which affected him now; and on Terry, who had cheated the whole game by virtue of his height and superior reach.

Halfway through the second game, Finn giggled out loud and immediately knew he'd made a mistake. Jono, who'd ignored him the whole time, now turned toward him with his face scrunched with anger, his fists clenched. "Fuck you, asshole!" he screamed at Finn, and grabbed a pool ball. He threw it viciously at Finn, who managed to duck enough that it struck the side of his head with less force than if it had hit him full on. Still, it made him cry out and it opened a small gash on his scalp. Finn doubled over and held his head. He heard Terry grab Jono and throw him into the wall.

"What the hell is wrong with you, you nasty shit?" Terry said. Finn looked up to see Terry's fist cocked to hit Jono. Jono didn't say anything, Terry had knocked the wind out of him.

"Get away from us and never talk to me again." Terry let go of Jono, who didn't say anything to either of them, he just gave Finn a bitter look and walked away.

Terry came over to Finn and looked at his head. "Are you okay?"

Finn said he thought he was. He felt very aware of Terry standing over him, the smell of Terry's T-shirt, and Terry's huge hands on his head.

"Hold on." Terry went to the front and came back with some wet paper towels, which he used to wipe away the blood on Finn's head.

"Aw, it's not big. You don't need stitches." Terry handed the towels over to him to hold against his head.

"I hate that guy," Finn said.

"Yeah, I do, too. I'm done with him. He's just getting worse and worse." Terry sat down at the table. "Do you

192

want to go home now?"

"Uh, maybe give me a few minutes." Finn didn't want his mum to see him bleeding, she'd freak out, and so would Maeve. Better to get home a bit late.

***

Terry had walked Finn home and then left. Finn was surprised that Maeve and his mum hadn't arrived home yet. Well, at least he would have time to shower and make sure the small gash on his head didn't show. He went into the bathroom and started the shower.

When he got out, he went to his room and lay in his bed and read for awhile, falling into a sleep before long. When he woke, the sky outside had darkened and he sat up with a jolt, afraid he'd missed his mum and Maeve coming home, as well as the plans he had that night with Terry. His clock said six o'clock, though. He got up and threw on some clothes and went out to the living room. No one had showed up.

Finn sat down and tried to think if his mum had said she had plans tonight, but he didn't remember any such conversation. He picked up the phone to call Siobhan's cell phone and heard the tone that indicated a message. His mum's voice told him that they had gotten stuck at the university library while she did some research, and then she thought she'd take Maeve to dinner and a cheap movie. He hung up the phone, puzzled that his mum would take Maeve to a movie on a school night. He dialed her number and got a busy signal.

Finn sat and stared at the wall for a while. Usually, Mum kept Maeve home as much as possible. Maeve easily felt stressed in traffic and crowds. He thought it so strange that she would keep Maeve out since eight o'clock that morning. He tried her number again. This time his mum answered.

"Mum, why are you taking Maeve to a movie on a school night?" he asked. He could barely hear her over the noise in the background.

"Well, we were already downtown, and she's had such a bad couple of days, I just thought it would be nice for her. She can sleep in tomorrow, I don't have a class."

"Well, what did the doctor say?"

"Finn, can we talk about that when I get home, we're surrounded by strangers right now."

"Yeah, I can hear that. Where are you?"

"At the food court at the mall."

"Maeve let you take her there?"

"Yes, but we have to hurry or she'll lose it."

"Okay," he answered. "I'll stay home tonight, and wait for you."

"Oh, no honey. Go out. We'll both be exhausted by the time we get home anyways. Go out, I know you had plans tonight."

"Are you sure?"

"Yes, really. We'll talk tomorrow. There's no big news. Honest."

He let her talk him into it a bit more, then agreed and hung up, feeling uneasy.

Finn walked over to Terry's. Terry lived in a small, one bedroom apartment with his grandmother. Terry's grandmother had taken Terry in at three years old. She'd treated Terry well, and always said hi to Finn, but now she just took care of Terry's basic needs, and seemed to have decided she had finished mothering him. She sat in her living room, an old brown and yellow TV tray in front of her, drinking instant coffee and rolling cigarettes on a huge, hand crank machine while she watched TV. She had a big black ashtray beside her that Terry would empty twice a day for her, or else she'd empty it into the small trash can next to her, and on more than one occasion Terry had come home to find the trash can smouldering.

"Hello, Terry's friend," she hacked as he stood in the hallway, waiting for Terry.

"Hello Mrs. Spiele," he answered politely.

"Are you boys going to get into trouble tonight?" She smiled at him, smoke streaming from every pore in her head.

"No, no, we're well-behaved."

She smiled at him, and took a sip of coffee. "Good boys get in trouble, too." She winked at him.

Terry came out of the bathroom and punched Finn on the arm as he walked by. Finn smiled at him. Terry grabbed his coat from the couch and gave his grandmother a kiss, leaning over the TV tray. She grabbed his hand firmly as he stood, and smiled at him.

"See you later, Gran."

"You boys have fun. And take the garbage down."

"Yep." Terry came toward him, slipping on his coat, and leaned into the small kitchen to grab a small bag of garbage. "Let's go out the back."

He asked Finn to hold the bag for a minute, while he took the twenty his grandmother had slipped him out of his palm and unfolded it, sticking it in his wallet.

They flipped the garbage into the dumpster in the alley. A rain soaked mattress mouldered up against the dumpster.

"Free mattress," Terry said, raising his eyebrows at Finn.

"Tempting, but I just don't have the blood encrusted sheets to go with it."

"True. You're going for a look, after all."

They walked off down the alley. Terry smoked a cigarette he'd gotten from his grandmother. "So, what'd your mum say happened at the doctor?"

Finn jolted a bit, surprised Terry had remembered that.

"Uh, well nothing yet. They weren't home when I left."

"Oh."

Finn looked down and shrugged. "I think she's stalling."

"Oh, no. I'm sure it's okay."

"We'll see. Will Jono be there tonight?"

"He better not be. I told Neka to stop inviting him over. He's such a shit."

"Why'd you guys start hanging out with him in the first place?"

"He didn't used to be so bad. He used to be a lot of fun, actually. But then he and Neka had this thing, and then she told him to fuck off, and then he started being a jerk. But I think we're all done with him, because of the shit he pulled last weekend."

Finn tried not to sound extremely pleased by this news. "What shit?"

"Aw, he got really drunk and tried to punch Luther. Then he puked in the fireplace. Neka was pissed at him."

"No doubt."

196

Chapter 9

Siobhan sat in her gynaecologist's office, fully dressed this time. She sat in the chair and looked at the 3-D medical posters on the wall. Maeve loved the posters when she came along, but today Siobhan had taken her to school, and she would go to her own class after this appointment. She felt anxious, wondering if the ultrasound had actually showed anything. Maybe she just had pelvic floor problems. She got up and took a small model of a uterus off the top of the cabinet over the sink. A layer of dust had settled on it and she ran it under water to clean it, then dried it and sat down with it. Did the doctors ever actually use these things?

The uterus opened up, and the inside had bright colours, and a hollow centre. Siobhan thought it might make an excellent place to stash a second set of keys. Or it would look great in a fish bowl, as decoration. *I must remember to ask how to get one of these.*

Someone knocked on the door, and Siobhan said, "Come in." A small, slender woman came in, younger than Siobhan.

"Hi, I'm Doctor Sterne, I'm filling in for Doctor Hardy, she's on maternity leave."

"Oh, I didn't know she was pregnant," Siobhan said, and shook the doctor's hand.

The doctor sat across from her, opened up Siobhan's file, and flipped through the pages.

"So, you've been having some discomfort. Is that all the time, or just occasionally?"

"Just occasionally. I feel pressure, down here" Siobhan said and pointed to just above her pubic bone, "and sometimes it feels like something's falling over."

The doctor looked at her with one eyebrow raised.

"Falling over?"

"Yeah. Please tell me it's not a prolapsed uterus. I have been so worried that it was."

"Well, let me look at the ultrasound report here."

"Okay."

"It's not a prolapsed uterus. You have an ovarian cyst."

"Oh." Siobhan hadn't thought of that. "And that's what's causing the falling feeling? I don't understand, aren't ovarian cysts small?"

"Usually, but yours is twelve centimetres."

What? Well that's tiny, I mean, how big is a centimetre?"

"Twelve centimetres is quite large. It's the size of a grapefruit." Dr. Sterne held up her hands in a circle to show Siobhan how big.

"Oh. Yeah, that's huge. How could I grow something so big and not feel it before?"

The doctor shrugged her shoulders.

"So, what do I do about it?" Siobhan asked.

"You need surgery. Right away. The cyst is irregular, which means it could be cancer."

Siobhan felt overwhelmed by both of those pieces of information. "Surgery? Right away? I can't. I can't have surgery right now. I have kids to take care of. And I can't just quit the semester."

"You'll have to make arrangements. Get a relative to take care of the kids, and talk to your professors."

"No, you don't understand. My daughter is very special needs, I don't have anyone to take care of her except my son, and he's only fifteen. I can't just leave him to watch her. And I can't just not finish the semester. I've already had to apply for extra funding, because I only take three classes a semester because of Maeve. I only have the summer left, and then I graduate. I really can't do it."

"You have to."

"No. How long will I be in the hospital for?" Siobhan frantically groped for a solution.

"Five days. It's a big operation."

"Right." Siobhan hunched over and put her head in her hands. How would she arrange such a thing? Maybe she could ask five people to watch them one night each. Could Finn even stay with her by himself? What laws would that break? She made up her mind.

"We have to wait until the end of the semester. I have to finish the semester, and I need to figure out what to do with the kids." Siobhan sat up and put a set look on her face. "It has to wait."

The doctor looked like she might argue more and opened her mouth. But Siobhan looked determined, and the doctor realised she would not change her mind.

The doctor composed herself, then asked Siobhan what date the semester would end.

"I'll book it for the next day, exactly, not a day later."

"Okay, thank you." Siobhan stood and shook her hand. She signed some consent forms at the front desk and left in a daze. She made her way automatically to school, and sat through two classes without taking any of it in, just doodling idly in her notebook.

She had told Finn a selective truth about Maeve's last appointment, but she would have to tell him the whole truth about this. And Maeve as well.

***

Siobhan got home, walked in, and flopped on her bed. She felt very tired, but she had to pick up Maeve soon, make dinner, dodge Finn's interrogation, and work on some research for a paper. She closed her eyes and let her mind wander, falling into a doze. She jolted awake, looked at the clock and realised that she had to go get Maeve. She pulled herself up, and fished under the bed for her sandals. Then she brushed her sleep mussed hair and left the apartment.

Maeve flew at her and grabbed her when the bell rang, and Siobhan pulled her aside so the other kids could get by.

"Did she have a good day?" Siobhan asked Jani.

"Oh, you know, she was a bit grumpy here and there, but she did her math questions in her math book, and here, look at this." Jani went to Maeve's desk and pulled out a small notebook. "She made this drawing this afternoon."

"Well, that's very nice." Siobhan bent over it, with Maeve beside her.

"I drew it for you, Mummy," Maeve said happily.

"Well, it's great." Siobhan picked it up and held it in front of her eyes, "Let's see, it's two fried eggs building an aeroplane?"

Maeve took the book very seriously from her and said, "It's polar bears on ice."

"Of course! I see it now." She gave Maeve a hug. "Let's go, and I'll make you a smoothie when we get home. Would you like that?"

Maeve just stood smiling and not responding.

"Maeve, say, 'Yay!' if you'd like that."

"Yay!" Maeve said.

When they got home, Siobhan made Maeve her drink and then sat down next to her.

"How was school today?" she asked Maeve, who sat reading a book.

Maeve made a truly miserable face and said, "Horrible!"

"Horrible? Why? What happened?"

"I don't remember."

"Well, how do you know you had a horrible day then?"

"I always do. School is horrible."

"But you used to love school. Remember, when you were littler, how much you loved it."

"No."

"Tell me, what is horrible about school?"

"I don't know."

"Well, think," Siobhan prodded her.

Maeve threw her head back in exasperation.

"Maeve," Siobhan prodded again.

"I'm the only invisible kid in my class," Maeve said with frustration.

"Invisible?" Siobhan sat and thought about what that meant. Then she knew. "Oh, Honey, you aren't actually invisible. You have an invisible disability. That means people can't see it when they look at you. They can't see your stroke, or your epilepsy, or your anxiety. That is good in some ways, it means people aren't going to judge you differently just by seeing you. But it also means that they might have a hard time understanding that you have a disability. It will always be hard for people to understand that they need to cut you some slack. I realise that you're the only kid who needs constant supervision, or has her own computer, or misses so much school, but at least half your classmates have disabilities. Just not the same as you."

"Whatever," Maeve said, and buried her face in

Siobhan's side.

Siobhan held her close, quiet for a minute. Then she sighed and said, "It's hard being you. Don't ever think I don't know that. You have a harder time at some things than most kids, and that will probably always be the case. I know it must feel very lonely and frustrating at school, because it's hard for you to understand people. And your seizures are scary for you and the people around you." Maeve tried to hide further in Siobhan's shirt. "If I could, I would change all that for you. If there had been a way for me to know about and stop your stroke, I would've done that. But it happened, and that's our life. That's your life. Most of us have something we struggle with." Siobhan tried to give her an encouraging hug. "But we should always remember all the stuff you're great at. You know so much about science, and dinosaurs, and dragons. You can sing well. You are a good, kind, funny kid, and Finn and I are lucky to have you. Next week, we're going to start you on some meds for your anxiety, and hopefully they'll help you feel better about school."

"Really?" Maeve said, her voice muffled.

"Really."

Maeve felt a bit better, and after a few minutes she sat up and finished her drink.

Siobhan got up and started dinner and when Finn got home he found her chopping onions while Maeve read in the living room. After greeting Maeve, he walked in an overtly casual manner into the kitchen and, making sure Maeve wouldn't hear him, asked Siobhan about her doctor's appointment. Siobhan hadn't told him the details of her recent discomfort, so all he knew was that she'd had an ultrasound and had learned the results that day. He kept trying to get more information out of her.

202

"I'm busy with dinner. We can talk after Maeve goes to bed," she said, and he knew he had to be content with that.

After dinner, Siobhan bathed Maeve and helped her floss and brush her teeth. In bed she read Maeve two books and sang to her, all while Finn made his impatient presence known with frequent trips back and forth down the hall. Siobhan pointedly ignored him.

Siobhan rolled over and slid her hand under Maeve's pillow, scratching her arm on something rough.

"Maeve, sit up," she said and then lifted the pillow. Underneath she found a tree branch, a wrapped tampon, a hairbrush, and a snow globe. She pulled them out and lined them up on top of the quilt with a sigh. "Maeve, when do you even collect all this stuff? We watch you constantly."

"I'm sorry, Mummy."

"It's alright, it's just something you've always done." Siobhan lay there, propped on one arm, examining Maeve's nest supplies. All of a sudden she laughed, and hugged Maeve close. "What?" Maeve asked, looking at her.

"Never mind. Go to sleep now. Everything will be okay. I should've named you Eris."

"Why?"

"It's from a book I read years ago. She's the goddess of chaos, and the *Principia Discordia* was a book that was very important to me when I was younger. You can read it when you're older."

"Okay. I can read it now."

"I don't think we need more chaos right now, Hon. Let's wait until you're in high school, okay?"

"Okay."

Siobhan got up and went into the living room where Finn sat pretending to read a book. Siobhan filled the kettle for tea, then came back to the living room.

"Okay, let's talk."

Finn put down his book in an exaggerated manner.

Siobhan leaned toward him and said, "Okay, first of all, everything is fine and will be fine. The doctor said that I had a bit of an ovarian cyst and I have to have an operation."

"When?" Finn asked.

"At the end of the semester, so about a month from now."

Finn looked at her steadily, and then got to his feet and went over to the computer, flicking it on. Siobhan thought of telling him to back away slowly, but she knew he would only research it later. *Might as well get this over with now.* She got up and busied herself in the kitchen.

Finn sat quietly reading and typing for awhile. After twenty minutes, he asked from the living room how large her cyst was.

"Twelve centimetres," Siobhan answered, trying to sound nonchalant.

"Twelve? Mum, that's over twice as big as average."

"Oh, is it?"

Finn didn't buy it. "Is it cancer?"

"No, no, it's not.".

Finn got up and came to stand in the doorway of the kitchen.

"How do you know? Did the doctor say that?"

Siobhan looked at him. His cheeks looked white and he looked tired. She knew he wouldn't go to bed until she levelled with him. She went over and hugged him.

"The doctor doesn't know, and she won't until they take it

204

out and look at it. But it isn't, I'll be fine, worrying won't change anything."

"Can't they do the operation sooner?"

"Finn, she wanted to, but I have to figure out what to do with you and Maeve while I'm in the hospital, and I need to finish this semester first. So I said we'd have to wait."

"I can look after Maeve."

"I know you can, but I think I need an adult, I don't think it's legal to leave you guys alone for that long, and I don't want you to have all that responsibility."

"Well, then who?"

"I don't know yet. I might ask Holly if you guys can go to sleep there for a few nights."

Finn thought about that quietly for a minute. "You could ask Uncle Thomas."

Siobhan honestly had not even thought of that. "Oh, I don't know. I don't think so."

"But he might do it, if we tell him why."

"I don't think that will work, he will likely be busy anyways," she saw the hope in his eyes, and she couldn't just say no, not right now. "I'll think about it, Finn." Later she could tell him no.

***

"Uncle Thomas?"

"Oh, hi Finn. I was thinking of calling you."

"Well, then, I should've waited!"

"No, no, I'm glad you called. Did you have a good Christmas?"

"Yeah, did you?"

"Sure did, went to a friend's for dinner, then the church. Prayed for your mum."

"Sounds nice. I'm not going to tell her that last part."

"Haha, okay. How's Maeve?"

"She's been having a rough time, we've been changing her meds. She just had a reaction to one, so we changed them again. She's having a lot of seizures."

"Aw, the poor kid. Give her a kiss for me. I'll try to come visit soon."

"Well, that's sort of why I'm calling."

"Oh?"

"Yeah. Mum doesn't know I'm doing this, but..."

"But what?"

"Mum has to have an operation in a couple of weeks. I think she's supposed to have it now, but she's stalling."

"An operation for what?"

"She has a huge ovarian cyst. It needs to come out."

"How huge?"

"Size of a softball." Uncle Thomas whistled.

"Yeah."

"Is it...is it cancer?"

"They won't know until they remove it."

"Uh-huh."

"So, anyways, we need someone to come stay with us. She'll be in the hospital a few days, and she can't leave me and Maeve alone."

"She doesn't have any friends to do it? That are close?"

"No, not that she'll ask. School and Maeve and me, we don't leave a lot of extra time for friends."

"No, no, I guess not. Okay. Okay, yeah. You'll have to let me know when."

"Yeah, I will. But there's one more thing."

"What?"

"Well, you'll need to act like you're coming down here anyways. She'll tell you not to come if she finds out I called."

"Oh, fuck, okay. Jeez, always so complicated with that woman."

"Tell me about it."

***

What are Finn and Mummy doing? They have big garbage bags. They're running around, putting stuff in them. I just want Mummy to come sit with me.

"I don't have time right now, Maeve," Mummy says.

"What are you doing?" I ask Finn.

"We're cleaning up, Maeve. Mum needs to have this place cleaned up before..."

"Before what?"

"Before the end of the semester."

"But I want Mummy to come read with me."

"She will later Maeve. You can help us by choosing to get rid of some toys."

"No! No, I won't!"

"But it would be a big help, Maeve."

All of a sudden, I am hitting Finn. Why am I hitting him?

I feel like it's not me. It isn't me. I want to stop.

"Maeve, Maeve, stop! What are you doing?" Finn says. He tries to hold my arms. I kick him. He tries to move away. I follow him.

Mummy is there. She tries to hold me. "Maeve, Maeve, what are you doing? Stop. Honey. Stop."

Mummy pulls me away. I hit her. I hit her.

Mummy pulls me down on the couch, she holds me. I can't hit her this way. I can hear screaming and crying.

"Shhhh. Shhhh."

Finn is crying. Mummy is holding me.

"Are you alright, Finn? What the hell made her do that?"

"I don't know, Mum. She just..."

"Maeve, are you okay?"

I can't say anything. I'm crying.

Chapter 10

Siobhan felt surprised and suspicious when Thomas just happened to phone two weeks before her surgery to ask if he could stay with her for a couple of weeks. He claimed he needed to retake his Industrial First Aid course for work. Maybe he told the truth, but Siobhan felt certain that he and Finn had connived a bit.

Of course, both denied it. Finn with his eyes unusually wide and innocent.

"Honestly, Mum, I would never do such a thing."

"Right."

Siobhan and Finn had worked very hard the week before the surgery and removed many bags of junk from the apartment. They had even taken a whole day while Maeve was at school and sifted through her mountain of toys and stuffies. They had to do it while Maeve could not watch them, because Maeve would not part with a single item.

Maeve's mood in the last month had plummeted, and she had grown prone to bursts of anger as well as periods of despondency. Siobhan had more and more kept Maeve with her, feeling that forcing her to go to school added to her stress level. She felt more empowered in making that decision by the excellent and exhaustive report that she'd given the school from the health centre assessment. Just knowing what your child needed did not go far with the school system. Professional directives helped enormously.

Siobhan had her last final scheduled for the next day, and Thomas would arrive that evening. Her surgery was scheduled for the day after. She had a ton of reading to do, and she needed to go shopping at some point, but Maeve would not leave her side at all. Siobhan sat on the couch, a book open on her lap, and Maeve wedged herself into Siobhan's side as much as possible, leaning on her and getting angry at Siobhan for reading.

"Mummy, you are obsessed with those books. You're obsessed with school."

"Maeve, I know you want me to pay attention to you, but I absolutely have to read this for my final tomorrow. Please, please go find something to do, and I'll watch a movie with you later."

"You always say that!" Maeve yelled at her.

"Maeve, please let Mummy finish this. Go do something, it'll be more fun than watching me read."

"Read to me now."

"No, go do something."

Maeve refused to move, she just sat there fuming and growling. Siobhan tried to ignore her, but that proved impossible as Maeve dug her fingers into Siobhan's arm. Siobhan lost her temper. "Maeve, go do something right now and leave me alone for awhile, I need to get this done!"

Maeve sat up and screeched at her, angry tears streaming down her face, "You only care about those books, not me!" Maeve stormed out of the room into their bedroom, slamming the door shut and screaming from the other side. Finn appeared out of his room and came into the living room.

"Is everything okay?" he asked.

Siobhan sighed and put down her book. "I just need her to..." and they both jumped as they heard a loud crash and more angry screaming. They both went to the door, but Maeve held it closed. Finn got there first, but he didn't want to push hard and hurt Maeve.

"Maeve, let us in," Siobhan said.

"No!" Maeve screamed, and they heard her throw something against the wall.

Siobhan moved Finn aside and methodically pushed the door open against Maeve's weight. Maeve screamed even louder at them.

When they got in, Siobhan saw that Maeve had kicked over her nightstand and pulled some drawers out of the dresser. Now she stood with some books in her hands, and threw them at the wall, screaming and crying. Siobhan grabbed her and held her, even though Maeve started hitting her, and pulled Maeve down on the bed. Finn knelt on the other side.

"Maeve, Maeve, stop, okay, stop," Siobhan said, over and over.

Finn rubbed her arm. "It's okay Maeve, it's okay."

Slowly Maeve wound down to crying. Siobhan held her and Finn sat near her. Finn picked up a book and read it to Maeve, and Maeve fell asleep listening to him, her head on Siobhan's arm.

"What is going on with her, Mum? Is it one of the new medicines?"

"It might be."

"Should we take her off them?"

"Well, we're just getting up to a full dose on the anxiety med now. We should wait and see if it will be any different when she's been on the full dose for awhile."

"I'm worried about her."

"I know." Siobhan reached out a hand to his shoulder.

"Her seizures aren't even controlled."

"I know. Let's wait a couple of weeks, and see how she's doing. Then I'll call the doctor."

"Okay."

"What I'm worried about is leaving her with you and your uncle for a few days. Especially while you're at school."

"Well, I can get my homework in advance and just stay home with them."

"We might have to do that, Finn. I don't want to, but I don't think either of them will handle it very well."

"Write me a note for school, I'll take it in tomorrow and talk to my teachers. I think the only one who won't like it is Mr. Addel."

"Well, I'll write a special note, just for him." Siobhan forced herself to sit up and she yawned. "Well, hopefully some rest will help her." Siobhan went back to the living room and her reading.

***

Thomas arrived the next in the late afternoon. Finn showed visible relief at his uncle's arrival, but Maeve grew very agitated and tried to hide behind Siobhan. She did not remember him. Siobhan slowly coaxed her out, but she remained close by and seemed reluctant to answer him at all.

Despite Siobhan's protests, Thomas insisted on ordering pizza for dinner.

"Maeve, do you like pizza?" Thomas asked her, and she nodded yes enthusiastically, so Siobhan stopped arguing. And when Thomas helped serve Maeve her pizza and opened her pop for her, the little girl relaxed and started to talk to him.

"So, Maeve, I'm going to stay here for awhile, is that okay?"

"Okay," Maeve answered. "You can sleep in our bed."

"Hmm, well, I think I'll sleep in Finn's bed and he can sleep with you until your Mum gets back."

"Where is she going?" Maeve asked, spraying some tomato sauce out of her mouth, her face covered in it already.

"I'm going to have an operation, remember?"

"For what?"

"I have a thing in me that needs to come out."

Maeve put down her pizza slowly, and wiped her hands on her shirt, leaving big grease stains on the front. She got up from her seat on the floor across the coffee table from Siobhan and went to stand on Siobhan's left side. She grabbed her mother's head and pulled it into her chest with an unbelievable strength. "Poor Mummy," she said, and rubbed Siobhan's forehead in a downwards motion that covered Siobhan's eyes. The other arm slipped around Siobhan's neck and cut off her air supply. Siobhan gasped a bit and pulled on Maeve's arm to loosen it.

"Thanks, Honey," Siobhan wheezed.

"I know what will help," Maeve said with happy inspiration, and she ran out of the room. She came back a minute later and said, "Finn, can you help me?"

Finn had started his fourth piece of pizza and didn't want to stop eating. "Help you what, Maeve?" he asked.

"Just come here," she beckoned with her arm. Finn sighed and got up and followed her.

"What's she up to?" Thomas asked Siobhan. Siobhan just shrugged. They could hear the kids talking in the bathroom.

Maeve came running back out with her arms full. She ran up and said to Siobhan, "Mum, hold these," and she dumped the arm load in Siobhan's lap abruptly. Siobhan tried to catch everything, but a box hit the floor.

Maeve knelt in front of Siobhan and started organising everything on the coffee table.

"See, Mum, we're already for your operation," and she lined up cotton balls, Buzz Lightyear band-aids, menstrual pads, and Siobhan's pumice stone.

"Oh, yes, I see that you'll be very ready to take care of me when I get back. Thank you."

Maeve smiled happily and opened a band-aid, which she stuck to Siobhan's knee.

After dinner, Siobhan put Maeve to bed and sent Finn off to study. Thomas helped her clean up, both of them silent.

"Well," Thomas said, stretching, "I'm going to go have a cigarette." He went to get his coat.

"I thought you quit," Siobhan said from the door of the kitchen.

"I did, but I fell off the wagon." Thomas slipped a ball cap on over his short hair.

"Well, don't let Maeve see, or you'll get a lecture."

"Okay, I'll be careful." He walked over to the to the sliding glass door.

"Wait, I'll come, too," Siobhan said, and he just looked at her for a moment, but then left the door open. Siobhan found a small blanket on the couch and wrapped that around her shoulders, then stepped out in her socks. She closed the door behind her. She took a deep breath of the cool air, then looked at the cigarette pack Thomas held. "Can I have one?"

"I thought you quit?"

"I did, but I still have one occasionally."

Thomas shrugged and slid one out for her. He held his

lighter out and she drew on the cigarette and then made a face. Thomas found it funny.

"Tastes good, does it?"

"Blah," she grimaced, but she kept smoking it.

They wandered over to the picnic table and sat next to each other.

"So, are you scared?" he asked after a minute of silence.

Siobhan, lost in thought, startled a bit at the question.

"Well, a bit, maybe. I'm more worried about you and the kids."

"We'll be okay."

"Maeve's had a really hard time lately. Her meds aren't working well, she's having a lot of seizures, and she's really depressed and moody."

"Can't you take her off the meds?"

"Not yet, they haven't reached the right levels in her body, and she needs to come off them as slowly as she went on. I'm going to wait a couple of weeks, then talk to her neurologist if nothing's changed."

"Sounds like a pain in the ass." Thomas stomped on his cigarette.

"It's never easy."

"Why is it so hard to find a medication that works?"

Siobhan shrugged, "It's the brain. They don't know tons of stuff about the brain. About normal brains, let alone abnormal brains. I've come to understand that a lot of medicine is really just informed guessing."

They sat silently again, and Siobhan finished her cigarette.

"Finn is going to stay home to help you."

"He doesn't need to."

"I think he does. You're not used to her. If she was

doing well, I might feel okay about it, but she's not, and there's just too much to know."

"I can do it."

"Aw, it's not a criticism. It's great that you actually came to help."

They fell silent again for awhile, both staring off into the dark. Thomas lit another cigarette and offered another to Siobhan, who thought about it for a minute and then took one quickly.

"If I could wait with this surgery, I would, but this will be my only chance for months, and I really had to talk the doctor into waiting even this long."

"Oh, yeah, you have to get it done." Thomas coughed and then spit off to the side. "So, it's not cancer, is it?"

"Naw. Well, I mean, they won't know until they look at it, but I doubt it."

"Well, what caused it then?"

"Hmmm, well, I have had two thoughts on that. Either it's a watermelon I grew from eating seeds, or it's my partially absorbed twin, who has been controlling me all these years, and when they remove him, I will suddenly adore Liberace and start voting conservative."

Thomas made a sound of disgust, followed quickly by a sigh of exasperation. "Why are you so fucking weird?'

"It's my evil twin, I'm telling you!"

Thomas shook his head at her. "So, you'll be done with school after the summer?"

"Yes."

"And you'll have what? A certificate?"

"No, a degree."

"Then what?"

"Well, I would like to work a bit, and then go on with it.

216

Education maybe. Law would be cool. I'm not exactly sure, it's taken all my energy and concentration so far just to get here. But I'd like to go on without getting more in debt."

"How would you do that?"

"Work part-time, and apply for different funding sources. I'll have to look into it."

"How much do you owe now?"

"Over $100,000."

"That's what Finn said. I was hoping he had that wrong. Are you crazy? Is it worth it?"

"Yes, it will be. I can't keep making just enough to get by. Maeve will need to be taken care of her whole life, even after I'm dead, and I don't want Finn thinking that's his job. I have to take this risk, make the investment in myself. I didn't plan on owing so much, it's just so far proven too much to go to school, raise Maeve and work as well. I only even manage because of Finn. It isn't fair to him."

"So, what will change?"

"I keep hoping that as Maeve gets older, she'll get better, and I'll find programs for her. But she keeps getting turned away from programs, because she's so complex. And she's been getting worse."

"Didn't you know that when you started? That that would happen? What do the doctors say will happen to her."

"No, I didn't know. No one knows. The doctors have never predicted what will happen, they don't know. A few years ago she seemed to be developing normally. A bit slower than most kids, but still within normal limits. They could not predict what would happen to her seizures. And her seizures, they steal time from her. Every day she has fewer accumulated hours of experience than the other kids. Her memory problems just make that worse. So she's ten chronologically now, but she's younger emotionally. What she needs is seizure control, but none of the medications work."

"So, what will happen?"

"I don't know. Right now, I'll concentrate on getting through this, finishing school, and then I'll just have to see what happens."

Thomas offered her another cigarette, which she took and lit. She felt agitated because saying all that out loud made everything seem impossible. She tried to only look at her life in small, manageable chunks, because taken as a whole it always felt completely overwhelming.

"Have you ever thought about putting her in foster care, at least for awhile, until you get this sorted out. Give you and Finn a break?"

"No. I love that little girl, and she needs me and she needs Finn. And while there are good social workers and foster parents, there are also horrible ones, and natural parents don't have much say in that system. Even getting a social worker to help her get services is a huge risk to me, one that I'm only now thinking of taking because I'm running out of options. No, I will not walk away from her because it's hard. It's not even her that makes it hard, it's the lack of services and support. It's the lack of funding in the schools, so that she doesn't get the support she needs. It's the disgusting fact that there are companies out there that make a profit running foster homes and group homes for kids like her. I've been told by a worker that a kid with her level of need, behaviour, and multiple diagnosis would mean four thousand a month for a foster family. And they would deserve it, don't get me wrong, but I get less than three hundred in disability for her.

That's just wrong. If I even got half that amount, I wouldn't be so in debt for school, and it would still save the government money."

"Okay, I just wanted to ask." Thomas had known when he asked what the answer would be.

"Poverty is a business. Tons of people make an excellent living off of servicing poverty, without changing one thing about it. Worse, we don't see the servicing of poverty, or welfare payments, as a subsidy for service providers, landlords, and businesses."

"What?"

"The social workers, the FAWs at welfare, the group home system, non-profits and charities, tons of people make a good living off of it, millions are paid into it. And people don't eat their welfare cheque, or live in it, they spend it. That's even more money going around.

Sure, people need mental health services and some kids need foster homes for other reasons, but a lot of it's financial. People need money. Despite the constant demonisation of poor people, whether they work or not, poverty isn't a moral failing, it's a lack of money. People need more money, that's the main answer. Better wages, better assistance, affordable education. The people that need the help get the least, and they get demonised, and all the people that benefit from it in other ways, get to feel superior.

I'm tired of people acting like it's a big fucking mystery, or like it's a new problem. Or worse, that they don't benefit from it themselves."

"It's not that simple," Thomas rebutted. "People use the system, try to take advantage of the people that work, and it's important we don't let them."

"Why?"

"Because you should have to work for what you get."

"So, you're willing to hurt lots of other people and their kids just to make sure this small group of people don't scam the system?"

"Well, blame *them*!"

"No. Look, the amount of welfare scamming is quite low, almost negligible, and most poor people do work, just for low pay. It's rich people that scam the system. If you're so interested in everyone having to work for what they get, then no one should inherit money. Most of the millionaires and billionaires out there inherited their money, and then made more money. They didn't get it by working hard, they're the lazy scammers. Hate them, and stop being suspicious of other poor people."

"Well, what about the druggies? What about them? They just do what they want to feed their habits. I remember from jail, how they'd steal from whoever, whatever they wanted. We should just jail them all. Do drugs, go to jail."

"Do you have any idea what jails cost? Much more than treatment, or housing. " Siobhan had risen and started pacing, in full-blown rant mode. "Instead, legalise all the drugs, make it a medical issue."

"But then we're saying it's alright what they do to themselves!" Thomas's voice raised.

"You can't make laws based on what you personally approve of. People, adult people, have a right to do what they want to their bodies, regardless of what you or I might feel. What if, by legalising it, all you got was the ability to stop fearing 'druggies'? Because they wouldn't have to steal or scam to get by. What if that allowed them the chance to focus on the other things in their lives, the chance to take a break from all of that? Wouldn't that be better for everyone? Allow everyone to see them as human again instead of scary monsters responsible for all of society's ills."

"It's just wrong to do that to your body."

"So is smoking, and eating big, fat Dorito laden sugar pop pizzas. That's a convenient morality."

"Things used to be better. Society is too lenient, we treat everyone like a victim, and nobody is responsible for what they do. It's all, 'feel bad for the druggie, feel bad for the criminal, and understand why they're there.' Fuck that, we each make choices, we each live with the consequences." Now Thomas stood, and they faced each other, the situation tense.

"Oh my god, things were *never* better. When people say things like, 'back before, in the day, things were better and more innocent,' they mean back before *they* knew about all the bad stuff. There has always been drug addiction, and alcoholism, and rape, and murder, and poverty, and war. When was this blissful time? All these problems have always existed, and people that question all of it have always existed, it isn't new. Tell me, when was any of this different."

"It wasn't like this where we grew up."

"We grew up in the middle of fucking nowhere, population twelve, and people were still drunk and beating each other and doing their daughters! Don't lie to yourself to back up your current bigotry!"

"I don't want to discuss this anymore!" Thomas shouted.

The sliding door slid cautiously open, and Finn stood there in his boxers. Both Siobhan and Thomas slammed back to the present.

"Um," Finn said, "are you two going to kill each other

now, so everyone can sleep? Or maybe you just want to come back in?"

Siobhan ran a hand through her hair. "Yeah, Hon, we'll be right in."

He looked at them for another moment and then closed the door.

Siobhan and Thomas collected themselves.

"Look, I think that for our sanity, for the kids' sanity, we should not talk about this again, until they've moved to another country, and it won't matter that we have beaten each other to death. Deal?" Siobhan said to him.

"I don't have any problem with that. Deal."

They went inside.

***

Siobhan got up at five in the morning. She got dressed sitting in the dark on the edge of the bed, hoping that only some of her clothing would end up inside out. She had orders not to eat or drink before the surgery, which caused her to think romantically about coffee and soft boiled eggs. She walked out to the living room, and went over to the bag on the couch that she had packed the night before and checked it to make sure she had everything, then sat in her chair for a bit. The room felt gloomy and foreign. She looked at the bookshelf in front of her, eyes squinted in the dimness. She tried to decide which books to take. She had many novels she had read for classes and planned on rereading when she had more time, but now she couldn't decide what she felt like reading.

She heard some footsteps in the hall and Thomas appeared from around the corner, wearing just his pants.

"Is it time to go?" he asked.

"Just about. I'll head for the bus in a few minutes. I'm just trying to figure out which books to take."

"I'll drive you, if it's okay to leave the kids here by themselves."

Siobhan hadn't expected a ride. "Yeah, it's fine. And a ride would be great."

"Okay, let me get ready," Thomas turned around and walked off.

Siobhan went back to staring at the bookcase.

Thomas came back after a few minutes, "Are you still just sitting there?"

"Yeah, I totally can't decide."

"Are you ready otherwise?"

"Yep, all ready."

"Well then, just grab a book and let's go."

"But I don't know what I want."

"Well, then, don't bring anything. Fuck, will you die without a book?"

"What a stupid question. Of course I will die without a book. I will totally die without one."

"Unbelievable."

"You choose one for me. Or two, pick two."

"I don't know anything about those books. I don't know what you want. I've never read any of them."

"Well, that's perfect, you're totally unbiased."

"Siobhan..."

"Aw, think of the orphans."

"Fine. If I pick two, then we can go?"

"Yes."

Thomas trudged over to the bookcases, which ran the whole length of the wall. He closed his eyes, waved his arm, and jabbed his finger forward. He pulled the book out, stepped sideways a few steps, and repeated the process.

"Here." He turned and held the two books out.

Siobhan didn't reach for them. She just read the covers and said, "Really? The Epic of Gilgamesh and Callahan's Crosstime Saloon? That's what you picked?"

Thomas groaned.

"They're perfect!" Siobhan plucked the books from him.

"Let's go. Maybe you can get a lobotomy today too, huh?" Thomas said.

"Ooh, you sounded just like Archie Bunker there."

"Get to the car."

Siobhan got up, smiling, and stuck the books in her bag, then opened the door for Thomas. After locking it, she handed him the keys. "You'll need these."

"Oh, yeah, thanks."

The morning felt cool but still nice, and the flower beds outside the apartment building had lots of new, spring flowers in them. Thomas had parked on the street right outside the front door, and the hood had little spots of dew all over it. Siobhan ran her finger around in the drops as she waited for Thomas to open the door. Her fingers came up wet and dirty. She wiped them on her skirt.

***

Siobhan woke feeling confused and parched after the surgery. The recovery room seemed too bright and busy. Monitors beeped and patients moaned.

Siobhan's back hurt, but she couldn't move. A nurse with short hair and glasses came across to her and leaned over her.

"Oh, you're awake already, that was fast. How do you

224

feel?"

"Thirsty," Siobhan croaked.

"Okay, I'll get you some ice chips." The nurse checked Siobhan's monitors and IV and walked off.

After some time, the nurse returned with a plastic cup with chips in it. She reached down and cranked the head of Siobhan's bed up a bit, which made Siobhan grimace. Siobhan took the cup and sucked up some ice, which felt good as she pressed it against the roof of her mouth.

"Your doctor will come by in awhile and tell you about the operation. If you need anything, push this button. I'll be nearby."

Siobhan nodded and closed her eyes, falling in and out of sleep, and eating ice. She had no idea how much time had gone by, and she couldn't see any windows anywhere. She thought she saw a clock on the wall her head faced, but she couldn't see the time. She wanted to phone the kids and tell them she had arrived safely on the other side.

She had drifted off again when she felt someone jostle her leg through the blanket. She opened her eyes and saw her doctor sitting there, still in scrubs.

"Hi Siobhan, are you awake enough to talk?"

"Yes."

"Okay. The operation went well. We removed the cyst and sent it off for testing. You have a mid-line incision from your belly button to your pubic bone. We didn't see anything else that made us want to perform a hysterectomy."

"Do I get to keep the cyst?"

"You want to keep it?"

"Yes. I want to take it home in a jar and put it on my bookshelf."

The doctor furrowed her eyebrows at Siobhan. "No, we don't usually do that. It needs to be biopsied."

"Darn. I was looking forward to having it."

"Sorry."

"Did you at least give me a scar shaped like a lightning bolt? I told the nurse before I went in that that's what I wanted."

"No, that really isn't something I would do."

"I wanted people to say, 'Well, she's fat, but she's fast,' when they saw me naked."

"Okay, well, sorry. Maybe next time."

"Yay."

"Oh, I phoned your son and told him everything's fine. You can talk to them tomorrow."

The nurse came and gave Siobhan more medicine in her IV. She started to drift again.

"Thank you, Doctor," she mumbled, but the doctor had left.

***

Thomas's first day with Maeve had not gone well. Maeve had become sullen and withdrawn when she'd awoken and they reminded her that Siobhan would not come home for several days. She'd had a good crying spell, and Thomas was totally unnerved by this. Finn found himself having to comfort both of them at the same time.

"It's okay, Maeve. Mum will phone later, and she'll be home in a few days."

"It's okay, Uncle Thomas. She doesn't hate you, she's just having trouble understanding where Mum is. She's completely forgotten about the surgery."

226

"Maeve, you can't sit under the coffee table the whole time Mum is gone, you need to come eat."

"She loves pancakes, Uncle Thomas. Just leave them and she'll eat them eventually."

Finn spent the whole morning as interpreter of actions and feelings for them. When Terry dropped by at one that afternoon, he saw the drawn expressions on everyone's faces. Thomas hid in the kitchen, and Finn sat cuddled up with Maeve on the couch, trying to cheer her with books.

"You know, Maeve, it's a really nice day out. Why don't you, me, and Finn take a walk to the Drive and get some ice cream?"

Maeve didn't want to go anywhere, but she did want ice cream. She allowed Finn to dress her. Thomas gratefully slipped Terry twenty dollars for the ice cream.

"Take your time," Thomas whispered to him.

Outside, Maeve perked up a bit as she stopped to pick every seed-covered dandelion on the way, turning a twenty minute walk into an hour long one. The boys didn't mind, they just enjoyed the warmth of the sun. Terry had stopped dying his hair black and now his blonde hair had grown in quite a lot. It looked even blonder in the sun.

"Neka phoned and invited us over for dinner," Terry told Finn. "I said we'd see her after your Mum comes home. I feel bad for her."

"Neka? Well, we can invite her out with us next week. Her and Luther."

"Yeah, let's do that."

"Or, you can go. I mean, not that you need my permission or anything. You don't have to not go just because I can't."

"Oh, well, thanks, but I don't feel like just hanging around there, drinking. I can't handle another one of

Neka's mystery drinks. And I can't stand maraschino cherries, which she puts in everything. She even put them in her beer." Terry made a face at that, and sounded so incredulous that Finn laughed at him.

"Do you think your mum had her surgery yet?" Terry asked a little further on.

"Well, unless they had some scheduling problem, yeah."

"Are you scared?"

Finn started to say no. He wanted to act like his mum, who never wanted anyone else to worry but herself. She had told him once, when he'd been feeling nervous about giving a presentation in English class, that he didn't have to feel like everything would work out all right, he just needed to act like it would. And if he learned to do that well enough, other people would believe it. And so would he, enough to get things done anyway.

"Yeah, I am. I don't want it to be cancer. I want her to be alright. I can't imagine what Maeve would do without her." Finn didn't want to look at Terry while he said this.

Terry bumped him with his arm. Finn once again felt very aware of the presence of his friend, just as he had when Terry had looked at his bleeding head. He could smell Terry's T shirt, and felt the bump of Terry's arm acutely even after the fact. He felt confused and conspicuous, and when Maeve ran up Finn hugged her to have something else to focus on.

"A white dragon has the attribute of ice," she told him, dandelion seeds in her hair.

"That's very interesting."

Finn took her hand and turned back to Terry. Terry took her other hand. "What kind of ice cream would a dragon eat?" Terry asked her.

"Dragons only eat villagers and sheep," she said.

"Oh," Terry said. "What are the other dragons' attributes?" Finn felt relief that Terry had asked, as this would keep Maeve talking for awhile, and would distract the conversation away from his mum.

***

Maeve made a huge mess of herself with ice cream. The ice cream covered her mouth, cheeks and nose, and ran over her fingers, staining her bright pink and blue. Finn made an attempt to clean her with a napkin, but her skin seemed to have formed a bond with the ice cream that would only alter with sandblasting or boiling. He gave up, and he and Terry just helped her up navigate the playground they had walked to, across from the ice cream store.

"My school won't let me do this because of my doctors," she told Terry. "My doctors worry too much."

"But you can go when Finn helps you," Terry said. He had had this conversation with her several times already. Finn felt grateful again that Terry treated Maeve kindly. Most people felt uncomfortable with her, like Uncle Thomas, who had trouble negotiating the subtleties of her deficits. Uncle Thomas kept going back and forth between wanting to treat her like she had no problems and acting like she had more serious delays than she had. But about the things she really liked, Maeve had a normal, almost gifted, aptitude. .

Finn and Terry brought her over to the sandbox and she grew very absorbed in making starfish molds with an old toy she found there. The boys settled at the edge and talked, lying back in the sun. Finn regularly glanced at

Maeve, shielding his eyes with his hands.

"Your uncle seems a lot different than your mum," Terry said.

"Oh, yeah. He's older than her, and really straight laced. He's also religious. They argue a lot."

"Well, your mum's pretty opinionated."

"And stubborn. But Uncle Thomas, he says weird stuff to her, sort of judging her for being a single mum, for not getting married, for not being what he thinks is normal."

"But he's not married, is he?"

"Oh, no. But he thinks it's different because she's a woman, and she has kids. He's one of those, 'Kids need a man and a woman to raise them,' types. He used to phone her about everything he heard on the news saying kids of single mums do worse at stuff. She'd get so furious at him." Finn smiled, remembering his mum once throwing the receiver of a cordless phone in the toilet and flushing repeatedly when she'd gotten really mad at Uncle Thomas. They'd had to go to the St. Vincent de Paul thrift store the next day to get a new phone.

"Is that true? Do kids of single mums do worse?" Terry asked. Finn rolled over and propped his head up with his hand.

"Well, Mum says the problem isn't single mums, it's the lack of resources they have, and that most of the kids she knew growing up had both a mum and dad, and they were usually miserable, so being a single parent isn't necessarily the problem. She thinks it's better to have one decent parent than two crappy ones. She won't get married or bring someone around to be our father just because."

Terry thought about that for a while. "It's true that the kids I know that have two parents aren't always better off.

I've been pretty happy with my grandma. And happy I didn't stay with my mum or dad that would've been really bad."

"Yeah. I'm really glad Mum doesn't drink or do drugs. That's hard."

"But she used to?"

"Uh huh. And Uncle Thomas did, too. He used to party, and he was in jail a few times. Mum said once that the difference between him and her is that he regrets all those times and she doesn't. So she's easier on herself, and others, than he is. It's probably also because he lives in a hillbilly town and she lives in the city. Also, she reads." Finn looked over at Maeve and asked if she felt okay, or did she want to go soon, but she completely ignored him. He shrugged and turned back to Terry.

"Have you met Neka's parents at all?" Terry asked him.

"No."

"I have, twice. Her mum is okay, but not very bright. Her step- dad's not mean, but he just doesn't care about Neka. He doesn't seem to notice her much."

"I can't imagine my mum putting up with that."

"No, I can't either."

Terry reached beside him and pulled out a long blade of grass, exposing the tender white end. He put this in his mouth.

"No, your mum wouldn't put up with that at all."

Finn looked at his friend, who stared up into the blue sky. Finn lay back down, and they fell silent for awhile. Maeve tapped sand out of the mold over and over. They could hear some other kids playing on a slide, their mother directing them in Chinese.

"Are you going to go to university?" Terry asked.

"Yes, I plan to."

"What will you take?"

"I'm not sure yet. Definitely a science."

"Not what your mum takes? What's she taking?"

"English Lit. And no, although it's interesting. I will probably take some of those courses. You need to, anyways. Mum's had to take some science."

"But she doesn't like science?"

"Mum? She loves science, but she says she's just not geared that way, and she only went to grade nine in school, so she doesn't have the background for it. Plus, she's really good at what she's taking."

"And you love science."

"Yep."

Finn looked at Maeve, her eyes lost in concentration, her cheeks still vividly pink and blue.

"Will you go to university?" Finn asked Terry.

Terry thought for a minute.

"I don't think so. My grades aren't great. And it's not too appealing to me, right now. I could maybe do a trade school. I don't know what, though. I don't have any skills, or any gifts."

"That's not true," Finn burst out, and then felt a bit embarrassed by his fervour.

Terry shielded his eyes with his hand and looked at Finn. "What's my skill, then?" he asked in a voice that already dismissed the answer.

"You're very good with people. People like you and they want to be liked by you. They always have. Even adults. Even when we were young."

"Is that all?" Terry looked at him condescendingly.

"Is that all? Isn't that everything? Doesn't everyone want that? I'd love it."

"Well, that's not a skill or a gift, not like being good at science or writing."

"Yeah, it is. You're charismatic. And you either have that or you don't."

"Well, what would I do with it. You don't just get paid because people like you."

"No, but it's important for stuff like acting, or being a politician, or a Baptist minister down in the states."

Terry looked at him like he had lost his mind. "A Baptist minister?"

"It's just an example," Finn shrugged. Then started laughing. Terry whacked him on the shoulder and laughed, too.

"Well, we'll see," Terry said.

The warm day floated on, and they floated with it.

***

Siobhan drove her nurses a crazy. She started to get up and walk around as soon as she woke the next morning, and kept getting up while they urged her to take it slow. Her back hurt lying in bed, and she felt very restless in the hospital room, which she shared with another woman. As much as Siobhan tried to seal her section off completely from the other woman's section by meticulously drawing the curtains, she still felt annoyed by every person who went to that side of the room, and would startle awake at the slightest sound. And every time the nurses came in, they disturbed the curtains, and the people on the other side would try to peek in.

Siobhan couldn't sleep, and they kept feeding her bland, mushy foods and asking if she had pooped. Siobhan kept asking the nurse for some food to actually chew, and the nurse kept saying, "I'll look into that for you," and the next meal would arrive all gelatinous and congealed.

On the second day, Siobhan had Finn sneak her in a spicy salad from a restaurant on the Drive. The nurse gave her shit for it.

"But I need real food, chewy food. And protein."

"Look, we can't let you eat that stuff until we know everything is working fine, because your doctor pulled your intestines out of your body during the operation and put them on your chest. Putting them back is tricky."

"Oh, fine. I'm fine though," Siobhan sulked, and dreamed about the shower she would have when she got home.

Siobhan started doing laps around the nurses' station, hunched over, a folded sheet pressed to her belly, she hobbled around and around them. She did it during the day. She did it during the night. She couldn't sleep and she hated staying in the hospital. She was constantly worried about the kids and Thomas. Worst of all, Maeve couldn't even visit her. "All visitors must be 12 or older," the sign said. Siobhan kept trying to persuade the nurses to let Maeve in.

On the third day, her doctor told her to leave.

"You were supposed to stay five or six days, but I think the nurses are plotting to kill you. Go home."

Siobhan waddled to the phone and called Thomas, then spent an hour trying to dress herself while she waited for him. He had to help her with her shoes.

Finn had to hold Maeve back from launching herself at Siobhan when she got home.

"Mum's all cut open, Maeve."

"Poor Mum," Maeve said, and led Siobhan to her bed

and tucked her in. Maeve got into bed with her and read her books, and Siobhan finally fell asleep and slept for twelve hours. Maeve would barely leave her, and spent her time laying next to Siobhan, reading books.

Siobhan woke the next morning with the old cat wrapped, sleeping, around her head, and Maeve laying sideways with her head shoved in Siobhan's armpit. Siobhan had to pee, urgently, but getting up posed a dilemma, as she didn't have a railing to grab like at the hospital. She needed a hand up.

"Finn," she whispered.

"Finn," a bit louder.

"Finn, Finn, Finn," she said louder and louder, fearing she'd pee any second.

He finally heard her and stumbled in her door, hair messed. "What?"

"Oh, help. I have to pee, and I have this child growing out of my armpit, and nothing to pull on to get up, and come here, please, quick," she said in a flurry.

Finn walked over and helped pull her up, then helped her walk to the bathroom, which she made just in time. Finn stood on the other side of the door and waited for her.

"Are you okay, Mum?" he asked through the door.

"Oh, yes, I'll be done in just a minute."

Finn heard her flush and wash her hands. She opened the door and leaned on him.

"Do you want to go back to bed?" he asked her.

"Mmmm, no. I want to sit up for a bit. What time is it?"

"Almost seven." Finn helped her to the living room, and helped her sit in her chair.

Siobhan saw that he'd made a bed out of couch cushions on the floor. "Oh, did you sleep out here? That must've been very uncomfortable. Why don't you go sleep in my bed with Maeve? I'll just watch a movie or read."

"No, I slept fine," he lied to her. "I'll make you some tea and toast."

Siobhan smiled at him.

"I'm glad you're home," Finn said to her.

"Me, too. How'd it go, while I was gone?"

"I'll tell you after I make you some food."

"Okay."

Finn turned on the TV for her and Siobhan flipped through the channels. Early morning TV did not offer much for entertainment, and Siobhan settled on old Bugs Bunny cartoons.

Finn came back and brought her tea and toast with peanut butter and jam. He settled down and watched with her.

"I don't understand, is Bugs Bunny magic or just really lucky?" he asked after a while.

"I think he's magic, which makes him really lucky. These cartoons are so old, and they've censored them so strangely. You can't see the anvil hit anyone on the head, just the resulting injury. What kid can't figure that out? And what kid ever thought they could drop an anvil on someone's head and it would be funny? It's so weird nowadays, what we think is harmful to kids. I mean this, this right here, it's quality entertainment. You learn to eat vegetables, spend time outside, fight greed, corruption, and Martians, and to cross-dress. All good stuff."

Siobhan looked over and saw Finn smiling with his eyes closed. "Go lay down. I'll be fine. I'll call if I need anything."

"Okay," Finn said. He got up and kissed her and

stumbled to the bedroom.

***

Maeve wouldn't leave Siobhan alone when she got up in the morning. She grabbed a blanket and sat at Siobhan's feet, leaning against her mum. If Siobhan hobbled to the bathroom, Maeve went with her. If Siobhan went to lie down, Maeve sat in the bed and read. For the first day, Finn and Thomas couldn't get her to get dressed, couldn't get her to really eat, couldn't get her to go outside the apartment for any reason. Siobhan told them to stop trying.

"She's fine here with me. Why don't you guys go out for awhile? Go for a little walk. Get me a coffee."

With worried looks on both their faces, they put jackets on and left.

"I thought they'd never leave," Maeve said with comic relief, and sat as close to Siobhan as possible. Siobhan couldn't lie on her side, so she just put her arm through Maeve's and rested her head against Maeve's little shoulder.

"Did you have a hard time while I was gone, Maeve?"

"Yes," Maeve said with absolute misery, "I had to sleep without you."

"I'm sorry. But I had to go to the hospital, and I'm sure your uncle and Finn tried their best to keep you happy."

"Uncle Thomas yelled at me."

"He did? About what?"

"I don't remember."

"Well, I'm sure he didn't mean anything, he's not used to kids. And even I yell sometimes. So do you."

"Yeah."

"I'm going to sleep for a bit. You read, okay?"

"Okay."

Maeve forgot to stay quiet and kept talking to Siobhan, but Siobhan drifted off anyway. When she woke up, she saw Maeve had fallen asleep beside her. Siobhan lay and watched Maeve's chest moving up and down. She heard voices in the living room. She rolled gingerly on her side and pushed herself up.

Thomas and Finn sat, coffees in hand, bags of cookies and pastries in front of them on the coffee table.

"Here's your coffee, Mum."

"Thank you. They wouldn't give me coffee at the hospital. Only tea, the evil bastards."

"Are you not supposed to drink it?" he looked at her with suspicion. He withdrew the coffee he'd held out to her.

"Oh, son, you do not want to play such a game with me right now. Need I remind you that I will get better and be able to wreak terrible vengeance upon you soon?"

"Mum?" he replied.

"Oh, geez. They didn't say I couldn't, they just gave me tea instead."

Finn examined her face and then relented. "Okay, but we'd better not have a forbidden salad incident again."

Siobhan stuck her tongue out, and then sat the coffee on a little bookcase beside her chair before she lowered herself into her, gingerly, with both hands on the armrests.

Thomas had ignored them and concentrated on his pastry, a fine sprinkle of crumbs trailing down his shirt.

"So, tell me about how it went while I was gone," Siobhan said to the two of them.

Thomas looked ill at ease as he busied himself shaking the crumbs off his shirt. Finn looked from his uncle to his mum and back again.

"Uh, fellas? Hello? I know I'm not suddenly speaking Swahili." Siobhan looked at them, a slight look of amusement crossing her face.

Finn coughed and sat up. "It went fine. Basically fine. For the most part."

"For the most part? What was the least part? Thomas?"

Thomas slid his hand under his ball cap and scratched his head. "Well, the first day was real tough. That little girl wouldn't stop crying, and she was mad that I was here and not you. The boys took her out for awhile, which made her happy, but when she came back, she started crying again."

"So, what did you do?"

Thomas straightened his hat and picked at his knee, his pastry sitting on his leg "I thought the best thing to do would be to distract her, so that's what we did. We went out."

Finn pointedly stared at his coffee as if he found it absorbing and informative.

"Oh, yeah? Where to?"

"To the aquarium, but she only liked that for a little bit, so we went to a movie," Thomas said.

"There were a lot of people at the aquarium," Finn added.

"Was the movie good?" Siobhan asked.

"We don't know, Maeve screamed when the sound started and we had to leave." Thomas sighed and took a drink of his coffee.

"Oh. I thought she'd gotten better about that," Siobhan said.

"So then we took her for pizza. And then to mini-golf, but she didn't golf, just me and Finn and Terry did."

"What did she do?" Siobhan asked.

"Ate cotton candy. And then she threw up on me, so we brought her home. Where she cried."

Siobhan looked at Thomas with amused sympathy. "Sounds pretty rough."

"The next day was a bit better," Finn said, trying to be cheerful, "but we just stayed home and watched movies."

"Yeah, that's easier for everyone. Did she have many seizures?"

"A couple, nothing too bad," Finn shrugged.

"I'm glad Finn was with me, though. Even just walking that girl around is a challenge. She has no idea where she is most of the time." Thomas said this like they'd think it new information.

"Oh, I know," Siobhan said, "and it's not that she doesn't know the rules of the road or anything. She does, she just doesn't remember to apply them, or where she is, or where she's going," Siobhan sighed. "It's hard to be Maeve. Finn could walk to school by himself in grade one, but Maeve, I don't know that she'll ever master it. I hope so, though."

Siobhan started to feel sleepy, and she leaned back in her chair and closed her eyes.

"Well, I'm going to hang around a few more days, I think. You still seem pretty slow, and Finn should go to school tomorrow," Thomas said.

"That's a good plan," Siobhan answered, half asleep, and dozed off, abusing them with her walrus snores.

"Geez, how does Maeve sleep next to that?" Thomas asked Finn.

Finn shrugged and smiled. "You get used to it."

The phone rang and Siobhan startled awake. She tried to sit up too quickly, and fell back, moaning and clutching her stomach.

240

"Mum, geez, just relax. I'll get it." Finn found the phone under the couch and answered it.

"Here, Mum. It's for you. Would you like me to ask them to call back?"

"No, no, Hon. I'm okay." Siobhan took the receiver from him. "Hello? Yes, this is her."

After a brief conversation, Siobhan handed the phone back to him.

"Who was it?" Finn asked.

"The doctor. My doctor. She got the report back on the cyst. It wasn't cancerous."

"They're sure?" Finn asked.

"Yes. She said it was just weird, fibrous tissue."

"That's good news, then," Thomas said. "Now you can get back to what passes as normal for you."

"Very droll, brother."

"I'm just pointing out the obvious."

"Yes, well, let's celebrate with more coffee."

Chapter 11

I wake up in the bed and I worry about where Mummy is. I roll over, and there she is. Her back is to me. I wiggle over to her and hug her back.

She moans a bit, but doesn't wake up. I lean over her and tickle her neck. She grabs my hand and holds it on her shoulder.

"Maf nop," Mum says.

"What?" I ask.

"Stop. Sleeping."

"I know. I'm waking you up."

"No. Day evil."

"The day isn't evil."

"Children evil."

"Children aren't evil."

"Something is evil, somewhere, and I'm staying here. Go watch TV." Mummy pulls the blanket over her head.

"Okay," I say. I go to the living room, and Finn is there, on cushions on the floor. Why is he sleeping in here? I lean over him to wake him up.

Finn opens his eyes and shouts. That freaks me out! He scares me. I try to get away from him. He makes me fall down on the floor.

"Aw, Maeve, I'm sorry, you just startled me. I'm not mad."

"You yelled at me."

"No, no. I was just surprised."

"What's wrong?" Mummy asks from the other room.

"Nothing, Mum, Maeve just startled me a bit." Finn gives me a hug. I feel better.

"Want to watch some SpongeBob with me?" Finn asks.

"Okay."

"Later would you like to hang outside with me and Terry?"

"Okay."

"Okay."

* * *

Thomas stood at the counter, folding little squares of dough over spoonfuls of potatoes and cheese. Making varaniki brought back all sorts of memories and he stood quietly, thinking about varaniki and family dinners, leaning slightly against the counter. Later he'd notice flour on his crotch.

The apartment felt quiet and calm. The boys had Maeve outside, and Siobhan had gone back to bed after eating some breakfast. In awhile, he'd make the kids lunch and take it out.

He planned to go home in a day or two, and part of him felt sad. Maeve had finally relaxed around him and he had taken her to the park the day before by himself, while Finn went to school and Siobhan read. Siobhan had given him some instructions and her cell phone, and he'd walked with Maeve, holding all the toys she'd brought. She'd told him all about dinosaurs and told him all about the dog she'd one day get. He noticed that she never asked him anything about himself, like where he lived, or what he did for work. He tried to tell her little bits, and she'd respond, "Oh, really?" and go right back to her interesting facts.

They'd played on the playground equipment together, Siobhan had said Maeve could go on if someone went with her. His bottom stuck a bit on the slide He remembered playing like that as a kid. It had been about thirty years since he'd sat on a slide or a swing. Were these things always so uncomfortable?

He didn't feel he knew Maeve any better, really, but while she prattled away on the walk home he decided he liked her, odd as she might seem. And he liked Finn. Maybe Siobhan had done okay.

Thomas finished the varaniki and put them on a tray in the freezer. Then he got out the bread and some cheese and meat and to make some sandwiches. Adding fruit and juice, he piled it all on a tray and went out the sliding glass door, where the boys sat at the picnic table. Maeve sat on the ground playing with her dinosaurs. The afternoon had warmth and sunshine, and they all looked relaxed. The boys stopped talking and thanked him for the sandwiches. He left the tray and went back in, closing the door behind him, but turning back to watch as they gave Maeve juice. Terry seemed like a good friend, but Thomas thought that maybe Finn thought too highly of him. Thomas worried about that. Maybe he'd have a talk to Finn about that before he left, and he drifted in thought, standing with his arms crossed, staring out at them vacantly.

He saw Finn rest his hand on Terry's shoulder and sort of lean against the taller boy. Thomas snapped back to attention. He watched. Finn didn't move back. Thomas had a bad feeling in his stomach, and he moved to open the door.

"Hello? Is anyone here?" Siobhan called from the bedroom. "Help, I need to pee!"

Thomas sucked in his cheeks, his hand on the door.

"Oh, no. Help!"

He turned and went to Siobhan's room. She lay in the bed, a look of panic on her face. "Ack, help me get up. I can't do it quickly yet."

"Sure thing." Thomas gave her his hand and pulled her up. She pushed past him in her panic for the toilet. He sat on the edge of her bed.

"What a relief. I hate not being able to sit up quickly," Siobhan said when she came back. With some effort she climbed back into bed.

Thomas just sat on the edge of her bed, his back to her.

"Where are the kids?" she asked, picking up her book.

"Oh, outside. Maeve's playing. Finn's hanging with that friend of his."

"Okay." Siobhan puzzled a bit over Thomas' tone, but he just sat, so she started reading.

He didn't move.

"Siobhan, do you think that boy..." he stopped.

Siobhan put down her book and looked at the back of his head.

"Do you think Finn's friend..." He stopped again.

"What if Finn is..."

"Is what?" Siobhan asked.

"Is."

"What?"

"What if he's."

"What? A Mormon?"

"No."

"Made of gelatin? Prone to sugar addiction? A secret hand puppet collector?"

"No! What if he's..."

"Oh my god, what?"

"You know what I'm asking!"

"Maybe, but I'm not going to make it easier on you. Say the word. Finish the damn question." Her knuckles flared white from her grip on the book.

Thomas closed his eyes and gritted his teeth.

"Queer, do you think he's queer?"

"Terry or Finn?"

"Either. Both."

"I'm sure I don't know."

"Don't you care? What if Terry makes Finn that way."

"Seriously?"

"Yes! Seriously!"

"Terry can't make Finn gay. Either Finn is gay or not gay. Or bi or not bi."

"But don't you want to, I mean, we can stop them from hanging out."

"I'm not going to do that."

"But, they could be..."

"What?"

"Fooling around. You know!"

"Look, I don't know if they are or they aren't fooling around, or if either of them is gay. It's not my business until one of them says something to me. I'm sure they don't even know yet."

"But, it could be dangerous."

"Finn has had the talk. He knows all the information. Fuck, the way that kid reads everything, he probably knows more than I do."

"But, he's just a kid."

"Yep. And they all have to work that out. I did. You did. He and Terry can work their own selves out."

"But I could just have a talk with him."

"Thomas, you're a total homophobe. You are exactly the wrong person to talk about that with either of them. Or any gay person. Anywhere."

"But just a small talk," he tried wheedling her.

Siobhan looked steadily at him. "Thomas, if you talk to either of them about this, in any way, I will beat you with a carp. Where I'll get one, I don't know, but I will find one."

Thomas gave her one last angry look, then stood up and left the bedroom. He grabbed a coat and left the apartment. Siobhan sighed as she heard the front door fall shut.

***

When he brought in the tray, Finn wondered where Thomas had gone. His mum sat in bed reading.

"Where's Uncle Thomas?"

"Probably out trying to buy holy water in bulk."

"What?"

"Never mind," she put her book down. "If he's not back by dinner, I'll help you cook the varaniki."

"Okay," Finn shrugged and went back outside.

Terry had removed his shirt, and Finn felt envious of his better physique. He didn't look nearly as young as Finn did. Finn sat next to him and tried not to look obvious about his admiration.

"Is your mum still in bed?" Terry asked, his eyes closed and his face turned towards the sun. "Yeah, but she's awake."

"She seems to be feeling better every day. How long until school starts up again for her?"

"A week and a bit. But it's summer classes, so they're at night."

"Are you going to miss your uncle much when he leaves?"

"A bit. It was nice having the help. And he's more domestic than I originally thought."

"He does like cooking and house cleaning."

"More than my mum, for certain." Finn laughed a bit at this. "Would you like to stay for dinner tonight?"

"Yeah, that would be nice. Gran has some friends in to play some card game tonight. They sit around and have old lady dirty talk that they think I don't get. It isn't even dirty."

"Well, that sounds uncomfortable," Finn said, and gave a fake shiver. "Have you ever had varaniki?"

"I've had pirogies before, and I..."

Finn stopped him by grabbing his arm. Terry looked at him, a bit surprised.

"Okay, this is very, very important. You must not say the word pirogi to either my mum or uncle." Finn said this slowly, as if talking to someone heavily medicated.

"Ooookkkkaaaayyyy," Terry said in response. "Why?"

"Because you will get such a lecture from them, on varanikis and pirogies, and the differences, and what exactly is wrong with people that buy them from the store, not making them like their mum did. It gets really fierce."

"Oh, okay. I will definitely watch what I say then."

Maeve had ignored them this whole time, playing with toy dinosaurs. Suddenly, she stood up, came over to them, and wedged herself between them. She leaned heavily against Terry. The boys looked at each other.

"Maeve, are you okay?" Finn asked her. She didn't answer. "Maybe she had a seizure."

"Should we take her inside?"

"Yeah, let's do that."

Terry scooped her up and followed Finn in. He put her on the couch and Finn covered her. She fell fast asleep.

"It's so weird that they can happen unnoticed like that," Terry said.

"Let's go to my room and let her sleep."

***

Thomas had found himself at the only sports bar in the area. He didn't drink any more. He hadn't had a drink in almost twenty years, since he'd joined AA. When the waitress came over, he ordered a pint of beer, and it came to the table cold, sweaty, and delicious looking. He put his hand on it. The glass felt right. He felt his dry fingertips sucking up the beads of sweat.

And he just sat there, watching the little bubbles in the head pop. He could smell it.

Siobhan didn't like AA. She thought they had a religious agenda. She'd told him that once she'd phoned them for a friend of hers, and the woman said she should come too, she'd just have to agree to give her control over to a higher power. Siobhan had told the woman that she didn't believe in god.

"And do you know what she said, Thomas?" Siobhan had told him over the phone. "She said, I can't even believe this, she said it didn't have to be god, my higher power could be a doorknob. Why the hell would I think a doorknob was a higher power? And why would they want you to go from giving all this power to booze, to giving it all to a doorknob? Shouldn't recovery be about your *own* power? About *you* finally taking control? It's totally ridiculous."

"Well, it works for me. God helped me quit drinking."

"No, he didn't, Thomas. That was you. Take the credit."

Siobhan didn't believe in anything he did. He didn't run around beating up gay guys, he just didn't want that life for Finn. He liked Finn. If Finn turned queer, everything would

249

feel awkward, Thomas would always think about him doing it with men, because that's all they thought about. But Siobhan only worried that the kids would think her cool and non-judgemental. All because of her own life choices. She didn't want to think that she had made bad choices, so she never made the kids think about what they did. Finn needed a father to set him straight. And since Siobhan did not seem interested in that, maybe he should step up.

He remembered having that same "everything goes" attitude, back when his life's ambition had not evolved beyond partying and doing what felt good. He'd partied himself into jail countless times, each time coming out more determined to flout the law, and what his father and family wanted. Whenever they looked down at him, and found him lacking, his jaw would grow more set. And then his father died, and instead of stepping up and helping Siobhan, he'd gone on partying, until there existed nothing between them. No relationship, no respect. When he'd straightened up and sought her out, wanting to reconnect, she didn't need him at all. His trying to get involved had just made her angry. He didn't want her to feel angry at him, but now her son had started down a bad path, and he could help Finn with that. Had to.

Thomas sat there, just holding the beer. After awhile, a seat opened on the patio and he took it so he could smoke. Thomas sat and held his beer and smoked until he'd justified many things to himself. He sat until the sun started to set, and the twilight came.

***

Siobhan had come out of her bedroom and helped Finn

and Terry make dinner.

"I have to hand it to Thomas, this kitchen has never looked so clean," Siobhan said.

"Well, I'm sure that will change not long after he leaves," Finn said.

"True, sad but true."

During dinner, Terry forgot and called the varanikis, pirogies. Siobhan gave him a look, and said, "Normally, I'd give you such a lecture, my boy, but it would take too long, and I have to give Maeve a bath. So I will give you the lecture at some further date, yet to be determined."

Terry laughed and promised he'd keep that in mind. "Will there be slides?"

"Don't mock, there might very well be, "Siobhan said. "You two clear the table, and then you can go watch a movie while I bathe Maeve."

The boys did as she asked, and Finn started a bath for Maeve.

"I can sit with her, Mum," he told Siobhan as she put the toilet lid down to sit there.

"No, hon, it's okay, go sit with Terry. I'll call if I need help."

"Okay," he said and went back to living room. The boys went through the movies, and soon Siobhan heard one start.

Maeve looked happy to have her mum help her bathe, and she told Siobhan all sorts of things that Siobhan didn't know about dragons. Siobhan washed Maeve's hair, and her face. Maeve sang her a song she made up. The bathroom was foggy and warm.

Siobhan sat happily with Maeve, heating up the water when asked, and swirling it around with her hands.

Shouting came from the living room. Siobhan heard

Thomas's voice, but the movie made it hard to hear him. Siobhan heard the boys say something back. She leaned over and pulled the door open a few inches, not wanting to let the cooler air of the hallway in.

"Hey, fellas, everything okay out there?" she called.

More shouting, from Thomas. She heard him say, "Out," and then a crash, and Finn yelling stop.

"Guys?" she called a bit more loudly, standing up, and stuck her head around the corner.

Thomas had pushed Terry down on the ground and had a hold of the front of the boy's shirt.

Siobhan shouted at Thomas, who ignored her, so she ran over and pushed him as hard as she could on the shoulder.

"Thomas, stop it right now!" She winced as she felt the strain on her healing stomach muscles. Thomas lost his balance a bit, and let go of Terry to stop himself from tripping as Siobhan moved him to the side.

Terry scrambled to his feet, looking scared and angry.

"What the hell is going on here?" Siobhan asked them. She looked at Finn.

"I don't know, Mum. He just came home and said we needed to talk and Terry had to go. Then he grabbed Terry."

"Are you okay, Terry?" she turned and asked him.

"Yeah," he answered, glaring at Thomas, who looked at the wall.

"Okay, go home now, we'll see you later."

"Okay," he said, and grabbed his jacket from next to the door and left.

"Finn, go sit with your sister, while I talk to your uncle."

252

"Okay," Finn said, looking wide-eyed between them.

Siobhan looked angrily at her brother, who wouldn't look back at her.

"Thomas," she started.

Finn shouted Maeve's name.

Siobhan turned away from Thomas, and her breathing stopped. She ran to the bathroom, where Finn struggled to hold Maeve out of the water. Water went all over the floor.

Damn, I'll have to mop that up. That's what happens when you don't watch her, water everywhere.

Chapter 12

Finn couldn't lift Maeve himself, and Siobhan could do little to help in her current condition. Thomas had followed her to the bathroom, and looked in over their heads at Maeve floating unconscious in the bathtub.

"Here, move, move, I'll get her out," he said, and stepped into the room. Finn moved over, and Thomas bent down and scooped Maeve up, water streaming down the front of him. Siobhan grabbed a towel that hung on the back of the door, and wrapped it around her. Thomas carried the girl into Siobhan's bedroom and laid her on the bed. He checked her breathing.

Her little chest went up and down, and he could hear breath sounds.

"Finn, was her head under water at all?" he asked.

"No, no, not that I saw. Is she okay?" Finn pushed by him and crouched beside the bed.

"Yes, I think she's fine. Her breathing is fine." He wiped a hand across her forehead, Siobhan pushed by him too, now, and covered Maeve with the quilt, then sat next to her on the bed. Both of them ignored Thomas.

He slowly exited the room, and went outside and lit a cigarette. He stepped up onto the seat of the picnic table and sat on the top, his cigarette dangling between his knees.

When he had finished that cigarette, he lit another.

After a while, Siobhan came out. Her face looked pale, and her eyes red, like she had a fever. He offered her a cigarette, which she took and smoked in silence, her arms folded across her chest, as she shuffled back and forth on bare feet.

She took a final drag and flicked the cigarette away. It skidded across cement and landed in a planter.

"Thank you for all your help. You can leave in the morning." She didn't look at him.

"Okay," he answered.

She walked away and went in to the apartment.

Thomas heard the door close.

He stayed on the picnic table.

Chapter 13

Finn hadn't seen Terry since his uncle had left two weeks ago. His mother had started her last semester of classes, and that meant he needed to watch Maeve most nights. He also felt bad that Thomas had attacked Terry like that, and he worried that Terry might blame him for it, so he hadn't called or emailed him.

He also felt embarrassed about what his uncle had said about the two of them that night. He hadn't told his mum about it. She already felt angry at her brother.

His mum had urged him to call Terry. She had offered to talk to him for Finn, but Finn had turned her down. Even though he didn't want to approach Terry, he knew that he would have to do it, and by himself. He just needed to choose the proper time.

Maeve hadn't had any bad effects from that night, but her seizures had increased and her mood had darkened considerably. Siobhan had decided to take her off the antidepressants, and had scheduled an appointment with the psychiatrist later that week.

"Let's get her seizures sorted first, then we can work on her mood. There's just so much going on with her meds right now, it's impossible to know what's causing what," she had said to Finn.

Maeve had grown prone to rages, and Siobhan took most of that. Twice in the past week they had stayed up all night with her as she attacked and attacked Siobhan, screaming and biting and hitting. Siobhan, still healing from surgery, wouldn't let him intervene, except to let him block the door when Maeve tried to run out of the apartment. The episodes could last hours, with all of them tired and sad after. Maeve would feel especially vulnerable, and would need to be cuddled after them.

All of them felt tense and tired. Siobhan felt at a complete loss, having never experienced these behaviour problems before. When she would find herself needing to hold Maeve down so she wouldn't run out the door in the middle of the night, or because she had picked up something to use to hit her, Siobhan would feel terrified that she would inadvertently hurt Maeve.

"I will try to push sooner for a social worker, Finn." "Will they take her?"

"Out of the house you mean? No, but they might help us access more services for her."

"I meant will they turn us down. Everyone turns her down."

"I don't know. We will have to find out. My biggest concern is that we'll end up with some zealot who has very restrictive views on child rearing, and we won't be able to get rid of them. I used to worry, when you were younger, that one would try to remove you. Being a single mum is a very vulnerable political position, but I'm not as worried now. I think we have to try. If her behaviour spills over into school she'll become known as a behaviour problem, and that's the last thing she needs."

When Siobhan left after dinner for class, Finn convinced Maeve to take her trike to the schoolyard with him and ride it around. The late spring air was warm, and her demeanour changed as she zoomed around on the pavement of the basketball court. Finn sat on a low retaining wall and read.

A shadow crossed over his book and Finn looked up, shielding his eyes. It was Jono. Finn jumped a bit. He had only seen the other boy in passing since the day at the pool hall.

"Where's your girlfriend?"

"Who?" Did he mean Neka?

"Pfft, Terry, your fucking protector."

"Um, I don't know. I'm here with my sister. I can tell him you were looking for him, when I see him."

"I'm not looking for him. I was just worried that you weren't safe without him."

"I'm fine, thanks for your concern."

"Is that your sister?" Jono gestured at Maeve, who had stopped her trike by the fence, and busily used a stick to collect spider webs, oblivious to everything else. For a kid who could not concentrate, she sure could concentrate.

"Yes," Finn answered, and braced himself for the insults.

"Cool trike."

"Oh. Thanks."

Jono shrugged. "Whatever." He turned to go, then stopped. "Look I'm sorry about throwing that ball at you."

"Okay, thanks."

Jono stomped off without looking back.

Maeve rode up to him on her trike and slammed on the brakes.

"Who was that?" she asked.

"Just some kid from school."

"Is he your friend?"

"No, not really. He's kind of mean to me. And everyone else."

"So, he's your bully?"

"Yeah, I guess."

"I had a bully when I was four."

"Oh, yeah?" Finn knew that she'd had an imaginary bully at one point. Only Maeve would have an imaginary bully.

"You should just say to him, 'Why can't we be friends?' and then share your lunch with him."

"That will work?"

"Yes." Her eyes had that wide open, earnest look she got when she had to explain things to others. Finn had to bite his lip to stop from smiling at her.

He looked at the sun in the sky. "It must be close to dinner time, Maeve, are you hungry?"

"No."

"Well, you never are, but let's go eat anyways."

"Can I ride my trike home?"

"Part way."

"Will Mum be home soon?"

"Not until later, you'll be asleep. But she'll be home when you get up."

"Okay."

"Maybe we'll go see Terry tonight, okay?"

"Is he your friend?"

"Yes. Well, I hope so."

***

Siobhan worried because she would graduate at the end of this semester, and she needed to find a job. All along she had thought she would work for awhile after graduation, and then continue to work as she went on with school. Before this year she had felt that working in conjunction with school would work as Maeve got older.

That was now impossible. Maeve's increasing seizure rate refused to respond to medication, and her mood and escalating behaviour issues made it all but impossible to plan any day-to-day activity. Right now, Finn could watch her in the evenings, because he went to school in the day and Siobhan went at night. In a few weeks, both kids would be out of school for the summer. Siobhan felt able to keep Maeve home as much as possible now, because at least one of them would be home for Maeve. But what would happen when Siobhan graduated and Finn's school started back up? She couldn't work all evenings in perpetuity, letting him shoulder more and more responsibility for a sister who seemed to grow worse and worse each day. And how could she find a job that could accommodate their erratic life? At most, she could work part-time, which meant that she could not take a job that paid minimum wage. Her options seemed few.

This semester marked the end of student loans. No matter how carefully she watched her budget, no matter how she cut back on expenses, she would need to find a job as soon as possible at the end of semester, or even sooner. She had not had to use welfare since Maeve had turned two, and she did not want to have to go back.

She kept checking the want ads in the student union building, but all of them wanted workers for evenings and weekends, and she had all evening classes. She needed daytime hours, so that Finn wouldn't have to spend all his time parenting Maeve.

She looked online, she looked in the newspapers. Her last paid job, at the student tutoring centre two years ago, seemed inadequate on her resume. She felt extremely lacking in recent work experience. That just figured, since before Maeve, she'd felt replete with work experience and lacking in education. Quitting high school had not presented much problem with the types of jobs she'd had back then, but after Maeve she'd determined to get on a better career path. Low level, minimum wage jobs would never provide the security Maeve needed.

Maeve barely went to school right now. When she did, Siobhan had to pick her up several times a week because of her seizures. If Maeve became violent with her at night or in the morning, she couldn't go to school. They waited for a counsellor at the youth mental health office, and had an interview set up to see if they would be accepted into the ministry agency that would help with therapies and a social worker.

Siobhan had trouble even conceiving of what job she could get that would accommodate all of that.

Now, after feeling for all of her time at school, that she'd made the right choices, that the sacrifices and the debt would pay off, now she felt scared, and without a path.

This year had taken it all away.

***

Finn is reading to me. I am laying with him in bed. I like it. I like to lean against him. I put my stuffies on the other side. I like to be in the middle.

I wish Mummy could read to me, but she's in school. Again. Finn says I can see her in the morning.

"This is the last story tonight, Maeve," Finn says to me.

"No, one more, please Finn."

I don't want Finn to go. I don't want to be alone.

"Okay, but then bedtime."

I hold onto Finn's arm while he reads the next book. I want the story to be a long one. I am worried the end will come. I'm worried Finn will leave the bedroom.

"Maeve, you're hurting me. Please back off a bit."

Now Finn's mad at me. Now he wants to leave me. I

didn't mean it! I didn't mean to hurt him. How can I fix it?

I hear a growl. Something is growling at Finn. Finn looks a little scared. I feel bad that he's scared.

"Maeve, it's okay. Relax, let go of my arm a bit, please, you're hurting me."

I don't know why he's telling me that. I don't know what is making that growling noise.

I'm dreaming this now. "Maeve, please. Please stop."

"Maeve, you're hurting."

"Maeve, you need to stay in your room."

The thing that growls is hurting Finn. I think I could help him. If I can stop dreaming. I feel like I can't help him now! I can't get to him from here.

I am crying. Finn is crying. I'm crying because he's crying. He yells at me. I want to stop the growling thing.

Mummy's face comes through my dream. Mummy holds me. She pulls me out of the dream. The growling thing goes away.

I am so tired now. I tried to save Finn. I want to tell her. Mummy lays down with me. She sings.

***

Siobhan felt relieved when they finally had their appointment with youth mental health services. They met with both the psychiatrist and the young woman who would meet with Maeve weekly.

Maeve played happily in the sandbox while Finn and Siobhan talked.

"She's become violent with us. She was never violent before."

"What are the episodes like?" the psychiatrist asked, writing notes on foolscap.

"She hits and screams. She kicks me. She tries to hit me with items around the house. Sometimes she tries to leave the apartment, which terrifies me. She can keep it up for hours, even in the middle of the night. I don't know why she is doing this all of a sudden. She never did it before, she's never had behaviour issues. I'm terrified that someone is going to phone the police, she's that loud."

"Has her mood improved with the anxiety medication?"

"Not that I can tell, no."

"Well, one of the side effects of the drug is bi-polar-like symptoms. It may be that she's manifested some. Regardless, if you haven't noticed an improvement by now, on this dose, it isn't working. We should wean her off."

Siobhan felt relief at this, even though it wouldn't help Maeve's anxiety.

"Would you like to try another medication for her?" the doctor asked her.

"No. Not right yet. We've been trying different meds for her seizures, and I'm worried about over-medicating her. Will coming off these meds help with the violence?"

"It might, if the medication is what's causing it. I can't promise."

"No, I understand. So, what do I do, then?"

"Well, didn't you say that you were going to apply to the ministry for a social worker?"

"Yes."

"Well, if stopping the medication doesn't work, maybe they can help with that."

"But I'm so worried about her hurting herself, or Finn. What do I do in the meantime?"

"You can give her some Ativan when she's escalating, to see if that calms her down."

"I've tried to when she's in full-blown meltdown, but not on the way to it. She won't take them at all when she's really in trouble. I can try giving them before, if I catch her escalating. Sometimes, it's just too fast."

Maeve came back in, happy with a juice box, and with cookie crumbs down her front. Siobhan hugged her, helped her collect her pile of stuff, and thanked everyone. She hoped taking Maeve off the medication would help.

***

Finn sat outside the school after his only exam. He generally had good enough marks that he hadn't had to take many finals. He only had to take the one for social studies, because Mr. Addle had given him a mark fractionally too low. The test had not proven difficult, though, and now Finn enjoyed the solitude of the mostly empty school ground. His face turned toward the sun, his eyes closed, he listened to the occasional distant laugh or voice, the intermittent hum of a lawnmower in the field, and birds flitting in the bushes. Soon he would go home and switch shifts with his mum as she headed to class. She was taking ancient architecture, which she hadn't known she had an interest in before taking it. She had started to critique every real or facade column they saw. She would point out the Doric columns, then explain the differences between them and Ionic or Corinthian. She had grown very personally insulted by columns that appeared confused. She always developed such weird pet peeves.

He just found her amusing. Who the hell cared about columns?

Behind him he heard the door open. A second later he heard Terry's voice.

"Hi."

Finn opened his eyes and gave Terry a nervous smile. "Hi."

"Did you have a test?"

"Yeah."

"I have one in a bit. Math."

"Are you nervous?"

"Not really. I understand it, I'm just not good with homework." Terry sat down next to him on the ground, with his long legs bent and his arms resting on his knees. "I wish I had a smoke, though."

"Actually, I think I have one."

Terry looked surprised, one eyebrow shot up.

"Yeah, I just found them the other day. I forgot I'd bought them." He fished around in his backpack and came up with his pencil case. He opened it and took out two slightly crooked cigarettes. "I bought them last fall. Do they go bad?"

Terry took one and straightened it with his fingers.

"Stale, not bad." He sniffed it. "Smells like a pencil."

Finn straightened the other. Terry lit his, took a drag and coughed. "Oh yeah, that's pretty old." He held out his lighter to Finn.

Finn looked at him for a minute, then put the the cigarette in his mouth and held it to the flame.

It tasted horrible.

Terry smiled. "You didn't inhale."

Finn tried again. His lungs seared, and he tried to quell the huge choking cough that ripped out of him. He clapped his hand over his mouth, but the force only redirected to his nose, spraying forth with a huge spray of snot.

Terry laughed uproariously, great whooping shrieks of laughter that made him curl up on the ground and hold his stomach. Finn smiled happily through teary eyes. He felt dizzy, and watched as Terry slowly wound down.

"Ah man, that was great," Terry finally said, wiping his face. "So, you want to hang out later?"

"I can't. I'm watching Maeve. But I'm free tomorrow, during the day."

"Okay. Let's do something then." Terry finished his cigarette and said, "I should go in."

"Okay. Good luck."

"Thanks."

Terry turned away.

"I'm sorry about my uncle," Finn said to his back.

"It's okay." Terry turned to him just slightly. "But what he said, I don't think..."

"He was just being stupid. He's got issues."

"That seems pretty clear."

"Yeah."

Finn watched him walk away. He still held the cigarette, which had burned down to the filter. He tossed it away.

***

Finn wants to take me to the park. He says the sun is shining. He says I can ride my trike.

But the bed feels safe. I can read and cuddle with my stuffies. I can hear Mummy in the living room on her computer.

I don't have to get dressed. I don't have school now. It's summer. In summer I can eat breakfast in bed. Not cereal, though.

Mummy is worried about getting a job. I think she should just ask the government for money. I don't want her to work. I want her to stay with me.

"Maeve get up, let's go do something. It's beautiful out,"

Finn says.

I hide in the bed.

"Should I leave you alone for just a bit and then you'll feel like it? I have to get some groceries. Mum has a test tonight."

I put my book on my face. I just want him to quit bugging me.

"Hon, why don't you just go out for awhile and do something. Maeve can stay with me," Mummy says.

"But you have your test tonight."

"It's okay, I just need to read for it. Maeve's reading, I'll read, it'll work."

"Okay, but I'll take your phone and you can phone if you need me."

"Yeah, yeah."

Mummy lays down next to me.

"What are you reading, Maeve?"

"Science!"

"I was just asking, Maeve. You don't need to yell."

I didn't mean to yell.

"I will go back and read in the living room."

"No."

"Do you want me to stay?"

"No."

"Maeve, what do you want?"

"I don't know!"

"Okay."

I feel Mummy get up. I hear her walk to the living room. She comes back and lays next to me again. I keep my book on my face. I can hear her breathing.

"Mum?"

"Yes, Honey?"

"Am I a medical miracle?"

Acknowledgements

This novel took four years to write, and during that time I whined at everyone I know to read it. I owe a great many people a debt of gratitude for their help, support, and feedback. Extremely personal novels are really hard to look at after you've written the words.

Thank you to my family, June Woods, Jodi Craney, Joe Craney, and Susan Park for all your support and help over the years. And for finally reading the manuscript, which you all kept promising to do for years. I love you all, but I still expect you buy the book. Okay, I'll give you twenty percent off, and I will concede one point of argument to each of you at some point in the next five years.

Thank you to Heather Kaytor, Martha Roberts, Theresa Hanley, and Jael Emberley for reading my second draft. You are tremendous and marvelous friends. For you all, one free copy of the book, and an airplane ride in a park of your choice.

I can't thank you, Diane Cliffe, enough for editing this novel. Your brilliant suggestions, humorous comments, and kind encouragement helped me move this novel from the never done pile to the actually done pile. You gave me motivation right when I needed it most.

Thank you to Filidh Publishing for being who I trust to publish my novel.

To Andrew Brechin, my partner of eight years, who chose to be father to my daughter. You are the kindest and most creative person I ever knew. I owe you so much more than words can ever repay. I am filled with sorrow that you did not live to see this novel in print. You are missed, and your love and support has had an incredible and profound effect upon my life. Thank you for being here. I love you.

And finally, to my beautiful daughter, Bronwyn, without whom there would be no story. You are, and will always be, the best influence I have ever had. You have made me a better person than I could've ever imagined. I am so proud of you, and I love you as big as all the stars.